W9-BJF-573

ARTEMIS FOWL

aurum potestas est

ARTEMIS FOWL is a child prodigy from Ireland who has dedicated his brilliant mind to criminal activities. When Artemis discovers that there is a fairy civilization below ground, he sees it as a golden opportunity. Now there is a whole new species to exploit with his ingenious schemes. But Artemis doesn't know as much as he thinks about the fairy People. And what he doesn't know could hurt him . . .

NEVER HAS A CRIMINAL MASTERMIND
RECEIVED SUCH PRAISE

'Reads like the fastest, punchiest comic strip
you've ever come across' – *Daily Telegraph*

'A hectic fusion of real, imaginary and fairy gadgetry.
From laser guns to mind wipers, through battery-powered craft
and anti-radiation suits, they make the world of
James Bond's Q look like child's play'
– *Guardian*

'Wickedly brilliant' – *Independent*

'Pacy, playful and very funny, an inventive mix of myth
and modernity, magic and crime'
– *Time*

'Colfer has the ability to make you laugh twice over: first in sheer
subversive joy at the inventiveness of the writing, and
again at the energy of the humour' – *Sunday Times*

'Funny, fast, cinematic adventure'
– *Financial Times*

'Fast, funny and very exciting'
– *Daily Mail*

'Full of action, weaponry, farting dwarves
and Chandleresque one-liners'
– *Evening Standard*

Books by Eoin Colfer

ARTEMIS FOWL
ARTEMIS FOWL AND THE ARCTIC INCIDENT
ARTEMIS FOWL AND THE ETERNITY CODE
ARTEMIS FOWL AND THE OPAL DECEPTION
ARTEMIS FOWL AND THE LOST COLONY
ARTEMIS FOWL AND THE TIME PARADOX
ARTEMIS FOWL AND THE ATLANTIS COMPLEX

AIRMAN
BENNY AND BABE
BENNY AND OMAR
HALF MOON INVESTIGATIONS
THE SUPERNATURALIST
THE WISH LIST

Graphic novels
ARTEMIS FOWL: THE GRAPHIC NOVEL
ARTEMIS FOWL AND THE ARCTIC INCIDENT: THE GRAPHIC NOVEL

And for younger readers
THE LEGEND OF SPUD MURPHY
THE LEGEND OF CAPTAIN CROW'S TEETH
THE LEGEND OF THE WORST BOY IN THE WORLD

Hack into the wicked world of Artemis Fowl
www.artemisfowl.co.uk

EOIN COLFER

ARTEMIS FOWL

AND THE OPAL DECEPTION

PUFFIN

PUFFIN BOOKS

UK | USA | Canada | Ireland | Australia
India | New Zealand | South Africa

Puffin Books is part of the Penguin Random House group of companies
whose addresses can be found at global.penguinrandomhouse.com.

www.penguin.co.uk   www.puffin.co.uk   www.ladybird.co.uk

First published by Puffin Books 2005
This edition published 2017

001

Text copyright © Eoin Colfer, 2005
Map illustrations by Kev Walker
All rights reserved

The moral right of the author has been asserted

Set in 13.5/16.3pt Perpetua

Printed in Great Britain by Clays Ltd, St Ives plc
A CIP catalogue record for this book is available from the British Library

ISBN: 978–0–241–33562–8

All correspondence to:
Puffin Books, Penguin Random House Children's
80 Strand, London WC2R 0RL

www.greenpenguin.co.uk

MIX
Paper from
responsible sources
FSC® C018179

Penguin Books is committed to a sustainable
future for our business, our readers and our
planet. This book is made from paper certified
by the Forest Stewardship Council.

For Sarah.
The pen is mightier than the word processor.

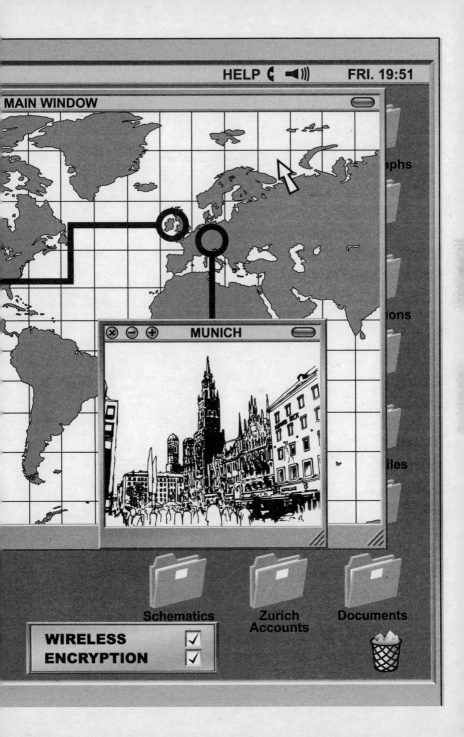

CONTENTS

PROLOGUE

The following article was posted on the fairy internet on the site www.horsesense.gnom. It is believed that this site is maintained by the centaur Foaly, technical consultant to the Lower Elements Police, although it has never been proved. Almost every detail of this account contradicts the official release from the LEP Press Office.

We've all heard the official explanation for the tragic events surrounding the Zito Probe investigation. The LEP's statement contained little in the way of concrete detail, preferring to fudge the facts and question the decisions of a certain female officer.

I know for an absolute fact that the officer in question, Captain Holly Short, behaved in an exemplary manner, and if it had not been for her skill as a field operative, many more lives would have been lost. Instead of scapegoating Captain Short, the Lower Elements Police should give her a medal.

Humans are at the centre of this particular case. Most humans aren't smart enough to find the leg holes in their trousers, but there are certain Mud Men clever enough to make me nervous. If they discovered the existence of an underground fairy city, they would certainly do their best to exploit the residents. Most men would be no match for superior fairy technology. But there are some humans who are almost smart enough to pass as fairies. One human in particular. I think we all know who I'm talking about.

In fairy history only one human has bested us. And it really sticks in my hoof that this particular human is little more than a boy. Artemis Fowl, the Irish criminal mastermind. Little Arty led the LEP a merry dance across the continents, until finally they used fairy technology to wipe our existence from his mind. But even as the gifted centaur Foaly pressed the mind-wipe button, he wondered if the fairy People were being fooled again. Had the Irish boy left something behind to make himself remember? Of course he had, as we were all to find out later.

Artemis Fowl does play a significant role in the following events, but for once he was not trying to steal from the People as he had completely forgotten we existed. No, the mastermind behind this episode is actually a fairy.

So who is involved in this tragic tale of two worlds? Who are the main fairy players? Obviously Foaly is the real hero of the piece. Without his innovations, the LEP would soon be beating the Mud Men back from our doors. He is the unsung hero who solves riddles of the ages, while the reconnaissance and retrieval teams swan about above ground, taking all the glory.

Then there's Captain Holly Short, the officer whose reputation is under fire. Holly is one of the LEP's best and brightest.

A natural-born pilot with a gift for improvisation in the field. She's not the best at taking orders, a trait that has landed her in trouble on more than one occasion. Holly was the fairy at the centre of all the Artemis Fowl incidents. The pair had almost become friends, when the Council ordered the LEP to mind-wipe Artemis, and just when he was becoming a nice Mud Boy too.

As we all know, Commander Julius Root has a role in proceedings. The youngest-ever full commander in the LEP. An elf who has steered the People through many a crisis. Not the easiest fairy to get along with, but sometimes the best leaders do not make the best friends.

I suppose Mulch Diggums deserves a mention. Until recently Mulch was imprisoned, but as usual he managed to wriggle his way out. This kleptomaniac, flatulent dwarf has played a reluctant part in many of the Fowl adventures. But Holly was glad to have his help on this mission. If not for Mulch and his bodily functions, things could have turned out a lot worse than they did. And they turned out badly enough.

At the very centre of this case lies Opal Koboi, the pixie who bankrolled the goblin gang's attempted takeover of Haven City. Opal was facing a lifetime behind laser bars. That is, if she ever recovered from the coma that claimed her when Holly Short foiled her plan.

For almost a year, Opal Koboi had languished in the padded-cell wing of the J. Argon Clinic, showing no response to the medical warlocks who tried to revive her. In all that time, she spoke not a single word, ate not a mouthful of food and exhibited *no response to stimuli. At first the authorities were suspicious. It is an act, they declared. Koboi is faking catatonia to avoid prosecution. But as the months rolled by, even the most sceptical were convinced. No one could pretend to be in a coma for almost a year. Surely not. A fairy would have to be totally obsessed . . .*

CHAPTER 1: TOTALLY OBSESSED

 THE J. Argon Clinic was not a state hospital. Nobody stayed there for free. Argon and his staff of psychologists only treated fairies who could afford it. Of all the clinic's wealthy patients, Opal Koboi was unique. She had set up an emergency fund for herself more than a year previously, *just in case* she ever went insane and needed to pay for treatment. It was a smart move. If Opal hadn't set up the fund, her family would undoubtedly have moved her to a cheaper facility. Not that the facility itself made much difference to Koboi, who had spent the past year drooling and having her reflexes tested. Doctor Argon doubted if Opal would have noticed a bull troll beating its chest in front of her.

The fund was not the only reason why Opal was unique. Koboi was the Argon Clinic's celebrity patient. Following the attempt by the B'wa Kell goblin triad to seize power, Opal Koboi's name had become the most infamous four syllables under the world. After all, the pixie billionairess had formed an alliance with disgruntled LEP officer Briar Cudgeon, and funded the triad's war on Haven. Koboi had betrayed her own kind, and now her own mind was betraying her.

For the first six months of Koboi's incarceration, the clinic had been besieged by media filming the pixie's every twitch. The LEP guarded her cell door in shifts, every staff member in the facility was treated to background checks and stern glares. Nobody was exempt. Even Doctor Argon himself was subjected to random DNA swabs to ensure that he was who he said he was. The LEP wasn't taking any chances with Koboi. If she escaped from Argon's clinic, not only would they be the laughing stock of the fairy world, but a highly dangerous criminal would be unleashed on Haven City.

But as time went by, fewer camera crews turned up at the gates each morning. After all, how many hours of drooling can an audience be expected to sit through? Gradually the LEP crews were downsized from a dozen to six and finally to a single officer per shift. Where could Opal Koboi go? the authorities reasoned. There were a dozen cameras focused on her twenty-four hours a day.

There was a subcutaneous seeker-sleeper under the skin of her upper arm and she was DNA swabbed four times daily. And even if someone did get Opal out, what could they do with her? The pixie couldn't even stand without help, and the sensors said her brainwaves were little more than flat lines.

That said, Doctor Argon was very proud of his prize patient, and mentioned her name often at dinner parties. Since Opal Koboi had been admitted to the clinic, it had become almost fashionable to have a relative in therapy. Almost every family on the rich list had a crazy uncle in the attic. Now, that crazy uncle could receive the best of care in the lap of luxury.

If only every fairy in the facility was as docile as Opal Koboi. All she needed was a few intravenous tubes and a monitor, which had been more than paid for by her first six months' medical fees. Doctor Argon fervently hoped that little Opal never woke up. Because once she did, the LEP would haul her off to court. And when she had been convicted of treason her assets would be frozen, including the clinic's fund. No, the longer Opal's nap lasted, the better for everyone, especially her. Because of their thin skulls and large brain volume, pixies were susceptible to various maladies such as catatonia, amnesia and narcolepsy. So it was quite possible that her coma would last for several years. And even if Opal did wake up, it was quite possible that her memory would stay locked up in some drawer in her huge pixie brain.

Doctor J. Argon did his rounds every night. He didn't perform much hands-on therapy any more, but he felt that it was good for the staff to feel his presence. If the other doctors knew that Jerbal Argon kept his finger on the pulse, then they were more likely to keep their own fingers on that pulse too.

Argon always saved Opal for last. It calmed him somehow to see the small pixie asleep in her harness. Often at the end of a stressful day, he even envied Opal her untroubled existence. When it had all become too much for the pixie, her brain had simply shut down, all except the most vital functions. She still breathed, and occasionally the monitors registered a dream spike in her brainwaves. But other than that, for all intents and purposes, Opal Koboi was no more.

On this fateful night, Jerbal Argon was feeling more stressed than usual. His wife was suing for divorce on the grounds that he hadn't said more than six consecutive words to her in over two years, the Council was threatening to pull his government grant because of all the money he was making from his new celebrity clients and he had a pain in his hip that no amount of magic could seem to cure. The warlocks said it was probably all in his head. They seemed to think that was funny.

Argon limped down the clinic's eastern wing, checking the plasma chart of each patient as he passed their room. He winced each time his left foot touched the floor.

The two janitor pixies, Mervall and Descant Brill, were outside Opal's room, picking up dust with static brushes. Pixies made wonderful employees. They were methodical, patient and determined. When a pixie was instructed to do something, you could rest assured that thing would be done. Plus they were cute, with their baby faces and disproportionately large heads. Just looking at a pixie cheered most people up. They were walking therapy.

'Evening, boys,' said Argon. 'How's our favourite patient?'

Merv, the elder twin, glanced up from his brush. 'Same old, same old, Jerry,' he said. 'I thought she moved a toe earlier, but it was just a trick of the light.'

Argon laughed, but it was forced. He did not like to be called Jerry. It was *his* clinic after all; he deserved some respect. But good janitors were like gold dust, and the Brill brothers had been keeping the building spotless and shipshape for nearly two years now. The Brills were almost celebrities themselves. Twins were very rare among the People. Mervall and Descant were the only pixie pair currently residing in Haven. They had featured on several TV programmes, including *Canto,* PPTV's highest-rated chat show.

LEP Corporal Grub Kelp was on sentry duty. When Argon reached Opal's room, the corporal was engrossed in a movie on his video goggles. Argon didn't blame him. Guarding Opal Koboi was about as exciting as watching toenails grow.

'Good film?' enquired the doctor pleasantly.

Grub raised the lenses. 'Not bad. It's a human Western. Plenty of shooting and squinting.'

'Maybe I'll borrow it when you're finished?'

'No problem, Doctor. But handle it carefully. Human disks are very expensive. I'll give you a special cloth.'

Argon nodded. He remembered Grub Kelp now. The LEP officer was very particular about his possessions. He had already written two letters of complaint to the clinic board about a protruding floor rivet that had scratched his boots.

Argon consulted Koboi's chart. The plasma screen on the wall displayed a constantly updated feed from the sensors attached to her temples. There was no change, nor did he expect there to be. Her vitals were all normal, and her brain activity was minimal. She'd had a dream earlier in the evening but now her mind had settled. And finally, as if he needed telling, the seeker-sleeper implanted in her arm informed him that Opal Koboi was indeed where she was supposed to be. Generally the seeker-sleepers were implanted in the head, but pixie skulls were too fragile for any local surgery.

Jerbal punched in his personal code on the reinforced door's keypad. The heavy door slid back to reveal a spacious room with gently pulsing floor mood lights. The walls were soft plastic, and gentle sounds of nature spilled from recessed speakers. At the moment a brook was splashing over flat rocks.

In the middle of the room, Opal Koboi hung suspended in a full body harness. The straps were gel-padded and adjusted automatically to any body movement. If Opal did happen to wake, the harness could be remotely triggered to seal like a net, preventing her from harming herself.

Argon checked the monitor pads, making sure they had good contact on Koboi's forehead. He lifted one of the pixie's eyelids, shining a pencil light at the pupil. It contracted slightly, but Opal did not avert her eyes.

'Well, anything to tell me today, Opal?' asked the doctor softly. 'An opening chapter for my book?'

Argon liked to talk to Koboi, just in case she could hear. When she woke up, he reasoned, he would have already established a rapport.

'Nothing? Not a single insight?'

Opal did not react. As she hadn't for almost a year.

'Ah well,' said Argon, swabbing the inside of Koboi's mouth with the last cotton bud in his pocket. 'Maybe tomorrow, eh?'

He rolled the cotton bud across a sponge pad on his clipboard. Seconds later, Opal's name flashed up on a tiny screen.

⊙ ⚭⍩⏁⅁⅌ • ⅋ ⊙ • ⊕◻⏁⅌ • ⅋⊹⊖⍉⚇

'DNA never lies,' muttered Argon, tossing the bud into a recycling bin.

With one last look at his patient, Jerbal Argon turned towards the door.

'Sleep well, Opal,' he said, almost fondly.

He felt calm again, the pain in his hip almost forgotten. Koboi was as far under as she had ever been. She wasn't going to wake up any time soon. The Koboi fund was safe.

It's amazing just how wrong one gnome can be.

Opal Koboi was not catatonic, but neither was she awake. She was somewhere in between, floating in a liquid world of meditation where every memory was a bubble of multicoloured light popping gently in her consciousness.

Since her early teens Opal had been a disciple of Gola Schweem, the cleansing coma guru. Schweem's theory was that there was a deeper level of sleep than that experienced by most fairies. The cleansing coma state could usually be reached only after decades of discipline and practice. Opal had reached her first cleansing coma at the age of fourteen.

The benefits of the cleansing coma were that a fairy usually awoke completely refreshed but also spent the sleep time thinking, or in this case plotting. Opal's coma was so complete that her mind was almost entirely separated from her body. She could fool the sensors and felt no embarrassment at the indignities of intravenous feeding and changing. The longest recorded consciously self-induced coma was forty-seven days. Opal had been under for eleven months and counting, though she wasn't planning to be counting much longer.

When Opal Koboi had joined forces with Briar Cudgeon and his goblins, she'd realized that she needed a back-up plan. Their scheme to overthrow the LEP had been ingenious, but there was always a chance that something could go wrong. In the event that it did, Opal had no intention of spending the rest of her life in prison. The only way she could make a clean getaway would be if everybody thought she was still locked up. So Opal had begun to make preparations.

The first was to set up the emergency fund for the Argon Clinic. This would ensure she was sent to the right place if she had to induce a cleansing coma. The second step was to get two of her most trusted personnel installed in the clinic, to help with her eventual escape. Then she began siphoning huge amounts of gold from her businesses. Opal did not wish to become an impoverished exile.

The final step was to donate some of her own DNA and to green light the creation of a clone that would take her place in the padded cell. Cloning was completely illegal and had been banned by fairy law for over five hundred years since the first experiments in Atlantis. It was by no means a perfect science. Doctors had never been able to create an exact fairy clone. The clones looked fine, but

14

they were basically shells with only enough brainpower
to run the body's basic functions. They were missing the
spark of true life. A fully grown clone resembled nothing
more than the original person in a coma. Perfect.

Opal had had a greenhouse lab constructed, far from
Koboi Laboratories, and had diverted enough funds to
keep the project active for two years, the exact time it
would take to grow a clone of herself to adulthood. Then,
when she wanted to escape from the Argon Clinic, a
perfect replica of herself would be left in her place. The
LEP would never know she was gone.

As things had turned out, she had been right to plan
ahead. Briar had proved treacherous, and a small group of
fairies and humans had ensured his betrayal led to her own
downfall. Now Opal had a goal to bolster her willpower:
she would maintain this coma for as long as it took,
because there was a score to be settled. Foaly, Root, Holly
Short and the human, Artemis Fowl. They were the ones
responsible for her defeat. Soon she would be free of
this clinic, and then she would visit those who had caused
her such despair, and give them a little despair of their
own. Once her enemies were defeated she could proceed
with the second phase of her plan: introducing the Mud
Men to the People in a way that could not be covered
up by a few mind wipes. The secret life of fairies was
almost at an end.

Opal Koboi's brain released a few happy endorphins.

The thought of revenge always gave her a warm, fuzzy feeling.

The Brill brothers watched Doctor Argon limp up the corridor.

'Moron,' muttered Merv, using his telescopic vacuum pole to chase some dust out of a corner.

'You said it,' agreed Scant. 'Old Jerry couldn't analyse a bowl of vole curry. No wonder his wife is leaving him. If he was any good as a shrink, he would've seen that coming.'

Merv collapsed the vacuum. 'How are we doing?'

Scant checked his moonometer. 'Ten past eight.'

'Good. How's Corporal Kelp?'

'Still watching the movie. This guy is perfect. We have to go tonight. The LEP could send someone smart for the next shift. And if we wait any longer, the clone will grow another two centimetres.'

'You're right. Check the spy cameras.'

Scant lifted the lid on what appeared to be a janitor's trolley, festooned as it was with mops, rags and sprays. Hidden beneath a tray of vacuum nozzles was a colour monitor split into several screens.

'Well?' hissed Merv.

Scant did not answer immediately, taking time to check all the screens. The video feed was from various micro-cameras that Opal had installed around the clinic before her incarceration. The spy cameras were actually genetically engineered organic material. So the pictures they sent were literally a live feed. The world's first living machines. Totally undetectable by bug sweepers.

'Night crew only,' he said at last. 'Nobody in this sector except Corporal Idiot over there.'

'What about the parking lot?'

'Clear.'

Merv held out his hand. 'OK, brother. This is it. No turning back. Are we in? Do we want Opal Koboi back?'

Scant blew a lock of black hair from one round pixie eye.

'Yes, because if she comes back on her own, Opal will find a way to make us suffer,' he said, shaking his brother's hand. 'So yes, we're in.'

Merv took a remote control from his pocket. The device was tuned to a sonix receiver planted in the clinic's gable wall. This in turn was connected to a balloon of acid which lay gently on the clinic's main power cube in the parking-lot junction box. A second balloon sat atop the back-up cube in the maintenance basement. As the clinic's janitors, it had been a simple matter for Merv and Scant to plant the acid balloons the previous evening. Of course the Argon Clinic was also connected to the main grid, but if the cubes did go down, there would be a two-minute interval before the main power kicked in.

There was no need for more elaborate arrangements — after all, this was a medical facility, not a prison.

Merv took a deep breath, flicked open the safety cover and pressed the red button. The remote control emitted an infrared command activating two sonix charges. The charges sent out sound waves bursting the balloons, and the balloons dumped their acidic contents on the clinic's power cubes. Twenty seconds later, the cubes were completely eaten away and the whole building was plunged into darkness. Merv and Scant quickly put on night-vision goggles.

As soon as the power failed, green strip lights began pulsing gently on the floor, guiding the way to the exits. Merv and Scant moved quickly and purposefully. Scant steered the trolley and Merv made straight for Corporal Kelp.

Grub was pulling the video glasses from over his eyes.

'Hey,' he said, disorientated by the sudden darkness. 'What's going on here?'

'Power failure,' said Merv, bumping into him with calculated clumsiness. 'Those lines are a nightmare. I've been telling Doctor Argon, but nobody wants to spend money on maintenance when there are fancy company cars to be bought.'

Merv was not waffling for the fun of it; he was waiting for the soluble pad of sedative he had pressed on to Grub's wrist to take effect.

'Tell me about it,' said Grub, suddenly blinking a lot more than he generally did. 'I've been lobbying for new lockers at Police Plaza . . . I'm really thirsty. Is anyone else thirsty?' Grub stiffened, frozen by the serum that was spreading through his system. The LEP officer would snap out of it in under two minutes, and be instantly alert. He would have no memory of his unconsciousness, and hopefully he would not notice the time-lapse.

'Go,' said Scant tersely.

Merv was already gone. With practised ease, he punched Doctor Argon's code into Opal's door. He completed this action faster than Argon ever could, due to hours spent practising on a stolen pad in his apartment. Argon's code changed every week, but the Brill brothers made certain that they were cleaning outside the room when Argon was on his rounds. The pixies generally had the complete code by midweek.

The battery-powered pad light winked green, and the door slid back. Opal Koboi swung gently before him, suspended in her harness like a bug in an exotic cocoon.

Merv winched her down on to the trolley. Moving briskly and with practised precision, he rolled up Opal's sleeve and located the scar in her upper arm where the seeker-sleeper had been inserted. He gripped the hard lump between his thumb and forefinger.

'Scalpel,' he said, holding out his free hand. Scant passed him the instrument. Merv took a breath, held it, and made a two-centimetre incision in Opal's flesh. He wiggled his index finger into the hole and rolled out the electronic capsule. It was encased in silicone and was roughly the size of a painkiller.

'Seal it up,' he ordered.

Scant bent close to the wound, placing a thumb at each end.

'Heal,' he whispered, and blue sparks of fairy magic ran rings round his fingers, sinking into the wound. In seconds, the folds of skin had zipped themselves together, with only a pale pink scar to show that a cut had been made. A scar almost identical to that which had already existed. Opal's own magic had dried up months ago, as she was in no position to complete a power-restoring ritual.

'Miss Koboi,' said Merv briskly. 'Time to get up. Wakey wakey.'

He unstrapped Opal completely from the harness. The unconscious pixie collapsed on to the lid of the cleaning trolley. Merv slapped her across the cheek, bringing a blush to her face. Opal's breathing rate increased slightly, but her eyes remained closed.

'Jolt her,' said Scant.

Merv pulled an LEP-issue buzz baton from inside his jacket. He powered it up and touched Opal on the elbow. The pixie's body jerked spasmodically, and Opal Koboi shot into consciousness, a sleeper waking from a nightmare.

'Cudgeon,' she screamed, 'you betrayed me!'

Merv grabbed her shoulders. 'Miss Koboi. It's us, Mervall and Descant. It's time.'

Opal glared at him, wild-eyed.

'Brill?' she said, after several deep breaths.

'That's right. Merv and Scant. We need to go.'

'Go? What do you mean?'

'Leave,' said Merv urgently. 'We have about a minute.'

Opal shook her head, dislodging the after-trance daze. 'Merv and Scant. We need to go.'

Merv helped her from the trolley's lid. 'That's right. The clone is ready.'

Scant peeled back a sealed-foil false bottom in the trolley. Inside lay a cloned replica of Opal Koboi, wearing an Argon Clinic coma suit. The clone was identical, down to the last follicle. Scant removed an oxygen mask from the clone's face, hauled it from its resting place and began cinching it into the harness.

'Remarkable,' said Opal, brushing the clone's skin with her knuckle. 'Am I that beautiful?'

'Oh yes,' said Merv. 'That and more.'

Suddenly Opal screeched. 'Idiots. Its eyes are open. It can see me!'

Scant closed the clone's lids hurriedly. 'Don't worry, Miss Koboi, it can't tell anyone, even if its brain could decipher what it sees.'

Opal climbed groggily into the trolley. 'But its eyes can register images. Foaly may think to check. That infernal centaur.'

'Don't fret, miss,' said Scant, folding the trolley's false bottom over his mistress. 'Very soon now, that will be the least of Foaly's worries.'

Opal strapped the oxygen mask across her face. 'Later,' she said, her voice muffled by the plastic. 'Talk, later.'

Koboi drifted into a natural sleep, exhausted by even this small exertion. It could be hours before the pixie regained sustained consciousness. After a coma of that length, there was even the risk that Opal would never be quite as smart as she once was.

'Time?' said Merv.

Scant glanced at his moonometer. 'Thirty seconds left.'

Merv finished cinching the straps exactly how they had been. Pausing only to dab sweat from his brow, he made a second incision with his scalpel, this time in the clone's arm, and inserted the seeker-sleeper. While Scant sealed the cut with a blast of magical sparks, Merv rearranged the cleaning paraphernalia over the trolley's false section.

Scant bobbed impatiently. 'Eight seconds, seven. By the gods, this is the last time I break the boss out of a clinic and replace her with a clone.'

Merv spun the trolley on its castors, pushing it through the open doorway.

'Five . . . four . . .'

Scant did one last check around, running his eyeballs across everything they had touched.

'Three . . . two . . .'

They were out, pulling the door behind them.

'One . . .'

Corporal Grub slumped slightly, then jerked to attention.

'Hey . . . what the —? I'm really thirsty! Is anyone else thirsty?'

Merv stuffed the night-vision goggles into the trolley, blinking a bead of sweat from his eyelid. 'It's the air in here. I get dehydrated all the time. Terrible headaches.'

Grub pinched the bridge of his nose. 'Me too. I'm going to write a letter, as soon as the lights come back.'

Just then the lights did come back, flickering on, one after another, down the length of the corridor.

'There we go,' grinned Scant. 'Panic over. Maybe now they'll buy us some new circuits, eh, brother?'

Doctor Argon came barrelling down the passageway, almost keeping pace with the flickering lights.

'Your leg is better then, Jerry?' said Merv.

Argon ignored the pixies, his eyes wide, his breath ragged.

'Corporal Kelp,' he panted. 'Koboi, is she? Has she . . .'

Grub rolled his eyes. 'Calm yourself, Doctor. Miss

Koboi is still suspended where you left her. Take a look.'

Argon flattened his palms against the wall, first checking the vitals.

'OK, no change. No change. A two-minute lapse, but that's OK.'

'I told you,' said Grub. 'And while you're here, I need to talk to you about these headaches I've been having.'

Argon brushed him aside. 'I need a cotton bud. Scant, do you have any?'

Scant slapped his pockets. 'Sorry, Jerry. Not on me.'

'Don't call me Jerry!' howled Jerbal Argon, ripping the lid from the cleaning trolley. 'There must be cotton buds in here somewhere,' he said, sweat pasting thin hair across a wide gnome's forehead. 'It's a janitor's box, for heaven's sake.' His blunt finger scrabbled through the trolley's contents, scraping across the false bottom.

Merv elbowed him out of the way before he could discover the secret compartment or spy screens. 'Here we are, Doctor,' he said, grabbing a tub of buds. 'A month's supply. Knock yourself out.'

Argon fumbled a single bud from the pack, discarding the rest.

'DNA never lies,' he muttered, punching his code into the keypad. 'DNA never lies.'

He rushed into the room, roughly swabbing the inside of the clone's mouth. The Brill brothers held their breath. They had expected to be out of the clinic before this happened. Argon rolled the cotton bud's tip across the sponge pad on his clipboard. A moment later, Opal Koboi's name flashed on to the board's mini-plasma screen.

Argon heaved a massive sigh, resting his hands on both knees. He threw the observers a shamefaced grin. 'Sorry. I panicked. If we lost Koboi, the clinic would never live it down. I'm just a little paranoid, I suppose. Faces can be altered, but . . .'

'DNA never lies,' said Merv and Scant simultaneously.

Grub reset his video goggles. 'I think Doctor Argon needs a little vacation.'

'You're telling me,' sniggered Merv, rolling the trolley towards the maintenance lift. 'Anyway, we better get going, brother. We need to isolate the cause of the power failure.'

Scant followed him down the corridor. 'Any idea where the problem could be?'

'I have a hunch. Let's try the parking lot, or maybe the basement.'

'Whatever you say. After all, you are the older brother.'

'And wiser,' added Merv. 'Don't forget that.'

The pixies continued down the corridor, their brisk banter masking the fact that their knees were shaking and their hearts were battering their ribcages. It wasn't until they had removed the evidence of their acid bombs and were well on their way home in the van that they began to breathe normally again.

Merv unzipped Koboi from her sealed hiding place back in the apartment he shared with Scant. Any worries they'd had about Opal's IQ taking a dip were immediately banished. Their employer's eyes were bright and aware.

'Bring me up to speed,' she said, climbing shakily from the trolley. Even though her mind was fully functioning, it would take a couple of days in an electro-massager to get her muscles back to normal.

Merv helped her on to a low sofa. 'Everything is in place. The funds, the surgeon, everything.'

Opal drank greedily, straight from a jug of core water on the coffee table. 'Good, good. And what of my enemies?'

Scant stood beside his brother. They were almost identical, except for a slight wideness in Merv's brow. He had always been the smart one.

'We have kept tabs on them, as you asked.'

Opal stopped drinking. 'Asked?'

'Instructed,' stammered Scant. 'Instructed, of course. That's what I meant.'

Koboi's eyes narrowed. 'I do hope the Brill brothers haven't developed any independent notions since I've been asleep.'

Scant stooped slightly, almost bowing. 'No, no, Miss Koboi. We live to serve. Only to serve.'

'Yes,' agreed Opal. 'And you live only as long as you *do* serve. Now, my enemies. They are well and happy, I trust.'

'Oh yes. Julius Root goes from strength to strength as LEP Commander. He has been nominated for the Council.'

Opal smiled, a vicious wolverine's smile. 'The Council. Such a long way to fall. And Holly Short?'

'Back on full active duty. Six successful reconnaissance missions since you induced your coma. Her name has been put on the list for promotion to major.'

'Major, indeed. Well, the least we can do is to make sure that promotion never comes through. I plan to wreck Holly Short's career, so she dies in disgrace.'

'The centaur Foaly is as obnoxious as ever,' continued Scant Brill. 'I suggest a particularly nasty . . .'

Opal raised a delicate finger, cutting him off. 'No. Nothing happens to Foaly just yet. He will be defeated by intellect alone. Twice in my life someone has outsmarted me. Both times it was Foaly. Just killing him requires no ingenuity. I want him beaten, humiliated and alone.' She clapped her hands in delighted anticipation. 'And then I will kill him.'

'We have been monitoring Artemis Fowl's communications. Apparently the human youth has spent most of the past year trying to find a certain painting. We have traced the painting to Munich.'

'A painting? Really?' Cogs turned in Opal's brain. 'Well, let's make sure we get to it before he does. Maybe we can add a little something to his work of art.'

Scant nodded. 'Yes. That's not a problem. I'll go tonight.'

Opal stretched out on the sofa like a cat in the sunlight. 'Good. This is turning out to be a lovely day. Now, send for the surgeon.'

The Brill brothers glanced at each other.

'Miss Koboi?' said Mervall nervously.

'Yes, what is it?'

'The surgeon. This kind of operation cannot be reversed, even by magic. Are you sure you wouldn't like to think –'

Opal leaped from the sofa. Her cheeks were crimson with rage.

'Think! You'd like me to think about it! What do you imagine I have been doing for the past year? Thinking! Twenty-four hours a day. I don't care about magic. Magic did not help me to escape, science did. Science will be my magic. Now, no more advice, Merv, or your brother will be an only child. Is that clear?'

Merv was stunned. He had never seen Opal in such a rage. The coma had changed her.

'Yes, Miss Koboi.'

'Now, summon the surgeon.'

'At once, Miss Koboi.'

Opal lay back on the sofa. Soon everything would be right in the world. Her enemies would shortly be dead or discredited. Once those loose ends were tied up, she could get on with her new life. Koboi rubbed the tips of her pointed ears. *What would she look like*, she wondered, *as a human?*

CHAPTER 2: THE FAIRY THIEF

 THIEVES have their own folklore. Stories of ingenious heists and death-defying robberies. One such legend tells of the Egyptian cat burglar, Faisil Mahmood, who scaled the dome of St Peter's basilica in order to drop in on a visiting bishop and steal his crozier.

Another story concerns confidence woman Red Mary Keneally, who dressed as a duchess and talked her way into the King of England's coronation. The palace denied the event ever took place, but every now and then a crown turns up at auction that looks very like the one in the Tower of London.

Perhaps the most thrilling legend is the tale of the lost Hervé masterpiece. Every primary-school child knows that Pascal Hervé was the French Impressionist who painted extraordinarily beautiful pictures of the fairy folk. And every art dealer knows that Hervé's paintings are second in value only to those of Van Gogh himself, commanding price tags of over 50 million euro.

There are fifteen paintings in the Hervé Fairy Folk series. Ten can be found in French museums and five are in private collections. But there are rumours of a sixteenth. Whispers circulate in the upper criminal echelons that another Hervé exists: *The Fairy Thief*, depicting a fairy in the act of stealing a human child. Legend has it that Hervé gave the picture as a gift to a beautiful Turkish girl he met on the Champs Élysées.

The girl promptly broke Hervé's heart, and sold the picture to a British tourist for twenty francs. Within weeks, the picture had been stolen from the Englishman's home. And since that time, it has been lifted from private collections all over the world. Since Hervé painted his masterpiece, it is believed that *The Fairy Thief* has been stolen fifteen times. But what makes these thefts different from the billion others that have been committed during this time is that the first thief decided to keep the picture for himself. And so did all the others.

The Fairy Thief has become something of a trophy for top thieves worldwide. Only a dozen know of its existence, and only a handful know of its whereabouts. The painting is to criminals what the Turner Prize is to artists. Whoever manages to successfully steal the lost painting is acknowledged as the master thief of his generation. Not many are aware of this challenge, but those who do know matter.

Naturally Artemis Fowl knew of *The Fairy Thief*, and recently he had learned of the painting's whereabouts. It was an irresistible test of his abilities. If he succeeded in stealing the lost masterpiece, he would become the youngest thief in history to have done so.

His bodyguard, the giant Eurasian Butler, was not best pleased with his young charge's latest project.

'I don't like this, Artemis,' said Butler in his bass gravelly tones. 'My instincts tell me it's a trap.'

Artemis Fowl inserted batteries in his hand-held computer game.

'Of course it's a trap,' said the fourteen-year-old Irish boy. '*The Fairy Thief* has been ensnaring thieves for years. That's what makes it interesting.'

They were travelling around Munich's Marienplatz in a rented Hummer H2. The military vehicle was not Artemis's style, but it would be consistent with the style of the people they were pretending to be. Artemis sat in the rear, feeling ridiculous, dressed not in his usual dark two-piece suit, but in normal teenager clothing.

'This outfit is preposterous,' he said, zipping his tracksuit top. 'What is the point of a hood that is not waterproof? And all these logos? I feel like a walking advertisement. And these *jeans* do not fit properly. They are sagging down to my knees.'

Butler smiled, glancing in the rear-view mirror. 'I think you look fine. Juliet would say that you were *bad*.'

Juliet, Butler's younger sister, was currently on a tour of the States with a Mexican wrestling troupe, trying to break into the big time. Her ring name was 'The Jade Princess'.

'I certainly feel *bad*,' admitted Artemis. 'As for these high-top trainers. How is one supposed to run quickly with soles ten centimetres thick? I feel as though I am on stilts. Honestly, Butler, the second we return to the hotel, I am disposing of this outfit. I miss my suits.'

Butler pulled on to Im Tal, where the International Bank was located.

'Artemis, if you're not feeling comfortable, perhaps we should postpone this operation?'

Artemis zipped the computer game into a backpack, which already contained a number of typical teenage items.

'Absolutely not. This window of opportunity has taken a month to organize.'

Three weeks previously, Artemis had made an anonymous donation to the St Bartleby's School for Young Gentlemen, on condition that the Third Year boys were taken on a trip to Munich for the European Schools' Fair. The principal had been happy to honour the donor's wishes. And now, while the other boys were viewing various technological marvels at an exhibition in Munich's Olympia Stadion, Artemis was on his way to the International Bank. As far as Guiney, the school's principal, was concerned, Butler was driving a poorly student back to his hotel room.

'Crane and Sparrow probably moves the painting several times a year. I certainly would. Who knows where it will be in six months?'

Crane & Sparrow was a firm of British lawyers who used their business as a front for an extremely successful burglary and fencing enterprise. Artemis had long suspected them of possessing *The Fairy Thief*. Confirmation had arrived a month earlier when a private detective, who was routinely employed to spy on Crane & Sparrow, reported that he had spotted them moving a painting tube to the International Bank. Possibly *The Fairy Thief*.

'I may not have this chance again until I am an adult,' continued the Irish youth. 'And there is no question of waiting that long. Franz Herman stole *The Fairy Thief* when he was eighteen years old. I need to beat that record.'

Butler sighed. 'Criminal folklore tells us that Herman stole the painting in 1927. He merely snatched a briefcase. There is rather more to contend with today. We must break open a safety deposit box in one of the world's most secure banks, in broad daylight.'

Artemis Fowl smiled. 'Yes. Many would say that it was impossible.'

'They would,' agreed Butler, slotting the Hummer into a parking space. 'Many sane people. Especially for someone on a school tour.'

They entered the bank through the lobby's revolving doors in full view of the CCTV. Butler led the way, striding purposefully across the gold-veined marble floor towards an enquiries desk. Artemis trailed behind, bobbing his head to some music on his portable disc player. In fact the disc player was empty. Artemis wore mirrored sunglasses that concealed his eyes but allowed him to scan the bank's interior unobserved.

The International Bank was famous in certain circles for having the most secure safety deposit boxes in the world, including Switzerland. It was rumoured that if the International Bank's deposit boxes were cracked open and the contents dumped on to the floor, perhaps one-tenth of the world's wealth would be heaped on the marble – jewels, bearer bonds, cash, deeds, art – at least half of it stolen from its rightful owners. But Artemis was not interested in any of these objects. Perhaps next time.

Butler stopped at the enquiries desk, casting a broad shadow across the slim-line monitor perched there. The thin man who had been working on the monitor lifted his head to complain, then thought better of it. Butler's sheer bulk often had that effect on people.

'How can I help you, Herr . . . ?'

'Lee. Colonel Xavier Lee. I wish to open my deposit box,' replied Butler in fluent German.

'Yes, Colonel. Of course. My name is Bertholt, and I will be assisting you today.' Bertholt opened Colonel Xavier Lee's file on his computer with one hand; the other was twirling a pencil like a mini-baton. 'We just need to complete the usual security check. If I may have your passport?'

'Of course,' said Butler, sliding a People's Republic of China passport across the desk. 'I expect nothing less than the most stringent security procedures.'

Bertholt took the passport in slim fingers, first checking the photograph, then placing it on a scanner.

'Alfonse,' snapped Butler at Artemis, 'stop fidgeting and stand up straight, son. You slouch so much that sometimes I think you don't have a spine.'

Bertholt smiled with an insincerity a toddler could have seen through.

'Alfonse, nice to meet you.'

'Dude,' said Artemis, with equal hypocrisy.

Butler shook his head. 'My son does not communicate well with the rest of the world. I look forward to the day he can join the army. Then we shall see if there is a man beneath all these moods.'

⊙ ⟩♌♈ · ⊞⬚ · ♌⊞⬚⟩ · ⦵⊖⚡ · ♌ ⊙ ·

Bertholt nodded sympathetically. 'I have a girl. Sixteen years old. She spends more on phone calls in a week than the entire family spends on food.'

'Teenagers, they're all the same.'

The computer beeped.

'Ah yes, your passport has been cleared. Now all I need is a signature.' Bertholt slid a handwriting tablet across the desk. A digi-pen was attached to the tablet by a length of wire. Butler took it, scrawling his signature across the line. The signature would match. Of course it would. The original writing was Butler's own, Colonel Xavier Lee being one of a dozen aliases the bodyguard had created over the years. The passport was also authentic, even if the details typed upon it weren't. Butler had purchased it years previously from a Chinese diplomat's secretary in Rio de Janeiro.

Once again the computer beeped.

'Good,' said Bertholt. 'You are indeed who you say you are. I shall bring you to the deposit box room. Will Alfonse be accompanying us?'

Butler stood. 'Absolutely. If I leave him here, he will probably get himself arrested.'

Bertholt attempted a joke. 'Well, if I may say so, Colonel, he's in the right place.'

'Hilarious, dude,' muttered Artemis. 'You should, like, have your own show.'

But Bertholt's comment was accurate. Armed security

men were dotted throughout the building. At the first sign of any impropriety, they would move to strategic points, covering all exits.

Bertholt led the way to a brushed-steel lift, holding his ID card up to a camera over the door.

The bank official winked at Artemis. 'We have a special security system here, young man. It's all very exciting.'

'I know. I think I'm going to faint,' said Artemis.

'No more attitude, son,' scolded Butler. 'Bertholt is simply trying to make conversation.'

Bertholt stayed civil in the face of Artemis's sarcasm. 'Maybe you'd like to work here when you grow up, eh, Alfonse?'

For the first time Artemis smiled sincerely, and for some reason the sight sent shivers down Bertholt's spine. 'Do you know something, Bertholt? I think some of my best work will be in banks.'

The awkward silence that followed was cut short by a voice from a tiny speaker below the camera.

'Yes, Bertholt, we see you. How many?'

'Two,' replied Bertholt. 'One key holder and one minor. Coming down to open a box.'

The lift door slid back to reveal a steel cuboid with no buttons or panels, just a camera elevated in one corner. They stepped inside and the lift was remotely activated. Artemis noticed Bertholt wringing his hands as soon as they began to descend.

'Hey, Bertholt? What's the problem? It's only a lift.'

Bertholt forced a smile. Barely a glint of tooth showed beneath his moustache. 'You don't miss much, do you, Alfonse? I don't like small spaces. And there are no controls in here, for security reasons. The lift is operated from the desk. If it were to break down, we would be relying on the guards to rescue us. This thing is virtually airtight. What if the guard had a heart attack, or went on a coffee break? We could all —'

The bank official's nervous rant was cut off by the hiss of the lift door. They had arrived at the deposit box floor.

'Here we are,' said Bertholt, mopping his forehead with a paper tissue. A section of the paper remained trapped in the worry lines of his forehead, and fluttered there like a windsock in the blast from the air conditioner. 'Safe, you see. Absolutely no need to worry. All is well.' He laughed nervously. 'Shall we?'

A bulky security guard was waiting for them outside the lift. Artemis noted the sidearm on his belt, and the earpiece cord winding along his neck.

'*Willkommen*, Bertholt, you made it in one piece. Again.'

Bertholt plucked the strand of tissue from his forehead. 'Yes, Kurt, I made it, and don't think the scorn in your voice goes unnoticed.'

Kurt sighed mightily, allowing the escaping air to flap his lips. 'Please pardon my phobic countryman,' he said to Butler. 'Everything terrifies him, from spiders to lifts. It's a wonder he ever gets out of bed. Now, if you could stand on the yellow square and raise both arms to shoulder level.'

There was a yellow square taped to the steel floor. Butler stepped on it, raising his arms. Kurt performed a body search that would have shamed a customs official, before ushering him through a metal-detector arch.

'He's clean,' he said aloud. The words would be picked up by the microphone on his lapel and relayed to the security booth.

'You next, boy,' said Kurt. 'Same drill.'

Artemis complied, slouching on to the square. He barely raised his arms from his sides.

Butler glared at him. 'Alfonse! Can't you do what the man says? In the army I would have you cleaning the latrines for this kind of behaviour.'

Artemis glared back. 'Yes, *Colonel*, but we're not in the army here, are we?'

Kurt slipped Artemis's pack from his back, rifling through the contents.

'What's this?' he asked, pulling out a toughened plastic frame.

Artemis took the frame, unfolding it with three deft movements. 'It's a scooter, dude. You may have heard of them. Transportation that doesn't pollute the air we breathe.'

Kurt snatched back the scooter, spinning the wheels and checking the joints.

Artemis smirked. 'Of course it's also a laser cutter, so I can break into your boxes.'

'You're a real smart alec, boy,' snarled Kurt, stuffing the scooter back in the bag. 'And what's this?'

Artemis turned on the video game. 'It's a game box. They were invented so teenagers wouldn't have to talk to grown-ups.'

Kurt glanced at Butler. 'He's a gem, sir. I wish I had one just like him.' He rattled a ring of keys on Artemis's belt. 'And what are these?'

Artemis scratched his head. 'Uh . . . keys?'

Kurt ground his teeth audibly. 'I know they're keys, boy. What do they open?'

Artemis shrugged. 'Stuff. My locker. My scooter lock. A couple of diaries. Stuff.'

The security guard examined the keys. They were everyday keys, and wouldn't open a complicated lock. But the bank had a no-key rule. Only safety deposit box keys were allowed through the metal detector.

'Sorry. The keys stay here.' Kurt unclipped the ring, placing the keys on a flat tray. 'You can pick them up on your way out.'

'Can I go now?'

'Yes,' said Kurt. 'Please do, but pass the bag through to your father first.'

Artemis handed the bag round the metal-detector arch to Butler. He passed through himself, setting off the buzzer.

Kurt followed him impatiently. 'Do you have anything else metallic on you? A belt buckle? Some coins?'

'Money?' scoffed Artemis. 'I wish.'

'What's setting off the detector, then?' said Kurt, puzzled.

'I think I know,' said Artemis. He hooked a finger inside his top lip, pulling it up. Two metal bands ran across his teeth.

'A brace. That would do it,' said Kurt. 'The detector is extremely sensitive.'

Artemis removed his finger. 'Should I take this out too? Rip it from my teeth?'

Kurt took the suggestion at face value. 'No. I think we're safe enough. Just go on through. But behave yourself in there. It's a vault, not a playground.' Kurt paused, pointing to a camera above their heads. 'Remember, I'll be watching.'

'Watch all you like,' said Artemis brazenly.

'Oh, I will, boy. You so much as spit on one of those doors, and I'll eject you from the premises. Forcibly.'

'Oh, for heaven's sake, Kurt,' said Bertholt. 'Don't be so theatrical. Those are not network television cameras, you know.'

Bertholt ushered them through to the vault door.

'I apologize for Kurt. He failed the special-forces exam and ended up here. Sometimes I think he would love someone to rob the place, just so he could see some action.'

The door was a circular slab of steel, at least five metres in diameter. In spite of its size, it swung easily at Bertholt's touch.

'Perfectly balanced,' explained the bank official. 'A child could open it, until five thirty, when it shuts for the night. Naturally the vault is time locked. Nobody can open the door until eight thirty a.m. Not even the bank president.'

Beyond the vault door were rows and rows of steel deposit boxes of all shapes and sizes. Each box had a single rectangular keyhole on its face, surrounded by a fibre-optic light. At the moment all the lights glowed red.

Bertholt took a key from his pocket; it was attached to his belt by a woven-steel cable.

'Of course the keys' shape is not the only important thing,' he said, inserting the key in a master keyhole. 'The locks are also operated by microchip.'

Butler took a similar key from his wallet. 'Are we ready?'

'Whenever you are, sir.'

Butler ran his fingers over several boxes until he reached number seven hundred. He inserted his key in the keyhole. 'Ready.'

⟊⟁⟐⟒⟐ ⟐⟐ ⟐⟒⟐⟐⟐ ⟐ ⟐⟐⟐⟐⟐⟐

'Very well, sir. On my mark. Three, two, one. Turn.'

Both men turned their keys simultaneously. The master key safeguard prevented a thief opening a box with a single key. If the two keys were not turned within one second of each other, the box would not open.

The light round both keys switched from red to green. The door on Butler's safety deposit box popped open.

'Thank you, Bertholt,' said Butler, reaching into the box.

'Of course, sir,' replied Bertholt, almost bowing. 'I'll be right outside. Even with the camera, there is a three-minute inspection rule. So I'll see you in one hundred and eighty seconds.'

Once the bank official had gone, Artemis shot his bodyguard a quizzical look.

'Alfonse?' he said out of the side of his mouth. 'I don't remember deciding on a name for my character.'

Butler set the stopwatch on his chronograph. 'I was improvising, Artemis. I thought the situation required it. And if I may say so, you make a very convincing obnoxious teenager.'

'Thank you, old friend. I try.'

Butler removed an architect's drawing from his deposit box, folding out the document until it was almost two metres square. He held it at arm's length, apparently studying the design inked on to the paper.

Artemis glanced upwards at the ceiling-mounted

camera. 'Raise your arms another five centimetres, and take a step to your left.'

Butler did so casually, covering the movements with a cough and a shake of the parchment.

'Good. Perfect. Stay right there.'

When Butler had rented the box on his last visit, he'd taken numerous photographs of the vault with a button camera. Artemis used these photos to render a digital reconstruction of the room. According to his calculations, Butler's present position provided him with a ten-square-metre box of cover. In that area his movements would be hidden by the drawing. At the moment, only his trainers could be seen by the security guards.

Artemis rested his back against a wall of security boxes, between two steel benches. He braced both arms against the benches, levering himself out of the oversized trainers. Carefully, the boy slid on to a bench.

'Keep your head down,' advised Butler.

Artemis rooted through his backpack for the video cube. Though the box did actually play a computer game, its primary function was as an X-ray panel with real-time viewing. The X-ray panels were in common usage among the criminal upper echelons, and it had been a relatively simple matter for Artemis to disguise one as a teenager's toy.

Artemis activated the X-ray, sliding it across the door of the deposit box beside Butler's. The bodyguard had rented his box two days after Crane & Sparrow. It stood to reason that the boxes would be close to one another, unless Crane & Sparrow had requested a specific number. In that case it was back to the drawing board. Artemis reckoned that this first attempt to steal *The Fairy Thief* had a forty per cent chance of success. These were not ideal odds, but he had no option but to go ahead. At the very least, he would learn more about the bank's security.

The game cube's small screen revealed that the first box was stuffed with currency.

'Negative,' said Artemis. 'Cash only.'

Butler raised an eyebrow. 'You know what they say, you can never have too much cash.'

Artemis had already moved on to the next box. 'Not today, old friend. But let's keep up the rental on our box, in case we ever need to return.'

The next box contained legal papers tied together with ribbons. The one after that was piled high with loose diamonds in a tray. Artemis struck gold on the fourth box. Figuratively speaking. Inside the deposit box was a long tube containing a rolled-up canvas.

'I think we have it, Butler. I think this could be it.'

'Time enough to get excited when the painting is hanging on the wall in Fowl Manor. Hurry up, Artemis, my arms are beginning to ache.'

Artemis steadied himself. Of course Butler was right. They were still a long way from possessing *The Fairy Thief*, if indeed this painting was Hervé's lost masterpiece. It could just as easily be some proud grandfather's crayon drawing of a helicopter.

Artemis moved the X-ray machine down to the bottom of the box. There were no manufacturer's markings on the door, but often craftsmen were proud and could not resist placing a signature somewhere, even if nobody but them knew it was there. Artemis searched for maybe twenty seconds before he found what he was looking for. Inside the door itself, on the rear panel, was engraved the word 'Blokken'.

'Blokken,' said the boy triumphantly. 'We were right.'

There were only six firms in the world capable of constructing deposit boxes of this quality. Artemis had hacked their computers and found International Bank on the Blokken client list. Blokken was a small family company in Vienna that also made boxes for several banks in Geneva and the Cayman Islands. Butler had paid their workshop a little visit and stolen two master keys. Of course the keys were of metal and would not escape the detector arch, unless for some reason metal had been allowed through.

Artemis reached two fingers into his mouth, dislodging the brace from his upper teeth. Behind the brace itself was a plastic retainer, and clipped to that were two keys. The master keys.

Artemis rotated his jaw for a few seconds.

'That feels better,' he said. 'I thought I was going to gag.'

The next problem was one of distance. There were over two metres between the deposit box and the master keyhole by the door. Not only was it impossible for one person to open the door unassisted, but whoever stood by the master keyhole would be visible to the security guards.

Artemis pulled his scooter from the backpack. He yanked one pin from its socket, detaching the steering column from the footpad. This was no ordinary scooter. An engineer friend of Butler's had constructed it from very specific blueprints. The footpad was completely regular, but the steering column telescoped at the touch of a spring-release button. Artemis unscrewed one hand-grip, reattaching it at the other end of the column. There was a slit in the end of each grip, into which Artemis screwed a master key. Now all he had to do was insert both keys into their corresponding keyholes, and turn them simultaneously.

Artemis slotted one key into Crane & Sparrow's box.

'Ready?' he asked Butler.

'Yes,' replied his bodyguard. 'Don't go one step further than you have to.'

'Three, two, one. Go.'

Artemis pressed the spring-release button on the steering column. He shuffled across the bench, pulling the telescoping pole behind him. As the boy moved, Butler swivelled his trunk so that Artemis remained shielded by the blueprint. He moved the plan just far enough to cover the master keyhole, without exposing Artemis's legless boots. However, the target box, complete with tele-scoping pole, was visible for the time it took Artemis to insert the second key.

The master keyhole was nearly a metre beyond the end of the steel bench. Artemis leaned as far as he could without losing his balance, slotting the key into its hole. It fitted snugly. Artemis shuffled back quickly. Now Butler could once again mask Crane & Sparrow's box. The entire plan hinged on the assumption that the guards would be concentrating on Butler and would not notice a slim pole extending towards the master keyhole. It would help that the pole was precisely the same colour as the deposit boxes.

Artemis returned to the original box, twisting the hand-grip. A pulley-and-cable system inside the pole twisted the other handgrip simultaneously. Both locks flashed green. Crane & Sparrow's box popped open. Artemis felt a moment of satisfaction. His contraption had worked. Then again, there was no reason why it shouldn't; all the laws of physics had been obeyed. Amazing how the tightest of electronic security could be defeated by a pole, a pulley and a brace.

'Artemis,' groaned Butler, 'keeping my arms up is becoming uncomfortable. So, if you wouldn't mind.'

Artemis cut short his mental celebration. They were not out of the vault yet. He turned the grips back to their original position, then yanked the bar towards him. Both keys popped from their holes. With the touch of a button, the pole snapped back to its original length. Artemis did not reassemble the scooter just yet. The pole might be needed to search other boxes.

Artemis studied the locker through the X-ray panel before opening the door any wider. He was searching for any wires or circuits that could trigger secondary alarms. There was one, a circuit-breaker attached to a portable klaxon. It would be extremely embarrassing for any thief if the authorities were alerted by the raucous wailing of a foghorn. Artemis smiled. It seemed as though Crane & Sparrow had a sense of humour. Maybe he would employ them as his lawyers.

Artemis unhooked the headphones from around his neck, popping off the earpieces. Once the wire inside was exposed, he twisted a length around each side of the breaker. Now he could safely pull the breaker apart without opening the circuit. Artemis pulled. The klaxon remained silent.

At last the box lay open before him. Inside, a single tube stood propped against the rear wall. The tube was fashioned from perspex and contained a rolled-up canvas. Artemis removed the tube, holding it up to the light. For several seconds he studied the painting through the transparent plastic. He could not risk opening the tube until they were safely back in the hotel. A hasty job now could cause accidental damage to the painting. He had waited years to obtain *The Fairy Thief*, and he could wait a few more hours.

'The brushwork is unmistakable,' he said, closing the box. 'Strong strokes. Thick blocks of light. It's either Hervé or a brilliant copy. I do believe we've done it, Butler, but I can't be sure without X-ray and paint analysis.'

'Good,' said the bodyguard, glancing at his watch. 'That can be done at the hotel. Pack up and let's get out of here.'

Artemis shoved the cylinder into his backpack, along with the reassembled scooter. He clipped the keys to his retainer and slotted the brace over his teeth.

The vault door slid open just as the Irish youth lowered himself into his trainers. Bertholt's head appeared in the gap.

'Everything all right in here?' asked the bank official.

Butler folded the blueprint and slotted it into his pocket.

'Fine, Bertholt. Excellent, in fact. You may escort us to the main level.'

Bertholt bowed slightly. 'Of course, follow me.'

Artemis was back in the role of argumentative teenager. 'Thanks so much, Berty. This has been a real blast. I just love spending my holidays in banks, looking at papers.'

All credit to Bertholt. His smile never wavered.

Kurt was waiting for them by the X-ray arch, his arms folded across a chest the size of a rhino's. He waited until Butler had gone past, then tapped Artemis's shoulder.

'You think you're really smart, don't you, boy?' he said, grinning.

Artemis grinned back. 'Compared to you? Definitely.'

Kurt bent over, hands on knees, until his eyes were level with Artemis's. 'I was watching you from the security booth. You didn't do a thing. Your kind never does.'

'How do you know?' asked Artemis. 'I could have been breaking into those safety deposit boxes.'

'I know all right. I know because I could see your feet the whole time. You barely moved an inch.'

Artemis grabbed his ring of keys from the tray, running after Butler to catch the lift. 'You win this time. But I'll be back.'

Kurt cupped a hand around his mouth. 'Bring it on,' he shouted. 'I'll be waiting.'

CHAPTER 3: NEARLY DEPARTED

 CAPTAIN Holly Short was up for a promotion. It was the career turnaround of the century. Less than a year had passed since she had been the subject of two Internal Affairs inquiries; but now, after six successful missions, Holly was the Lower Elements Police Reconnaissance squad's golden fairy. The Council would soon meet to decide whether or not she would be the first female major in LEPrecon's history. And to tell the truth, the prospect did not appeal to her one bit. Majors rarely got to strap on a set of wings and fly between land and stars. Instead they spent their time sending junior officers topside on missions. Holly had made up her mind to turn down the promotion if it were offered to her. She could live with a smaller pay cheque if it meant she could still see the surface on a regular basis.

Holly decided it would be wise to tell Commander Julius Root what she planned to do. After all, it was Root who had stood by her through the inquiries, and it was Root who had recommended her for promotion in the first place. The commander would not take the news well. He never took any kind of news well; even good news was received with a gruff 'Thank you' and a slammed door.

Holly stood outside Root's office on that morning, working up the courage to knock. And even though, at one metre exactly, she was just below the average fairy height, Holly was glad of the extra centimetre granted by her spiky auburn hair. Before she could knock, the door was yanked open and Root's rosy-cheeked face appeared in the doorway.

'Captain Short!' he roared, his buzz-cut grey hair quivering. 'Get in here!' Then he noticed Holly standing beside the door. 'Oh, there you are. Come in, we have a puzzle that needs solving. It involves one of our goblin friends.'

Holly followed Root into the office. Foaly, the LEP's technical adviser, was already there, close enough to the wall plasma screen to singe his nose hairs.

'Howler's Peak video,' explained Root. 'General Scalene escaped.'

'Escaped?' echoed Holly. 'Do we know how?'

Foaly snapped his fingers. 'D'Arvit! That's what we should be thinking about, instead of standing around here playing I Spy.'

'We don't have time for the usual sarcastic small talk, Foaly,' snapped Root, his complexion deepening to burgundy. 'This is a PR disaster. Scalene is public enemy number two, second only to Opal Koboi herself. If the journos get wind of this, we'll be the laughing stock of Haven. Not to mention the fact that Scalene could round up a few of his goblin buddies and reactivate the triad.'

Holly crossed to the screen, elbowing Foaly's hindquarters out of the way. Her little talk with Commander Root could wait. There was police work to be done. 'What are we looking at?'

Foaly highlighted a section of the screen with a laser pointer.

'Howler's Peak, goblin correctional facility. Camera eighty-six.'

'Which shows?'

'The visiting room. Scalene went in, but he never came out.'

Holly scanned the camera location list. 'No camera in the room itself?'

Root coughed, or it may have been an actual growl. 'No. According to the third Atlantis Convention on Fairy Rights, detainees are entitled to privacy in the visiting room.'

'So we don't know what went on in there?'

'Not as such, no.'

'What genius designed this system anyway?'

In spite of the seriousness of the situation, Root chuckled. He never could resist needling the smug centaur.

'Our horsy friend here designed Howler's Peak automated security system all on his own.'

Foaly pouted, and when a centaur pouts his bottom lip almost reaches his chin. 'It's not the system. The system is foolproof. Every prisoner has the standard subcutaneous seeker-sleeper in his head. Even if a goblin manages to miraculously escape, we can remotely knock him out, then pick him up.'

Holly raised her palms. 'So what's the problem?'

'The problem is that the seeker-sleeper is not broadcasting. Or, if it is, we're not picking up the signal.'

'That *is* a problem.'

Root lit a noxious fungal cigar. The smoke was instantly whipped away by an air recycler on his desk. 'Major Kelp is out with a mobile unit, trying to get a fix on a signal.'

Trouble Kelp had recently been promoted to Root's second in command. He was not the kind of officer who liked sitting behind a desk, unlike his little brother, Corporal Grub Kelp, who would have liked nothing better than to be stuck behind a nice safe desk for the remainder of his career. If Holly were forced into promotion, she hoped she could be half the major that Trouble was.

Holly returned her attention to the plasma screen. 'So, who was visiting General Scalene?'

'One of his thousand nephews. A goblin by the name of Boohn. Apparently that means "of noble brow" in Goblin cant.'

'I remember him,' said Holly. 'Boohn. Customs and Excise think he's one of the goblins behind the B'wa Kell smuggling operation. There's nothing noble about him.'

Foaly opened a folder on the plasma screen with his laser pointer.

'Here's the visitors' list. Boohn checks in at seven fifty, Lower Elements Mean Time. At least I can show you that on video.'

A grainy screen showed a bulky goblin in the prison's access corridor nervously licking his eyeballs, while the security laser scanned him. Once it was confirmed that Boohn wasn't trying to smuggle anything in, the visitors' door popped open.

Foaly scrolled down the list. 'And look here. He checks out at eight fifteen.'

Boohn left swiftly, obviously uncomfortable in the facility. The parking-lot camera showed him reverting to all fours for the dash to his car.

Holly scanned the list carefully. 'So you're saying that Boohn checked out at eight fifteen?'

'I just said that, didn't I, Holly?' replied Foaly testily. 'I'll say it again slowly. Eight fifteen.'

Holly snatched the laser pointer. 'Well, if that's true, how did he manage to check out again at eight twenty?'

It was true. Eight lines down on the list, Boohn's name popped up again.

'I saw that already. It's a glitch,' muttered Foaly, 'that's all. He couldn't leave twice. It's not possible. We get that sometimes, a bug, nothing more.'

'Unless it wasn't him the second time.'

The centaur folded his arms defensively. 'Don't you think I thought of that? Everyone who enters or leaves Howler's Peak is scanned a dozen times. We take at least eighty facial points of reference with each scan. If the computer says Boohn, then that's who it was. There's no way a goblin beat my system. They barely have enough brainpower to walk and talk at the same time.'

Holly used the pointer to review the entry video of Boohn. She enlarged his head, using a photo-manipulation program to sharpen the image.

'What are you looking for?' asked Root.

'I don't know, Commander. Something. Anything.'

It took a few minutes, but finally Holly got it. She knew immediately that she was right. Her intuition was buzzing like a swarm of bees at the base of her neck.

'Look here,' she said, enlarging Boohn's brow. 'A scale blister. This goblin is shedding.'

'So?' said Foaly grumpily.

Holly reopened Boohn's exit file. 'Now look. No blister.'

'So he burst the blister. Big deal.'

'No. It's more than that. Going in, Boohn's skin was almost grey. Now he's bright green. He even has a camouflage pattern on his back.'

Foaly snorted. 'A lot of good camouflage is in the city.'

'What's your point, Captain?' asked Root, stubbing out his cigar.

'Boohn shed his skin in the visitors' room. So where's the skin?'

There was silence for a long moment as the others absorbed the implications of this question.

'Would it work?' asked Root urgently.

Foaly was almost dumbstruck. 'By the gods, I think it would.'

The centaur pulled out a keyboard, his thick fingers flying across the Gnommish letters. A new video box appeared on the screen. In this box, another goblin was leaving the room. It looked a lot like Boohn. A lot, but not exactly. Something wasn't quite right. Foaly zoomed in on the goblin's head. At high magnification it was clear that the goblin's skin was ill-fitting. Patches were missing altogether, and the goblin seemed to be holding folds together across his waist.

'He did it. I can't believe it.'

'This was all planned,' said Holly. 'This was no opportunistic act. Boohn waits until he's shedding. Then he visits his uncle and they peel off his skin. General Scalene puts on the skin and just walks out the front door, fooling all your scanners on the way. When Boohn's name shows up again, you think it's a glitch. Simple, but completely ingenious.'

Foaly collapsed into a specially designed office chair. 'This is incredible. Can goblins do that?'

'Are you kidding?' said Root. 'A good goblin seamstress can peel a skin without a single tear. That's what they make their clothes from, when they bother wearing any.'

'I know that. I meant, could goblins think of this all on their own? I don't think so. We need to catch Scalene and find out who planned this.'

Foaly dialled a connection to the Koboi cam in the Argon Clinic. 'I'm going to check Opal Koboi is still under. This sort of thing is just her style.' A minute later, he swivelled to face Root. 'Nope. Still in dreamland. I don't know if that's good or bad. I'd hate to have Opal back in circulation, but at least we'd know what we were up against.'

A thought struck Holly, draining the blood from her face.

'You don't think it could be him, do you? It couldn't be Artemis Fowl?'

'Definitely not,' said Foaly. 'It's not the Mud Boy. Impossible.'

Root wasn't convinced. 'I wouldn't be throwing that word around so much if I were you. Holly, as soon as we catch Scalene, I want you to sign out a surveillance pack and spend a couple of days on the Mud Boy's trail. See what he's up to. Just in case.'

'Yes, sir.'

'And you, Foaly. I'm authorizing a surveillance upgrade. Whatever you need. I want to hear every call Artemis makes and read every letter he sends.'

'But, Julius. I supervised his mind wipe myself. It was a sweet job. I scooped out his fairy memories cleaner than a goblin sucking a snail out of its shell. If we were to turn up at Artemis's front door dancing the cancan, he still wouldn't remember us. It would take some kind of planted trigger to initiate even partial recall.'

Root did not appreciate being argued with. 'One, don't call me Julius. Two, do what I say, horsy boy, or I'll have your budget slashed. And three, what in Frond's name is the cancan?'

Foaly rolled his eyes. 'Forget it. I'll organize the upgrades.'

'Wise move,' said Root, plucking a vibrating phone from his belt. He listened for several seconds, grunting affirmatives into the speaker.

'Forget Fowl for the moment,' he said, closing the

phone. 'Trouble has located General Scalene. He's in E37. Holly, you're with me. Foaly, you follow us in the tech shuttle. Apparently the general wants to talk.'

Haven City was waking up for morning trade. Although to call it 'morning' was a bit misleading, as there was only artificial light this far underground. By human standards, Haven was barely more than a village, having fewer than ten thousand inhabitants. But in fairy terms, Haven was the largest metropolis since the original Atlantis, most of which lay buried beneath a three-storey shuttle dock in the new Atlantis.

Commander Root's LEP cruiser cut through the rush-hour traffic, its magnetic field automatically shunting other vehicles out of the way into slots on the slow lane. Root and Holly sat in the back, wishing the journey away. This situation was becoming stranger by the minute. First of all, Scalene escapes, and now his locater shows up and he wants to talk to Commander Root.

'What do you make of this?' asked Root eventually. One of the reasons he made such a fine commander was that he respected his officers' opinions.

'I don't know. It could be a trap. Whatever happens, you can't go in there alone.'

Root nodded. 'I know. Even I am not that stubborn. Anyway, Trouble will probably have the situation secured by the time I get there. He doesn't like waiting around for

62

the brass to arrive. Like someone else I know, eh, Holly?'

Holly half grinned, half grimaced. She had been reprimanded more than once for ignoring the order to wait for reinforcements.

Root raised the soundproof barrier between them and the driver.

'We need to talk, Holly. About the major thing.'

Holly looked her superior in the eyes. There was a touch of sadness in them.

'I didn't get it,' she blurted, unable to hide her relief.

'No. No, you *did* get it. Or you *will*. The official announcement is tomorrow. The first female major in Recon history. Quite an achievement.'

'But, Commander, I don't think that —'

Root silenced her with a wave of his finger. 'I want to tell you something, Holly. About my career. It's actually a metaphor for *your* career, so listen carefully and see if you can figure it out. Many years ago, when you were still wearing one-piece baby suits with padded backsides, I was a hotshot Recon jock. I loved the smell of fresh air. Every moment I spent in the moonlight was a golden moment.'

Holly had no trouble putting herself in the commander's shoes. She felt exactly the same way about her own surface trips.

'So I did my job as well as I could, a little bit too well as it happened. One day I went and got myself promoted.'

Root clamped a purifier globe around the end of a cigar

so that the smell would not stink up the car. It was a rare gesture.

'Major Julius Root. It was the last thing I wanted, so I marched into my commander's office and told him so. I'm a field fairy, I said. I don't want to sit behind a desk filling out e-forms. Believe it or not, I got quite agitated.'

Holly tried to look amazed, but couldn't pull it off. The commander spent most of his time in an agitated, red-faced state, which explained his nickname, 'Beetroot'.

'But my commander said something that changed my mind. Do you want to know what that was?'

Root ploughed on with his story without waiting for an answer.

'My commander said: "Julius, this promotion is not for you, it's for the People."' Root raised one eyebrow. 'Do you see what I'm getting at?'

Holly knew what he meant. It was the flaw in her argument.

Root placed a hand on her shoulder. 'The People need good officers, Holly. They need fairies like you to protect them from the Mud Men. Would I prefer to be zipping around under the stars with the wind in my nostrils? Yes. Would I do as much good? No.'

Root paused to suck deeply on his cigar, and the glow illuminated the purifier globe. 'You're a good Recon officer, Holly, one of the best I've seen. A bit impulsive at times, not much respect for authority, but an intuitive officer nonetheless. I wouldn't dream of taking you off the front lines if I didn't think you could serve the LEP better below ground. Do you understand?'

'Yes, Commander,' said Holly glumly. He was right, even if her selfish side wasn't ready to accept it just yet. At least she had the Fowl surveillance to look forward to, before her new job anchored her in the Lower Elements.

'There is a perk to being a major,' said Root. 'Sometimes, just to relieve the boredom, you can give yourself an assignment. Something on the surface. In Hawaii maybe, or New Zealand. Look at Trouble Kelp. He's a new breed of major, more hands-on. Maybe that's what the LEP needs.'

Holly knew that the commander was trying to soften the blow. As soon as the major's acorns were on her lapel, she wouldn't get above ground as much as she did now. If she was lucky.

'I'm putting my neck on the block here, Holly, recommending you for major. Your career so far has been eventful, to say the least. If you intend turning the promotion down, tell me now and I'll withdraw your name.'

Last chance, thought Holly. *Now or never.*

'No,' she said. 'I won't turn it down. How could I? Who knows when the next Artemis Fowl will turn up?'

In Holly's ears, her voice sounded distant, as though someone else was speaking. She imagined the bells of

lifelong boredom clanging behind her every word. A desk
job. She had a desk job.

Root patted her on the shoulder, his huge hand
knocking the air from her lungs.

'Cheer up, Captain. There *is* life below ground, you
know.'

'I know,' said Holly with an utter lack of conviction.

The police cruiser pulled in beside E37. Root opened
the car door and began to disembark, then stopped.

'If it makes any difference,' he said quietly, almost
awkwardly, 'I'm proud of you, Holly.' And he was gone,
out of the door and into the throng of LEP officers training
their weapons on the chute entrance.

It does make a difference, thought Holly, watching Root
instantly take command of the situation. *A big difference.*

The chutes were natural magma vents that stretched from
the Earth's core to the planet's surface. Most emerged
underwater, supplying warm streams that nurtured deep-
sea life, but some filtered their gases through the network
of cracks and fissures that riddled surface dry land. The
LEP used the power of magma flares to propel their
officers to the surface in titanium eggs. A more leisurely
shuttle trip could be taken in a dormant chute. E37
emerged in downtown Paris, and until recently had been
the chute used by goblins in their smuggling operations.
Closed to the public for many years, the chute's terminal

had fallen into disrepair. Currently, E37's only occupants were the members of a movie company that was making a TV film about the B'wa Kell rebellion. Holly was being portrayed by three-time AMP winner Skylar Peat, and Artemis Fowl was to be completely computer generated.

When Holly and Root arrived, Major Trouble Kelp had three squads of tactical LEP arranged around the terminal's entrance.

'Fill me in, Major,' ordered Root.

Kelp pointed to the entrance. 'We have one way in, and no way out. All the secondary entrances have long since subsided, so if Scalene is in there, he has to get through us to go home.'

'Are we sure he's there?'

'No,' admitted Major Kelp. 'We picked up his signal. But whoever helped him to escape could have sliced open his head and removed the transmitter. All we know for sure is that someone is playing games with us. I sent in a couple of my best Recon sprites, and they came back with this.' Trouble handed them a sound wafer. The wafers were the size of a thumbnail and were generally used to record short birthday greetings. This one was in the shape of a birthday cake. Root closed his fingers around the wafer. The heat from his hand would power its microcircuits.

A sibilant voice issued from the tiny speaker, made even more reptilian by the cheap wiring.

'Root,' said the voice, 'I would speak to you. I would tell you a great secret. Bring the female, Holly Short. Two only, no more. Any more, and many will die. My comrades will see to it . . .' The message ended with a traditional birthday jingle, its cheeriness at odds with the message.

Root scowled. 'Goblins. Drama queens, the lot of them.'

'It's a trap, Commander,' said Holly without hesitation. 'We were the ones at Koboi Labs a year ago. The goblins hold us responsible for the rebellion's failure. If we go in there, who knows what's waiting for us?'

Root nodded approvingly. 'Now you're thinking like a major. We're not expendable. So what are our options, Trouble?'

'If you don't go in, many will die. If you do, *you* might.'

'Not a nice set of options. Don't you have anything good to tell me?'

Trouble lowered his helmet's visor and consulted a mini-screen on the perspex. 'We managed to get the terminal's security scanners back on line and ran substance and thermal scans. We found a single heat source in the access tunnel, so Scalene is alone, if it's him. Whatever he's doing in there, he doesn't have any known form of weaponry or explosives. Just a few beetle bars and some good old H_2O.'

'Any magma flares due?' asked Holly.

Trouble ran his index finger along a pad on his left glove, scrolling down the screen on his visor. 'Nothing for a couple of months. That chute is intermittent. So Scalene is not planning to bake you.'

Root's cheeks glowed like two heating coils. 'D'Arvit!' he swore. 'I thought our goblin troubles were over. I'm tempted just to send in tactical and take a chance that Scalene is bluffing.'

'That would be my advice,' said Trouble. 'He doesn't have anything in there that could harm you. Give me five fairies, and we'll have Scalene in a wagon before he knows he's been arrested.'

'I take it the sleeper half of the seeker-sleeper is not working?' said Holly.

Trouble shrugged. 'We have to suppose it's not. The seeker-sleeper didn't function until now, and when we got here the wafer was left out for us. Scalene knew we were coming. He even left a message.'

Root punched his palm with a fist. 'I have to go in. There's no immediate danger inside, and we can't assume that Scalene hasn't come up with a way to carry out his threat. I don't have a choice, not really. I won't order you to come with me, Captain Short.'

Holly felt her stomach lurch, but she swallowed the fear. The commander was right. There was no other way. This was what being an LEP officer was all about. Protecting the People.

'You don't have to, Commander. I volunteer.'

'Good. Now, Trouble, let Foaly and his shuttle through the barricade. We may have to go in, but we don't have to go in unarmed.'

Foaly had more weaponry crammed into the back of a single shuttle than most human police forces had in their entire arsenal. Every centimetre of wall space had a power cable screwed into it or a rifle dangling from a hook. The centaur sat in the centre, fine-tuning a Neutrino handgun. He tossed it to Holly as she entered the van.

She caught it deftly. 'Hey, careful with that.'

Foaly snickered. 'Don't worry. The trigger hasn't been coded yet. Nobody can fire this weapon until its computer registers an owner. Even if this weapon did fall into goblin hands, it would be useless to them. One of my latest developments. After the B'wa Kell rebellion, I thought it was time to upgrade our security.'

Holly wrapped her fingers round the pistol's grip. A red scanner light ran the length of the plastic butt, then switched to green.

'That's it. You're the owner. From now on, that Neutrino 3000 is a one-female gun.'

Holly hefted the transparent gun in her fist. 'It's too light. I prefer the 2000.'

Foaly brought the gun's specifications up on a wall screen. 'It's light, but you'll get used to it. On the plus side, there are no metal parts. It's powered by kinetics, the motion of your body, with a back-up mini-nuke cell. Naturally, it's linked to a targeting system in your helmet. The casing is virtually impregnable and, if I do say so myself, it's a cool piece of hardware.'

Foaly passed a larger version of the gun to Root. 'Every shot is registered on the LEP computer, so we can tell who fired, when they fired and in what direction. That should save Internal Affairs a lot of computer time.' He winked at Holly. 'Something you'll be glad to hear.'

Holly leered back at the centaur. She was well known to IA. They had already conducted two inquiries into her professional conduct, and they would just love the opportunity to conduct a third. The one good thing about being promoted would be the looks on their faces when the commander pinned those major's acorns to her lapel.

Root holstered his weapon. 'OK. Now we can shoot. But what if we get shot?'

'You won't get shot,' insisted Foaly. 'I've hacked into the terminal scanners, and I've planted a couple of sensors of my own too. There's nothing in there that can harm you. Worst-case scenario, you trip over your own feet and get a sprained ankle.'

Root's complexion reddened all the way down his neck. 'Foaly, do I have to remind you that your sensors have been fooled before? In this very terminal, if I remember correctly.'

'OK, OK. Take it easy, Commander,' said Foaly under his breath. 'I haven't forgotten about last year. How could I, with Holly reminding me every five minutes?'

The centaur lifted two sealed suitcases on to a workbench. He keyed in a number sequence on their security pads, and popped the lids.

'These are the next-generation Recon suits. I was planning to unveil them at the LEP conference next month, but with a real live commander going into action, you'd better have them today.'

Holly pulled a jumpsuit from the case. It glittered briefly, then turned the colour of the van walls.

'The fabric is actually woven from cam foil, so you are virtually hidden all the time. It saves you using your magical shield,' explained Foaly. 'Of course the function can be turned off. The wings are built into this suit. A completely retractable whisper design, a brand new concept in wing construction. They take their power from a cell on your belt, and of course each wing is coated with mini-solars for above-ground flights. The suits also have their own pressure equalizers, so you can go directly from one environment to another without getting the bends.'

Root held the second suit in front of him. 'These must cost a fortune.'

Foaly nodded. 'You have no idea. Half of my research budget for last year went on developing these suits. They won't replace the old suit for five years at least. These two are the only operational models we have, so I would appreciate having them back. They are shockproof, fire-resistant, invisible to radar and relay a continuous stream of diagnostic information back to Police Plaza. The current LEP helmet sends us basic vitals data, but the new suit sends a second stream of information that can tell us if your arteries are blocked, diagnose fractured bones and even detect dry skin. It's a flying clinic. There's even a bullet-proof plate on the chest, in case a human shoots at you.'

Holly held the suit in front of a green plasma screen. The cam foil instantly turned emerald.

'I like it,' she said. 'Green is my colour.'

Trouble Kelp had commandeered some spotlights left on-site by the movie company, and he directed them into the shuttle port's lower level. The stark light picked out every floating speck of dust, giving the entire departures area an underwater feel. Commander Root and Captain Short edged into the room, weapons drawn and visors down.

'What do you think of the suit?' asked Holly, automatically keeping track of the various displays on the inside of her visor. LEP trainees often had difficulties developing the double focus needed to watch both the terrain and their helmet screens. This often resulted in an action known as 'filling the vase', which was how LEP officers referred to throwing up in one's helmet.

'Not bad,' replied Root. 'Light as a feather, and you wouldn't even know you were wearing wings. Don't tell Foaly I said that, his head is swelled enough as it is.'

'No need to tell me, Commander,' said Foaly's voice in his earpiece. The speakers were a new, gel-vibration variety, and it sounded as though the centaur were in the helmet with him. 'I'm with you every step of the way, from the safety of the shuttle, of course.'

'Of course,' said Root dourly.

The pair advanced cautiously past a line of check-in booths. Foaly had assured them that there was no possible danger in this area of the terminal, but the centaur had been wrong before. And mistakes in the field cost lives.

The film company had decided that the actual dirt in the terminal was not authentic enough, so they had sprayed piles of grey foam in various corners. They had even added a doll's head to one mound. A poignant touch, or so they thought. The walls and escalator were blackened with fake laser burns.

'Quite a shooting match,' said Root, grinning.

'Slightly exaggerated. I doubt if half a dozen shots were fired.'

They proceeded through the embarkation area into the docking zone. The original shuttle used by the goblins in their smuggling runs had been resurrected, and it lay in the docking bay. The shuttle had been painted gloss black to make it seem more menacing, and a goblinesque decorated prow had been added to its nose.

'How far?' said Root, into his mike.

'I'm transferring the thermal signature to your helmets,' replied Foaly.

Seconds later, a schematic appeared in their visors. The plan was slightly confusing as, in effect, they were looking down on themselves. There were three heat sources in the building. Two were close together, moving slowly towards the chute itself. Holly and the commander. The third figure was stationary in the access tunnel. Metres past the third figure, the thermo scan was whited out by the ambient heat from E37.

They reached the blast doors, two metres of solid steel that separated the access tunnel from the rest of the terminal. Shuttles and titanium eggs would glide in on a magnetized rail, to be dropped into the chute itself. The doors were sealed.

'Can you open these remotely, Foaly?'

'But of course, Commander. I have managed, quite ingeniously, to marry my operating system with the terminal's old computers. That wasn't as easy as it sounds –'

'I'll take your word for it,' said the commander, cutting Foaly off. 'Just push the button, before I come out there and push it with your face.'

'Some things never change,' muttered Foaly, pushing the button.

*

The access tunnel smelled like a blast furnace. Ancient swirls of melted ore hung from the roof and the ground underfoot was cracked and treacherous. Each footfall punctured a crust of soot, leaving a trail of deep foot-prints. There was another set of footprints – leading to the shadowy figure huddled on the ground, a short distance from the chute itself.

'There,' said Root.

'Got him,' said Holly, resting the bullseye of her laser sight on the figure's trunk.

'Keep him covered,' ordered the commander. 'I'm going down.'

Root advanced along the tunnel, keeping well out of Holly's line of fire. If Scalene did make a move, Holly would need a clear shot. But the general, if it were him, squatted immobile, his spine curled along the tunnel wall. His frame was covered by a full-length hooded cape.

The commander turned on his helmet PA so he could be heard above the howl of core wind.

'You there. Stand facing the wall. Place your hands on your head.'

The figure did not move. Holly had not expected it to. Root stepped closer, always cautious, knees bent, ready to dive to one side. He poked the figure's shoulder with his Neutrino 3000.

'On your feet, Scalene.'

The poke was sufficient to knock the figure sideways. The goblin keeled over, landing face up on the tunnel floor. Soot flakes fluttered around him like disturbed bats. The hood flopped to one side, revealing the figure's face, most importantly the eyes.

'It's him,' said Root. 'He's been mesmerized.'

The general's slitted eyes were bloodshot and vacant. This was a serious development, as it confirmed that somebody else had planned the escape, and Holly and Root had walked into a trap.

'I recommend we leave,' said Holly. 'Immediately.'

'No,' said Root, leaning over the goblin. 'Now that we're here, we might as well take Scalene back with us.'

He placed his free hand on the goblin's collar, preparing to haul him to his feet. Later, Holly would record in her report that it was at this precise moment that things began to go terribly wrong. What had been a routine — albeit strange — assignment suddenly became an altogether more sinister affair.

'Do not touch me, elf,' said a voice. A hissing, goblin voice. Scalene's voice. But how could that be? The general's lips had not moved.

Root reared back, then steadied himself. 'What's going on here?'

Holly's soldier's sense was buzzing at the base of her neck. 'Whatever it is, we won't like it. We should go, Commander, right now.'

⊗♁ɕ⋅ ♁ɕ⋅ ⊗☐⋅ ⚬δ♌◊⊙⋅ ⊗◗ββ

Root's features were thoughtful. 'That voice came from his chest.'

'Maybe he had surgery,' said Holly. 'Let's get out of here.'

The commander reached down, flipping Scalene's cape aside. There was a metal box strapped to the general's chest. The box was thirty centimetres square, with a small screen in the centre. There was a shadowy face on the screen, and it was talking.

'Ah, Julius,' it said in Scalene's voice. 'I knew you'd come. Commander Root's famous ego would not allow him to stay out of the action. An obvious trap, and you walked straight into it.'

The voice was definitely Scalene's, but there was something about the phrasing, the cadence. It was too sophisticated for a goblin. Sophisticated, and strangely familiar.

'Have you figured it out yet, Captain Short?' said the voice. A voice that was changing. Slipping into a higher register. The tones were no longer male, not even goblin. *That's a female talking*, thought Holly. *A female that I know*.

A face appeared on the screen. A beautiful and malicious face, its eyes bright with hate. Opal Koboi's face. The rest of the head was swathed in bandages, but the features were only too visible.

Holly began to speak rapidly into her helmet mike.

'Foaly, we have a situation here. Opal Koboi is loose. I repeat, Koboi is loose. This whole thing is a trap. Cordon off the area, five-hundred-metre perimeter, and bring in the medical warlocks. Someone is about to get hurt.'

The face on the screen laughed, tiny pixie teeth glinting like pearls.

'Talk all you want, Captain Short. Foaly can't hear you. My device has blocked your transmissions as easily as I blocked your seeker-sleeper and the substance scan that I assume you ran. Your little centaur friend can see you, though. I left him his precious lenses.'

Holly immediately zoomed in on Opal's pixelated face. If Foaly got a shot of the pixie, he would figure out the rest.

Again Koboi laughed. Opal was genuinely enjoying herself.

'Oh, very good, Captain. You were always a smart one. Relatively speaking, of course. Show Foaly my face and he will initiate an alert. Sorry to disappoint you, Holly, but this entire device is constructed from stealth ore and is practically invisible to the artificial eye. All Foaly will see is a slight shimmer of interference.'

Stealth ore had been developed for space vehicles. It absorbed every form of wave or signal known to fairy or man and so was virtually invisible to everything but the naked eye. It was also incredibly expensive to manufacture. Even the small amount necessary to cover Koboi's device would have cost a warehouse full of gold.

Root straightened quickly. 'The odds are against us here, Captain. Let's move out.'

Holly didn't bother with relief. Opal Koboi wouldn't make things that easy. There was no way they were just walking out of here. If Foaly could hijack the terminal's computers, then so could Koboi.

Opal's laugh stretched to an almost hysterical screech.

'Move out? How very tactical of you, Commander. You really need to expand your vocabulary. Whatever next? Duck and cover?'

Holly peeled back a Velcro patch on her sleeve, revealing a Gnommish keyboard. She quickly accessed her helmet's LEP criminal database, opening Opal Koboi's file in her visor.

'Opal Koboi,' said Corporal Frond's voice. The LEP always used Lili Frond for voice-overs and recruitment videos. She was glamorous and elegant, with flowing blond tresses and inch-long manicured nails that were absolutely no use in the field. 'LEP enemy number one. Currently under guard in the J. Argon Clinic. Opal Koboi is a certified genius, scoring over three hundred on the standardized IQ test. She is also a suspected mega-lomaniac, with an obsessive personality. Studies indicate that Koboi may be a pathological liar and suffer from mild schizophrenia. For more detailed information please consult the LEP central library on the second floor of Police Plaza.'

Holly closed the file. An obsessive genius and a pathological liar. Just what they needed. The information didn't help a lot; what it told her she pretty much already knew. Opal was loose, she wanted to kill them and she was smart enough to figure out how to do it.

Opal was still enjoying her triumph.

'You don't know how long I have waited for this moment,' the pixie said, then paused. 'Actually, you *do* know. After all, you were the ones who wrecked my plan. And now I have you both.'

Holly was puzzled. Opal may have had serious mental issues, but that could not be confused with stupidity. Why would she prattle on? Was she trying to distract them?

The same thought occurred to Root. 'Holly! The doors!'

Holly whirled round, to see the blast doors sliding across, their engines masked by core wind. If those doors closed, they would be completely cut off from the LEP, and at the mercy of Opal Koboi.

Holly targeted the magnetic rollers along the doors' upper rim, sinking blast after blast from her Neutrino into their mechanisms. The doors jerked in their housings but did not stop. Two of the rollers blew out, but the massive portals' momentum carried them together. They connected with an ominous bong.

'Alone at last,' said Opal, sounding for all the world like an innocent college fairy on her first date.

Root pointed his weapon at the device belted round Scalene's middle, as if he could somehow hurt Koboi.

'What do you want?' he demanded.

'You know what I want,' replied Opal. 'The question is, how am I going to get it? What form of revenge would be the most satisfying? Naturally, you will both end up dead, but that's not enough. I want you to suffer as I did, discredited and despised. One of you at least – the other will have to be sacrificed. I don't really care which.'

Root retreated to the blast doors, motioning for Holly to follow.

'Options?' he whispered, his back to Koboi's device.

Holly raised her visor, wiping a bead of sweat from her brow. The helmets were air conditioned, but sometimes sweating had nothing to do with temperature.

'We have to get out of here,' she said. 'The chute is the only way.'

Root nodded. 'Agreed. We fly up far enough to clear Koboi's blocker signal, then alert Major Kelp.'

'What about Scalene? He's mesmerized to the gills, he can't look after himself. If we do escape, Opal is not going to leave him around as evidence.'

It was basic criminal logic. Your typical 'take over the world' types were not averse to knocking off a few of their own if it meant a clean getaway.

Root actually growled. 'It really tugs my beard to put us in harm's way over a goblin, but that's the job. We take Scalene with us. I want you to sink a few charges into that box round his waist, and when the buzzing stops I throw him over my shoulder and we're off up E37.'

'Understood,' said Holly, lowering the setting on her weapon to minimum. Some of the charge would be transferred to Scalene, but it wouldn't do much more than dry up his eyeballs for a couple of minutes.

'Ignore the pixie. Whatever she says, keep your mind on the job.'

'Yes, sir.'

Root took several deep breaths. Somehow it calmed Holly to see the commander as nervous as she was. 'OK. Go.'

The two elves turned and strode rapidly towards the unconscious goblin.

'Have we come up with a little plan?' said Koboi mockingly from the small screen. 'Something ingenious, I hope. Something I haven't thought of?'

Grim-faced, Holly tried to shut out the words, but they wormed their way into her thoughts. Something ingenious? Hardly. It was simply the only option open to them. Something Koboi hadn't thought of? Doubtful. Opal could conceivably have been planning this for almost a year. Were they just about to do exactly what she wanted?

'Sir . . .' began Holly, but Root was already in position beside Scalene.

Holly fired six charges at the small screen. All six impacted on Koboi's pixelated features. Opal's image disappeared in a storm of static. Sparks squeezed between the metal seams and acrid smoke leaked through the speaker grid.

Root hesitated for a moment, allowing any charge to disperse, then he grabbed Scalene firmly by the shoulders.

Nothing happened.

I was wrong, thought Holly, releasing a breath she did not realize she'd been holding. *I was wrong, thank the gods. Opal has no plan.* But it wasn't true, and Holly didn't really believe it.

The box around Scalene's midriff was secured by a set of octo-bonds, eight telescoping cables often used by the LEP to restrain dangerous criminals. They could be locked and unlocked remotely and, once cinched, could not be removed without the remote or an angle grinder. As soon as Root leaned over, the octo-bonds released and whiplashed around the commander's torso, freeing Scalene and drawing the metal box tight to Root's own chest.

Koboi's face appeared on the reverse side of the box. The smokescreen had been just that: a smokescreen.

'Commander Root,' she said, almost breathless with malice, 'it looks like you're the sacrifice.'

'D'Arvit!' swore Root, beating the metal box with the butt of his pistol. The cords tightened until Root's breath came in agonized spurts. Holly heard more than one rib crack. The commander fought the urge to sink to his feet. Magical blue sparks played around his torso, automatically healing the broken bones.

Holly rushed forward to help, but before she could reach her superior officer an urgent beeping began to emanate from the device's speaker. The closer she got, the louder the beep.

'Stay back,' grunted Root. 'Stay back. It's a trigger.'

Holly stopped in her sooty tracks, punching the air in frustration. But the commander was probably right. She had heard of proximity triggers before. Dwarfs used them in the mines. They would set a charge in the tunnels, activate a proximity trigger and then set it off from a safe distance, using a stone.

Opal's face reappeared on the screen.

'Listen to your Julius, Captain Short,' advised the pixie. 'This is a moment for caution. Your commander is quite right – the tone you hear is indeed a proximity trigger. If you come too close, he will be vaporized by the explosive gel packed into the metal box.'

'Stop lecturing and tell us what you want,' snarled Root.

'Now, now, Commander, patience. Your worries will be over soon enough. In fact they are already over, so why don't you just wait quietly while your final seconds tick away.'

Holly circled the commander, keeping the beep constant, until her back was to the chute.

'There's a way out of this, Commander,' she said. 'I just need to think. I need a minute to sort things out.'

'Let me help you to *sort things out,*' said Koboi mockingly, her childlike features ugly with malice. 'Your LEP comrades are currently trying to laser their way in here, but of course they will never make it in time. And you can bet that my old school chum, Foaly, is glued to his video screen. So what does he see? He sees his good friend Holly Short apparently holding a gun on her commander. Now why would she want to do that?'

'Foaly will figure it out,' said Root. 'He beat you before.'

Opal tightened the octo-bonds remotely, forcing the commander to his knees. 'Maybe he *would* figure it out, at that. If he had time. But unfortunately for you, time is almost up.'

On Root's chest, a digital readout flickered into life. There were two numbers on the readout. A six and a zero. Sixty seconds.

'One minute to live, Commander. How does that feel?'

The numbers began ticking down.

The ticking and the beeping and Opal's snide sniggers drilled into Holly's brain.

'Shut it down, Koboi. Shut it down, or I swear I'll . . .'

Opal's laughter was unrestrained. It echoed through

the access tunnel like the attack screech of a harpie.

'You will what? Exactly? Die beside your commander?'

More cracks. More ribs broken. The blue sparks of magic circled Root's torso like stars caught in a whirlwind.

'Go now,' he grunted. 'Holly, I am ordering you to leave.'

'With respect, Commander. No. This isn't over yet.'

'Forty-eight,' said Opal, in a happy, sing-song voice. 'Forty-seven.'

'Holly! Go!'

'I'd listen if I were you,' said Koboi. 'There are other lives at stake. Root is already dead — why not save someone who can be saved?'

Holly moaned. Another element in an already overloaded equation.

'Who can I save? Who's in danger?'

'Oh, no one important. Just a couple of Mud Men.'

Of course, thought Holly, *Artemis and Butler. Two others who had put a stop to Koboi's plan.*

'What have you done, Opal?' said Holly, shouting above the proximity trigger and core wind.

Koboi's lip drooped, mimicking a guilty child.

'I'm afraid I may have put your human friends in danger. At this very moment they are stealing a package from the International Bank in Munich. A little package I prepared for them. If Master Fowl is as clever as he is supposed to be, he won't open the package until he reaches the Kronski Hotel and can check for booby traps. Then a bio-bomb will be activated, and "Bye bye, obnoxious humans". You can stay here and explain all this. I'm sure it won't take more than a few hours to sort it out with Internal Affairs. Or you can try to rescue your friends.'

Holly's head reeled. The commander, Artemis, Butler. All about to die. How could she save them all? There was no way to win.

'I will hunt you down, Koboi. For you, there won't be a safe inch on the planet.'

'Such venom. What if I gave you a way out? One chance to win.'

Root was on his knees now, blood leaking from the corner of his mouth. The blue sparks were gone, he was out of magic.

'It's a trap,' he gasped, every syllable making him wince. 'Don't be fooled again.'

'Thirty,' said Koboi. 'Twenty-nine.'

Holly felt her forehead throb against the helmet pads. 'OK. OK, Koboi. Tell me quickly. How do I save the commander?'

Opal took a deep, theatrical breath. 'On the device. There's a sweet spot. Two-centimetre diameter. The red dot below the screen. If you hit that spot from outside the trigger area, then you overload the circuit. If you miss, even by a hair, you set off the explosive gel. It's a sporting chance – more than you gave me, Holly Short.'

Holly gritted her teeth. 'You're lying. Why would you give me a chance?'

'Don't take the shot,' said Root, strangely calm. 'Just get out of range. Go and save Artemis. That's the last order I'll ever give you, Captain. Don't you dare ignore it.'

Holly felt as though her senses were being filtered through a metre of water. Everything was blurred and slowed down.

'I don't have any choice, Julius.'

Root frowned. 'Don't call me Julius! You always do that just before you disobey me. Save Artemis, Holly. Save him.'

Holly closed one eye, aiming her pistol. The laser sights were no good for this kind of accuracy. She would have to do it manually.

'I'll save Artemis next,' she said.

She took a deep breath, held it, and squeezed the trigger.

Holly hit the red spot. She was certain of it. The charge sank into the device, spreading across the metal face like a tiny bush fire.

'I hit it,' she shouted at Opal's image. 'I hit the spot.'

Koboi shrugged. 'I don't know. I thought you were a fraction low. Hard luck. I mean that sincerely.'

'No!' screamed Holly.

The countdown on Root's chest ticked faster than

before, flickering through the numbers. There were only moments left now.

The commander struggled to his feet, raising the visor on his helmet. His eyes were steady and fearless. He smiled gently at Holly. A smile that laid no blame. For once there wasn't even a touch of feverish temper in his cheeks.

'Be well,' he said, and then an orange flame blossomed in the centre of his chest.

The explosion sucked the air from the tunnel, feeding on the oxygen. Multicoloured flames roiled like the plumage of battling birds. Holly was shunted backwards by a wall of shock waves, the force impacting on every surface inch facing the commander. Microfilaments blew in her suit as they were overloaded with heat and force. The camera cylinder on her helmet popped right out of its groove, spinning into E37.

Holly herself was borne bodily into the chute, spinning like a twig in a cyclone. Sonix sponges in her earpieces sealed automatically as the sound of the explosion caught up with the blast. The commander had disappeared inside a ball of flame. He was gone, there was no doubt about it. Even magic could not help him now. Some things are beyond fixing.

The contents of the access tunnel, including Root and Scalene, disintegrated into a cloud of shrapnel and dust, particles ricocheting off the tunnel walls. The cloud surged down the path of least resistance, which was, of course, directly after Holly. She barely had time to activate her wings and climb a few metres before flying shrapnel drilled a hole in the chute wall below her.

Holly hovered in the vast tunnel, the sound of her own breathing filling her helmet. The commander was dead. It was unbelievable. Just like that, at the whim of a vengeful pixie. Had there been a sweet spot on the device? Or had she actually missed the target? She would probably never know. But to the LEP observers it would seem as though she had shot her own commander.

Holly glanced downwards. Below her, fragments from the explosion were spiralling towards the Earth's core. As they neared the revolving magma sphere, the heat ignited each one, utterly cremating all that was left of Julius Root. For the briefest moment the particles twinkled, gold and bronze, like a million stars falling to earth.

Holly hung there for several minutes, trying to absorb what had happened. She couldn't. It was too awful. Instead, she froze the pain and guilt, preserving it for later. Right now she had an order to follow. And she would follow it, even if it were the last thing she ever did, because it had been the last order Julius Root would ever give.

Holly increased the power to her wings, rising through the massive charred chute. There were Mud Men to be saved.

CHAPTER 4: NARROW ESCAPES

Munich

 MUNICH during working hours was like any other major city in the world: utterly congested. In spite of the U-Bahn, an efficient and comfortable rail system, the general population preferred the privacy and comfort of their own cars, with the result that Artemis and Butler were stuck on the airport road in a rush-hour traffic jam that stretched all the way from the International Bank to the Kronski Hotel.

Master Artemis did not like delays. But today he was too focused on his latest acquisition, *The Fairy Thief*, still sealed in its perspex tube. Artemis itched to open it, but the previous owners, Crane & Sparrow, could somehow have booby-trapped the container. Just because there were no visible traps didn't mean that there couldn't be an invisible one. An obvious trick would be to vacuum-pack the canvas, then inject a corrosive gas that would react with oxygen and burn the painting.

It took almost two hours to reach the hotel, a journey that should have taken twenty minutes. Artemis changed into a dark cotton suit, then called up Fowl Manor's number on his mobile phone's speed dial. But before he connected, he linked the phone by firewire to his Powerbook so he could record the conversation. Angeline Fowl answered on the third ring.

'Arty,' said his mother, sounding slightly out of breath, as though she had been in the middle of something. Angeline Fowl did not believe in taking life easy, and was probably halfway through a Tai Bo workout.

'How are you, Mother?'

Angeline sighed down the phone line. 'I'm fine, Arty, but you sound like you're doing a job interview, as usual. Always so formal. Couldn't you call me "Mum" or even "Angeline"? Would that be so terrible?'

'I don't know, Mother. "Mum" sounds so infantile. I am fourteen now, remember?'

Angeline laughed. 'How could I forget? Not many teenage boys ask for a ticket to a genetics symposium for their birthday.'

Artemis had one eye on the perspex tube. 'And how is Father?'

'He is wonderful,' gushed Angeline. 'I am surprised

how well he is. That prosthetic leg of his is marvellous, and so is his outlook. He never complains. I honestly think that he has got a better attitude towards life now than he had before he lost his leg. He's under the care of a remarkable therapist. He says the mental is far more important than the physical. In fact, we leave for the private spa in Westmeath this evening. They use this marvellous seaweed treatment, which should do wonders for your father's muscles.'

Artemis Fowl Senior had lost a leg before his kidnap by the Russian Mafiya. Luckily Artemis had been able to rescue him with Butler's help. It had been an eventful year. Since Artemis Senior's return, he had been making good on his promise to turn over a new leaf and go straight. Artemis Junior was expected to follow suit but was having trouble abandoning his criminal ventures. Although sometimes, when he looked at his father and mother together, the idea of being a normal son to loving parents didn't seem such a far-fetched one.

'Is he doing his physiotherapy exercises twice a day?'

Angeline laughed again, and suddenly Artemis wished he were home.

'Yes, *Grandad*. I am making sure of that. Your father says he'll run the marathon in twelve months.'

'Good, I'm glad to hear it. Sometimes I think you two would spend your time wandering around the grounds, holding hands, if I didn't check up on you.'

His mother sighed, a rush of static through the speaker. 'I'm worried about you, Arty. Someone your age shouldn't be quite so . . . responsible. Don't worry about us, worry about school and friends. Think about what you really want to do. Use that big brain of yours to make yourself and other people happy. Forget the family business, living is the family business now.'

Artemis didn't know how to reply. Half of him wanted to point out that there really would be no family business if it weren't for him secretly safeguarding it. The other half of him wanted to get on a plane home and wander the grounds with his family.

His mother sighed again. Artemis hated the fact that just talking to him could make her worry.

'When will you be home, Arty?'

'The trip ends in three more days.'

'I mean, when will you be home for good? I know Saint Bartleby's is a family tradition, but we want you home with us. Principal Guiney will understand. There are plenty of good day schools locally.'

'I see,' said Artemis. Could he do it? he wondered. Just be part of a normal family. Abandon his criminal enterprises. Was it in him to live an honest life? 'The holidays are in a couple of weeks. We can talk then,' he said. Delaying tactics. 'To be honest, I can't concentrate now. I'm not feeling very well. I thought I might have food poisoning, but it turns out to be just a twenty-four-hour bug. The local doctor says I will be fine tomorrow.'

'Poor Arty,' crooned Angeline. 'Maybe I should put you on a plane home.'

'No, Mother. I'm feeling better already. Honestly.'

'Whatever you like. I know bugs are uncomfortable, but it's better than a dose of food poisoning. You could have been laid low for weeks. Drink plenty of water, and try to sleep.'

'I will, Mother.'

'You'll be home soon.'

'Yes. Tell Father I called.'

'I will, if I can find him. He's in the gym, I think, on the treadmill.'

'Goodbye, then.'

'Bye, Arty, we'll talk more about this on your return,' said Angeline, her voice low and slightly sad. Sounding very far away.

Artemis ended the call and immediately replayed it on his computer. Every time he spoke to his mother he felt guilty. Angeline Fowl had a way of awakening his conscience. This was a relatively new development. A year ago he might have felt a tiny pinprick of guilt at lying to his mother, but now even this minor trick he was about to play would haunt his thoughts for weeks.

Artemis watched the sound-wave meter on his computer screen. He was changing, no doubt about it. This kind of self-doubt had been increasing over the past several months . . . ever since he had discovered mysterious mirrored contact lenses in his own eyes one morning. Butler and Juliet had been wearing the same lenses. They had tried to find out where the lenses came from, but all that Butler's contact in that field would say was that Artemis himself had paid for them. Curiouser and curiouser.

The lenses remained a mystery. And so did Artemis's feelings. On the table before him was Hervé's *The Fairy Thief,* an acquisition that established him as the foremost thief of the age, a status he had longed for since the age of six. But now that his ambition was literally in his grasp, all he could think about was his family.

Is now the time to retire? he thought. *Aged fourteen and three months, the best thief in the world. After all, where can I go from here?* He replayed a section of the phone conversation: 'Don't worry about us, worry about school and friends. Think about what you really want to do. Use that big brain of yours to make yourself and other people happy.'

Maybe his mother was right. He should use his talents to make others happy. But there was a darkness in him, a hard surface in his heart that would not be satisfied with the quiet life. Maybe there were ways to make people happy that only he could achieve. Ways on the far side of the law. Over the thin blue line.

Artemis rubbed his eyes. He could not come to a

conclusion. Perhaps living at home full time would make the decision for him. Best to continue with the job at hand. Buy some time, and then authenticate the painting. Even though he felt some guilt about stealing the master-piece, it was not nearly enough to make him give it back. Especially to Messrs Crane & Sparrow.

The first task was to deflect any enquiries from the school as to his activities. He would need at least two days to authenticate the painting, as some of the tests would need to be contracted out.

Artemis opened an audio manipulation program on his Powerbook and set about cutting and pasting his mother's words from the recorded phone call. When he had selected the words he wanted and had put them in the right order, he smoothed the levels to make the speech sound natural.

When Principal Guiney turned on his mobile phone after the visit to Munich's Olympia Stadion, there would be a new message waiting for him. It would be from Angeline Fowl, and she would not be in a good mood.

Artemis routed the call through Fowl Manor, then sent the edited sound file by infrared to his own mobile phone.

'*Principal Guiney,*' said the voice, unmistakably Angeline Fowl's, which the caller ID would confirm, '*I'm worried about Arty. He has a dose of food poisoning. His outlook is marvellous, he never complains but we want him home with us. You understand. I put Arty on a plane home. I am surprised he got a dose of food poisoning under your care. We will talk more on your return.'*

That took care of school for a few days. The dark half of Artemis felt an electric thrill at the subterfuge, but his growing conscience felt a tug of guilt at using his mother's voice to weave his web of lies.

He banished the guilt. It was a harmless lie. Butler would escort him home, and his education would not suffer through a few days' absence. As for stealing *The Fairy Thief*, theft from thieves was not real crime. It was almost justifiable.

Yes, said a voice in his head, unbidden. *If you give the painting back to the world.*

No, replied his granite-hearted half. *This painting is mine until someone can steal it away. That's the whole point.*

Artemis banished his indecision and turned off his mobile phone. He needed to focus completely on the painting and a vibrating phone at the wrong moment could cause his hand to jitter. His natural inclination was to pop the stopper on the perspex tube's lid. But that could be more than foolish, it could be fatal. There were any number of little gifts that Crane & Sparrow could have left for him.

Artemis took a chromatograph from the rigid suitcase that contained his lab equipment. The instrument would take a sample of the gas inside the tube and process it. He chose a needle nozzle from a selection, screwing it on to the rubber tube protruding from the chromatograph's flat end. He held the needle carefully in his left hand. Artemis was ambidextrous, but his left hand was slightly steadier. With care, he poked the needle through the tube's silicone seal into the space round the painting. It was essential that the needle be moved as little as possible so that the container's gas could not leak out and mingle with the air. The chromatograph siphoned a small sample of gas, sucking it into a heated injection port. Any organic impurities were driven off by heating, and a carrier gas transported the sample through a separation column and into a flame ionization detector. There, individual components were identified. Seconds later, a graph flashed up on the instrument's digital readout. The percentages of oxygen, hydrogen, methane and carbon dioxide matched a sample taken earlier from downtown Munich. There was a five per cent slice of gas that remained unidentified. But that was normal. This was probably caused by complex pollution gases or equipment sensitivity. Mystery gas aside, Artemis knew that it was perfectly safe to open the tube. He did so, carefully slitting the seal with a craft knife.

Artemis put on a set of surgical gloves, teasing the painting from the cylinder. It plopped on to the table in a tight roll, but sprang loose almost immediately; it hadn't been in the tube long enough to retain the shape.

Artemis spread the canvas wide, weighing the corners

with smooth gel sacs. He knew immediately that this was no fake. His eye for art took in the primary colours and the layered brushwork. Hervé's figures seemed to be composed of light. So beautifully were they painted, the picture seemed to sparkle. It was exquisite. In the picture, a swaddled baby slept in its sun-drenched cot inside an open window. A fairy with green skin and gossamer wings had alighted on the window sill and was preparing to snatch the baby from its cradle. Both of the creature's feet were on the outside of the sill.

'It can't go inside,' muttered Artemis absently, and was immediately surprised. How did he know that? He didn't generally voice opinions without some evidence to back them up.

Relax, he told himself. It was simply a guess. Perhaps based on a sliver of information he had picked up on one of his Internet trawls.

Artemis returned his attention to the painting itself. He had done it. *The Fairy Thief* was his, for the moment at any rate. He selected a surgical scalpel from his kit, scraping the tiniest sliver of paint from the picture's border. He deposited the sliver in a sample jar and labelled it. This would be sent to the Technical University of Munich, where they had one of the giant spectrometers necessary for carbon dating. Artemis had a contact there. The radiocarbon test would confirm that the painting, or at least the paint, was as old as it was supposed to be.

He called to Butler, in the suite's other room.

'Butler, could you take this sample over to the university now? Remember, only give it to Christina, and remind her that speed is vital.'

There was no answer for a moment, then Butler came charging through the door, his eyes wide. He did not look like a man coming to collect a paint sample.

'Is there a problem?' asked Artemis.

Two minutes earlier, Butler had been holding his hand to the window, lost in a rare moment of self-absorption. He glared at the hand, almost as if the combination of sunlight and staring would make the skin transparent. He knew that there was something different about him. Something hidden below the skin. He felt strange this past year. Older. Perhaps the decades of physical hardship were taking their toll on him. Though he was barely forty, his bones ached at night and his chest felt as though he was wearing a Kevlar vest all the time. He was certainly nowhere near as fast as he had been at thirty-five, and even his mind seemed less focused. More inclined to wander . . . *Just as it is doing now*, the bodyguard scolded himself silently.

Butler flexed his fingers, straightened his tie and got back to work. He was not at all happy with the security of the hotel suite. Hotels were a bodyguard's nightmare. Service lifts, isolated upper floors and totally inadequate escape routes made the principal's safety almost impossible to guarantee. The Kronski was luxurious, certainly, and the staff efficient, but that was not what Butler looked for in a hotel. He looked for a ground-floor room, with no windows and a fifteen-centimetre-thick steel door. Needless to say, rooms like this were impossible to find, and even if he could find one, Master Artemis would undoubtedly turn up his nose at it. Butler would have to make do with this third-storey suite.

Artemis wasn't the only one with a case of instruments. Butler opened a chrome briefcase on the coffee table. It was one of a dozen such cases that he held in safety deposit boxes around the world. Each case was full to bursting with surveillance equipment, counter-surveillance equipment and weaponry. Having one in each country meant that he did not have to break Customs laws on each overseas trip from Ireland.

He selected a bug sweeper and quickly ran it around the room, searching for listening devices. He concentrated on the electrical appliances: phone, television, fax machine. The electronic waffle from those items could often drown a bug's signal, but not with this particular sweeper. The Eye Spy was the most advanced sweeper on the market and could detect a pinhole mike half a mile away.

After a minute he was satisfied, and he was on the point of returning the device to the case when it registered a tiny electrical field. Nothing much, barely a single flickering blue bar on the indicator. The first bar solidified, then turned bright blue. The second bar began to flicker. Something electronic was closing in on them. Most men would have discounted the reading; after all, there were several thousand electronic devices within a square mile of the Kronski Hotel. But normal electronic fields did not register on the Eye Spy, and Butler was not most men. He extended the sweeper's aerial and panned the device around the room. The reading spiked when the aerial was pointing at the window. A claw of anxiety tugged at Butler's intestines. Something airborne was coming closer at high speed.

He dashed to the window, ripping the net curtains from their hooks and flinging the window wide open. The winter air was pale blue, with remarkably few clouds. Jet trails criss-crossed the sky like a giant's game of noughts and crosses. And there, twenty degrees up, a gentle spiralling curve, was a tear-shaped rocket of blue metal. A red light winked on its nose and white-hot flames billowed from its rear end. The rocket was heading for the Kronski, no doubt about it.

It's a smart bomb, Butler said to himself, without one iota of doubt. *And Master Artemis is the target.*

Butler's brain began flicking through his list of alternatives. It was a short list. There were only two choices really: get out or die. It was *how* to get out that was the problem. They were three storeys up, with the exit on the wrong side. He spared a moment to take one last look at the approaching missile. It was unlike anything he'd ever seen. Even the emission was different from conventional weapons, with hardly any vapour trail. Whatever this was, it was brand new. Somebody must very badly want Artemis dead.

Butler turned from the window and barged into Artemis's bedroom. The young master was busy conducting his tests on *The Fairy Thief*.

'Is there a problem?' asked Artemis.

Butler did not reply, because he didn't have time. Instead he grabbed the teenager by the scruff of the neck and hoisted him on to his own back.

'The painting!' Artemis managed to shout, his voice muffled by the bodyguard's jacket.

Butler grabbed the picture, unceremoniously stuffing the priceless masterpiece into his jacket pocket. If Artemis had seen the century-old oil paint crack, he would have sobbed. But Butler was paid to protect only one thing, and it was not *The Fairy Thief*.

'Hang on extremely tightly,' advised the massive bodyguard, hefting a king-size mattress from the bed.

Artemis held on tightly as he'd been told, trying not to think. Unfortunately his brilliant brain automatically analysed the available data: Butler had entered the room at speed and without knocking, therefore there was danger of some kind. His refusal to answer questions meant that the danger was imminent. And the fact that he was on Butler's back, hanging on tightly, indicated that they would not be escaping the aforementioned danger through conventional exit routes. The mattress would indicate that some cushioning would be needed . . .

'Butler,' gasped Artemis. 'You do know that we're three storeys up?'

Butler may have answered, but his employer did not hear him, because by then the giant bodyguard had propelled them through the open double windows and over the balcony railing.

For a fraction of a second, before the inevitable fall, the air currents spun the mattress round and Artemis could see back into his own bedroom. In that splinter of a moment, he saw a strange missile corkscrew through the bedroom door and come to a complete halt, directly over the empty perspex tube.

There was some kind of tracker in the tube, said the tiny portion of his brain that wasn't panicking. *Someone wants me dead.*

Then came the inevitable fall. Ten metres. Straight down.

Butler automatically spread his limbs in a skydiving 'X', bearing down on the four corners of the mattress to stop it flipping. The trapped air below the mattress slowed their fall slightly, but not much. The pair went straight down, fast, G-force increasing their speed with every centimetre.

Sky and ground seemed to stretch and drip like oil paints on a canvas, and nothing seemed solid any more. This impression came to an abrupt halt when they slammed into the extremely solid tiled roof of a maintenance shed at the hotel's rear. The tiles seemed almost to explode under the impact, though the roof timbers held, just. Butler felt as though his bones had been liquidized, but he knew that he would be OK after a few moments' unconsciousness. He had been in worse collisions before.

His last impression before his senses deserted him was the feel of Master Artemis's heartbeat through his jacket. Alive then. They had both survived. But for how long? If their assassin had seen his attempt fail, then maybe he would try again.

Artemis's impact was cushioned by Butler and the mattress. Without them he would certainly have been killed. As it was, the bodyguard's muscle-bound frame was dense enough to break two of his ribs. Artemis bounced a full metre into the air before coming to rest on the unconscious bodyguard's back, facing the sky.

Each breath was short and painful, and two nubs of bone rose like knuckles from his chest. Sixth and seventh ribs, he guessed.

Overhead, a block of iridescent blue light flashed from his hotel window. It lit the sky for a split second, its belly busy with even brighter blue flares that wriggled like hooked worms. No one would pay much attention; the light could easily have come from an oversized camera flash. But Artemis knew better.

Bio-bomb, he thought. *Now how do I know that?*

Butler must be unconscious or else he would be moving, so it was up to Artemis to foil their attacker's next murderous attempt. He tried to sit up, but the pain in his chest was ferocious and enough to knock him out for a second. When he awoke, his entire body was slick with sweat. Artemis saw that it was too late to escape; his assassin was already here, crouched, catlike, on the shed wall.

The killer was a strange individual, no bigger than a child but with adult proportions. She was female, with pretty, sharp features, cropped auburn hair and huge hazel eyes, but that didn't mean any mercy would be forthcoming. Butler had once told him that eight of the top ten paid hitters in the world were women. This one wore a strange jumpsuit that shifted colours to suit the background, and those large eyes were red from crying.

Her ears are pointed, thought Artemis. *Either I'm in shock, or she's not human.*

Then he made the mistake of moving again, and one of his broken ribs actually punched through the skin. A red stain blossomed on his shirt and Artemis gave up the fight to stay conscious.

It had taken Holly almost ninety minutes to reach Germany. On a normal mission it would have taken at least twice that long, but Holly had decided to break a few LEP regulations. Why not? she reasoned. It wasn't as if she could get into any more trouble. The LEP already thought she had killed the commander, and her communications were blocked so she could not explain what had really happened. No doubt she was classified as rogue and a Retrieval squad was already on her tail. Not to mention the fact that Opal Koboi was probably keeping electronic tabs on her. So there was no time to lose.

Ever since the goblin gangs had been caught smuggling human contraband through disused chutes, sentries had been posted in each surface shuttle port. Paris was guarded by a sleepy gnome who was only five years from retirement. He was awakened from his afternoon nap by an urgent communiqué from Police Plaza. There was a rogue Recon jock on the way up. Detain for questioning. Proceed with caution.

Nobody really expected that the gnome would have any success. Holly Short was in peak physical condition and had once lived through a tussle with a troll. The gnome sentry couldn't remember the last time he'd been in shape, and he had to lie down if he got a hangnail. Nevertheless the sentry guarded the shuttle bay gamely until Holly blew past him on her way to the surface.

Once in the air, she peeled back a Velcro patch on her forearm and ran a search on her computer. The computer found the Kronski Hotel and flashed up three route options. Holly chose the shortest one, even though it meant passing over several major human population centres. More LEP regulations smashed to bits. At this point she really didn't care. Her own career was beyond salvaging, but that didn't matter. Holly had never been a career elf anyway. The only reason she hadn't already been booted out of the LEP was the commander. He had seen her potential, and now he was gone.

The earth flashed by below. European smells drifted through her helmet filters. The sea, baked earth, vines and the tang of pure snow. Generally this was what Holly lived for, but not today. Today she felt none of the usual above-ground euphoria. She simply felt alone. The commander had been the closest thing to family she had left. Now he was gone too. Perhaps because she had missed the sweet spot. Had she effectively killed Julius herself? It was too awful to think about, and too awful to forget.

Holly opened her visor to clear the tears. Artemis Fowl must be saved. As much for the commander as for himself. Holly closed her visor, kicked up her legs and opened the throttle to maximum. Time to see what these new wings of Foaly's could do.

In a little more than an hour Holly sped into Munich's airspace. She dropped to thirty metres, activating her helmet's radar. It would be a shame to make it this far, only to be pasted by an incoming aircraft. The Kronski showed up as a red dot in her visor. Foaly could have sent a live satellite feed, or at least the most recent video footage, but she had no way to contact the centaur – and even if she did, the Council would order her back to Police Plaza immediately.

Holly zeroed in on the red dot in her visor. That was where the bio-bomb would be headed, so she had to go there too. She dropped lower until the Kronski's roof was just under her toes, then touched down on the rooftop. She was on her own now. This was as far as the on-board tracker could take her. She would have to locate Artemis's room on her own.

Holly chewed her lip for a moment, then typed a command into the keypad on her wrist. She could have used voice command, but the software was touchy and she did not have time for computer error. In seconds, her on-board computer had hacked into the hotel computer and was displaying a guest list and schematic. Artemis was in room 304. Third storey on the south wing of the hotel.

Holly sprinted across the roof, activating her wings as she ran. She was seconds away from saving Artemis. Having a mythological creature drag him from his hotel room might be a bit of a shock, but not as much of a shock as being vaporized by a bio-bomb.

She stopped dead. A guided missile was arcing in from the horizon, towards the hotel. It was of fairy manufacture, no doubt about that, but new. Slicker and faster, with bigger tail rockets than she'd ever seen on a missile. Opal Koboi had obviously been making upgrades.

Holly spun on her heels, racing for the other side of the hotel. In her heart she knew she was too late, and the realization hit her that Opal had set her up again. There never was any hope of rescuing Artemis, just as there had never been any chance of rescuing the commander.

Before her wings even had a chance to kick in, there was a bright blue flash from beyond the lip of the roof, and a slight shudder underfoot as the bio-bomb detonated. It was the perfect weapon. There was no structural damage, and the bomb casing would consume itself, leaving no evidence that it had ever been there.

Holly dropped to her knees in frustration, peeling off her helmet to gulp in breaths of fresh air. The Munich air was laced with toxins, but it still tasted better than the below-ground filtered variety. But Holly did not notice the sweetness. Julius was gone. Artemis was dead. Butler was dead. How could she go on? What was the point? Tears dropped from her lashes, running into tiny cracks in the concrete.

Get up! said her core of steel. The part of her that made Holly Short such an excellent officer. *You are an LEP officer. There is more at stake here than your personal grieving. Time enough to cry later.*

In a minute. I'll get up in a minute. I just need sixty seconds.

Holly felt as though the grief had scooped out her insides. She felt hollow, numb. Incapacitated.

'How touching,' said a voice. Robotic and familiar.

Holly did not even look up. 'Koboi. Have you come to gloat? Does murder make you happy?'

'Hmm?' said the voice, seriously considering the question. 'You know, it does. It actually does make me happy.'

Holly sniffled, shaking the last tears from her eyes. She decided not to cry again until Koboi was behind bars.

'What do you want?' she asked, rising from the concrete roof. Hovering at head height was a small bio-bomb. This model was spherical, about the size of a melon, and equipped with a plasma screen. Opal's happy features were plastered across the monitor.

'Oh, I just followed you from the chute because I wanted to see what total despair looks like. It's not very fetching, is it?'

For a few moments the screen displayed Holly's own distraught face, before flashing back to Opal.

'Just detonate, and be damned,' growled Holly.

The bio-bomb rose a little way, slowly circling Holly's head.

'Not just yet. I think there's a spark of hope in you yet. So, I would like to extinguish that. In a moment I will detonate the bio-bomb. Nice, isn't it? How do you like the design? Eight separate boosters, you know.

It's what happens after the detonation that's important.'

Holly's law-enforcer curiosity was piqued in spite of the circumstances. 'What happens then, Koboi? Don't tell me, world domination.'

Koboi laughed, the volume distorting the sound through the bomb's micro-speakers. 'World domination? You make it sound so unattainable. The first step is simplicity itself. All I have to do is put humans in contact with the People.'

Holly felt her own troubles instantly slip away. 'Put humans into contact with the People? Why would you do that?'

Opal's features lost their merry cast. 'Because the LEP imprisoned me. They studied me like an animal in a cage, and now we shall see how they like it. There will be a war, and I will supply the humans with the weapons to win. And after they have won, my chosen nation will be the most powerful on Earth. And I, inevitably, will become the most powerful person in that nation.'

Holly almost screamed. 'All this for a childish pixie's revenge.'

Seeing Holly's discomfort cheered Opal immediately. 'Oh no, I'm not a pixie any more.' Koboi slowly unwound the bandages circling her head to reveal two surgically rounded humanoid ears. 'I'm one of the Mud People now. I intend to be on the winning side. And my new daddy has an engineering company. And that company is sending down a probe.'

'What probe?' shouted Holly. 'What company?'

Opal wagged a finger. 'Oh no, enough explaining. I want you to die desolate and ignorant.' For one moment her face lost its false merriment and Holly could see the hatred in her huge eyes. 'You cost me a year of my life, Short. A year of a brilliant life. My time is too special to be wasted, especially answering to pathetic organizations like the LEP. Soon I will never have to answer to anyone ever again.'

Opal raised one hand into camera shot; it was clutching a small remote. She pressed the red button. And, as everyone knows, the red button can mean only one thing. Holly had milliseconds to come up with a plan. The monitor fizzled out, and a green light on the missile's console winked red. The signal had been received. Detonation was imminent.

Holly jumped up, hooking her helmet over the spherical bomb. She put her weight on the helmet, bearing down on it. It was like trying to submerge a football. LEP helmets were composed of a rigid polymer that could deflect solinium flares. Of course the rest of Holly's suit was not rigid and could not protect her from the bio-bomb, but maybe the helmet would be enough.

The bomb exploded, spinning the helmet into the air. Pure blue light gushed from the underside of the helmet, dissipating across the cement. Ants and spiders hopped once, then their tiny hearts froze. Holly could feel her own heart speed up, battling against the deadly solinium. She held on for as long as she could, then the concussion wave flung her off. The helmet spun away and the fatal light was free.

Holly flipped her wing control to rise, reaching for the skies. The blue light was after her like a wall of death. It was a race now. Had she gained enough time and distance to outrun the bio-bomb?

Holly felt her lips dragged back across her teeth. G-force rippled the skin on her cheeks. She was counting on the fact that the bio-bomb's active agent was light; this meant that it could be focused to a certain diameter. Koboi would not want to draw attention to her device by wiping out a city block. Holly alone was her target.

Holly felt the light swipe her toes. A dreadful feeling of nothingness crept up her leg before the magic banished it. She streamlined her body, arcing her head back and folding her arms across her chest, willing the mechanical wings to accelerate her to safety.

Suddenly the light dissipated, flashed out, leaving only a dozen squirrelly flares in its wake. Holly had outrun the deadly light, with only minor injuries. Her legs felt weakened, but that sensation would recede shortly. Time enough to worry about that later. Now she had to return to the Lower Elements and somehow warn her comrades what Opal was planning.

Holly glanced down at the roof. Nothing remained now to suggest that she'd ever been there, except the remains of her helmet, which spun like a battered top. Generally, inanimate objects were not affected by bio-bombs, but the helmet's reflective layer had bounced the light around so much internally that it had overheated. And once the helmet had shorted out, so had all Holly's bio-readings. As far as the LEP or Opal Koboi were concerned, Captain Short's helmet was no longer broadcasting her heartbeat or respiratory rate. She was officially dead. And being dead had possibilities.

Something caught Holly's eye. Far below, in the centre of a cluster of maintenance buildings, several humans were converging on one hut. With her bird's-eye view, Holly could see that the hut's roof had been blown out. There were two figures lying in the roof timbers. One was huge, a veritable giant. The other closer to her own size. A boy. Artemis and Butler. Could they have survived?

Holly threw her legs up behind her, diving steeply towards the crash site. She did not shield, conserving her magic. It looked likely that every spark of healing power she possessed would be needed, so she would have to trust to speed and her revolutionary suit to keep her hidden.

The other humans were metres away, picking their way through the debris. They looked curious rather than angry. Still, it was vital that Holly get Artemis away from here, if he were alive. Opal could have spies anywhere, and a back-up plan just waiting to spring into deadly operation. It was doubtful whether they could cheat death again.

She landed on the shed's gable end and peered inside. It was Artemis all right, and Butler. Both breathing. Artemis was even conscious, though clearly in pain. Suddenly a red rose of blood spread across his white shirt, his eyes rolled back and he began to buck. The Mud Boy was going into shock, and it looked as if a rib had punctured the skin. There could be another one in his lung. He needed healing. Now.

Holly dropped to Artemis's chest and placed a hand on the nubs of bone protruding under his heart.

'Heal,' she said, and the last sparks of magic in her elfin frame sped down her arms, intuitively targeting Artemis's injuries. The ribs shuddered, twisted elastically, then rejoined with a hiss of molten bone. Steam vented from Artemis's shuddering body as the magic flushed impurities from his system.

Even before Artemis had finished shaking, Holly was wrapping herself around the boy as much as possible. She had to get him away from here. Ideally she would have taken Butler too, but he was too bulky to be shielded by her slim frame. The bodyguard would have to look out for himself, but Artemis had to be protected. Firstly because he was undoubtedly the prime target, and secondly because she needed his devious brain to help her defeat Opal Koboi. If Opal intended to join the world of men, then Artemis was the ideal foil for her genius.

Holly locked her fingers behind Artemis's back, hoisting his limp body into an upright position. His head lolled on her shoulder, and she could feel his breath on her cheek. It was regular. Good.

Holly bent her legs until her knees cracked. She would need all the leverage she could get to mask their escape. Outside, the voices grew closer, and she felt the walls shake as someone inserted a key in the door.

'Goodbye, Butler, old friend,' she whispered. 'I'll be back for you.'

The bodyguard groaned once, as though he had heard. Holly hated to leave him, though she had no choice. It was either Artemis alone or no one, and Butler himself would thank her for what she was doing.

Holly gritted her teeth, tensed every muscle in her body, and opened the throttle wide on her wings. She took off out of that shed like a dart from a blowpipe, kicking up a fresh cloud of dust in her wake. Even if someone had been staring straight at her, all they would have seen was a dust and sky-coloured blur, with possibly one loafered shoe poking out. But that must have been their eyes playing tricks, because shoes couldn't fly. Could they?

CHAPTER 5: MEET THE NEIGHBOURS

 FOALY could not believe what was happening. His eyes were sending information to his brain, but his brain refused to accept it. Because if he were to accept this information, he would have to believe that his friend Holly Short had just shot her own commander and was now attempting to escape to the surface. This was completely impossible, though not everybody was equally reluctant to accept this.

The centaur's mobile tech shuttle had been commandeered by Internal Affairs. This operation now fell under their jurisdiction because an LEP officer was suspected of a crime. All LEP personnel had been ejected from the shuttle, but Foaly was allowed to stay simply because he was the only one able to operate the surveillance equipment.

Commander Ark Sool was an LEP gnome who went after suspect police fairies. Sool was unusually tall and thin for a gnome, like a giraffe in a baboon's skin. His dark hair was slicked straight back in a no-nonsense style and his fingers and ears boasted none of the golden adornments generally so beloved of the gnome families. Ark Sool was the highest-ranked gnome officer in Internal Affairs; he believed that the LEP was basically a bunch of loose cannons, presided over by a maverick. And now the maverick was dead, killed apparently by the biggest loose cannon in the bunch. Holly Short may have narrowly avoided criminal charges on two previous occasions. She would not escape this time.

'Play the video again, centaur,' he instructed, tapping the worktop with his cane. Most annoying.

'We've looked at this a dozen times,' protested Foaly. 'I don't see the point.'

Sool silenced him with a glare from his red-rimmed eyes. 'You don't see the point? The centaur doesn't see the point? I don't see where that's an important factor in the current equation. You, Mister Foaly, are here to press buttons, not to offer opinions. Commander Root placed far too much value on your opinions, and look where that got him, eh?'

Foaly swallowed the dozen or so acidic responses that

were queuing on his tongue. If he were excluded from this operation now, he could do nothing to help Holly.

'Play the video. Yessir.'

Foaly cued the video from E37. It was damning stuff. Julius and Holly hovered around General Scalene for several moments. They appeared to be quite agitated. Then, for some reason, incredible as it sounded, Holly shot the commander with some kind of incendiary bullet. At this point they lost all video feeds from both helmets.

'Back the tape up twenty seconds,' ordered Sool, leaning in close to the monitor. He poked his cane into the plasma screen. 'What's that?'

'Careful with the cane,' said Foaly. 'These screens are expensive. I get them from Atlantis.'

'Answer the question, centaur. What is that?' Sool prodded the screen twice, just to show how little he cared about Foaly's gizmos.

The Internal Affairs commander was pointing to a slight shimmer on Root's chest.

'I'm not sure,' admitted Foaly. 'It could be heat distortion, or maybe equipment failure. Or perhaps just a glitch. I'll have to run some tests.'

Sool nodded. 'Run your tests, though I don't expect you'll find anything. Short is a burnout, simple as that. She always was. I nearly had her before, but this time it's cut and dried.'

Foaly knew he should bite his tongue, but he had to

defend his friend. 'Isn't this all a bit convenient? First we lose sound, so we don't know what was said. Then there's this fuzzy patch that could be anything, and now we're expected to believe that a decorated officer just up and shot her commander, an elf who was like a father to her.'

'Yes, I see your point, Foaly,' said Sool silkily. 'Very good. Nice to know you're thinking on some level. But let's stick to our respective jobs, eh? You build the machinery and I operate it. For example, these new Neutrinos that our field personnel are armed with?'

'Yes, what about them?' said Foaly suspiciously.

'They are personalized to each officer, am I right? Nobody else can fire them. And each shot is registered?'

'That is correct,' admitted Foaly, all too aware where this was leading.

Sool waved his cane like an orchestra conductor. 'Well then, surely all we have to do is check Captain Short's weapons log to see if she fired a shot at the precise time indicated on the video. If she did, then the film is authentic, and Holly Short did indeed murder her commander, regardless of what we can or cannot hear.'

Foaly ground his horsy teeth. Of course it made perfect sense. He had thought of it half an hour ago, and he already knew what the cross-referencing would reveal. He pulled up Holly's weapons log, reading out the relevant passage.

'Weapon registered at zero nine forty, HMT. Six

pulses at zero nine fifty-six, and then one level-two pulse fired at zero nine fifty-eight.'

Sool slapped the cane into his palm in triumph. 'One level-two pulse fired at zero nine fifty-eight. Exactly right. Whatever else happened in that chute, Short fired on her commander.'

Foaly leaped out of his specially tailored office chair. 'But a level-two pulse couldn't cause such a big explosion. It practically caved in the entire access tunnel.'

'Which is why Short isn't in custody right now,' said Sool. 'It will take weeks to clear out that tunnel. I've had to send a Retrieval team through E1, in Tara. They will have to travel overground to Paris and pick up her trail from there.'

'But what about the explosion itself?'

Sool grimaced, as though Foaly's question was a bitter nugget in an otherwise delicious meal. 'Oh, I'm sure there's an explanation, centaur. Combustible gas, or malfunction or just bad luck. We'll figure that out. For now, my priority, *and yours*, is to bring Captain Short back here for trial. I want you to liaise with the Retrieval team. Feed them constant updates on Short's position.'

Foaly nodded without enthusiasm. Holly was still wearing her helmet. And the LEP helmet could verify her identity and relay a constant stream of diagnostic information back to Foaly's computers. They had no sound or video, but there was plenty of information to track Holly, wherever she might go in the world, or under it. At the moment, Holly was in Germany. Her heart rate was elevated, but otherwise she was OK.

Why did you run, Holly? Foaly asked his absent friend silently. *If you're innocent, why did you run?*

'Tell me where Captain Short is now,' demanded Sool.

The centaur maximized the live feed from Holly's helmet on the plasma screen.

'She's still in Germany – Munich, to be precise. She's stopped moving now. Maybe she will decide to come home.'

Sool frowned. 'I seriously doubt it, centaur. She's a bad egg, through and through.'

Foaly ground his teeth. Good manners dictated that only a friend referred to another fairy by species, and Sool was no friend of his. Or anyone's.

'We can't say that for sure,' said Foaly through his clenched teeth.

Sool leaned even closer to the plasma screen, a slow smile stretching his tight skin.

'Actually, centaur, you're wrong there. I think we can safely say for sure that Captain Short won't be coming back. Recall the Retrieval team immediately.'

Foaly checked Holly's screen. The life signs from her helmet were all flatlining. One second she was stressed but alive, and the next she was gone. No heartbeat, no brain activity, no temperature reading. She couldn't have simply taken off the helmet, as there was an infrared connection between each LEP officer and helmet. No, Holly was dead, and it hadn't been natural causes.

Foaly felt the tears brimming on his eyelids. Not Holly too.

'Recall the Retrieval team? Are you insane, Sool? We have to find Holly. Find out what happened.'

Sool was unaffected by Foaly's outburst. If anything, he appeared to enjoy it.

'Short was a traitor and she was obviously in collusion with the goblins. Somehow her nefarious plan backfired and she has been killed. I want you to activate the remote incinerator in her helmet immediately, and we'll close the book on a rogue officer.'

Foaly was aghast. 'Activate the remote incinerator! I can't do that.'

Sool rolled his eyes. 'Again with the opinions. You don't have authority here, you just obey it.'

'But I'll have a satellite picture in thirty minutes,' protested the centaur. 'We can wait that long, surely.'

Sool elbowed past Foaly to the keyboard. 'Negative. You know the regulations. No bodies are left exposed for the humans to find. It's a tough rule, I know, but necessary.'

'The helmet could have malfunctioned!' said Foaly, grasping at straws.

'Is it likely that all the life-sign readings could have

flatlined at the same moment through equipment failure?'

'No,' admitted Foaly.

'And just how unlikely is it?'

'About one chance in ten million,' said the technical adviser miserably.

Sool picked his way around the keyboard. 'If you don't have the stomach for it, centaur, I'll do it myself.' He entered his password and then detonated the incinerator in Holly's helmet. On a rooftop in Munich, Holly's helmet dissolved in a pool of acid. And, in theory, so did Holly's body.

'There,' said Sool, satisfied. 'She's gone, and now we can all sleep a little easier.'

Not me, thought Foaly, staring forlornly at the screen. *It will be a very long time before I sleep easy again.*

TEMPLE BAR, DUBLIN, IRELAND

Artemis Fowl woke from a sleep haunted by nightmares. In his dreams, strange, red-eyed creatures had ripped open his chest with scimitar tusks and dined on his heart. He sat up in an undersized cot, both hands flying to his chest. His shirt was caked in dried blood, but there was no wound. Artemis took several deep, shuddering breaths, pumping oxygen through his brain. 'Assess the situation,' Butler always told him. 'If you find yourself in unfamiliar territory, become familiar with it before opening your mouth. Ten seconds of observation could save your life.'

Artemis looked around, his eyelids fluttering like camera shutters. Absorbing every detail. He was in a small boxroom, about three metres square. One wall was completely transparent and appeared to look out over the Dublin quays. From the position of the Millennium Bridge, the room had to be somewhere in the Temple Bar area. The chamber itself was constructed from a strange material: some kind of silver-grey fabric – rigid, but malleable – with several plasma screens on the opaque walls. It was all extremely high-tech but seemed to be years old, and almost abandoned.

In the corner, a girl sat, hunched, on a folding chair. She cradled her head in both hands, her shoulders twitching gently with sobs.

Artemis cleared his throat. 'Why are you crying, girl?'

The girl jerked upright, and it became immediately obvious that this was no normal girl. In fact, she appeared to belong to a totally different species.

'Pointed ears,' Artemis noted, with surprising composure. 'Prosthetic or real?'

Holly almost smiled through her tears. 'Typical Artemis Fowl. Always looking for options. My ears are very real, as you well know . . . knew.'

Artemis was silent for several moments, processing the wealth of information in those few sentences.

128

'Real pointed ears? Then you are of another species, not human. Possibly a fairy?'

Holly nodded. 'I am a fairy. Actually an elf. I'm what you would call a leprechaun too, but that's just a job.'

'And fairies speak English, do they?'

'We speak all languages. The gift of tongues, it is part of our magic.'

Artemis knew that these revelations should send his world spinning on its axis, but he found himself accepting her every word. It was as though he had always suspected the existence of fairies, and this was simply confirmation. Although, strangely, he could not remember ever having even thought about fairies before this day.

'And you claim to know me? Personally, or from some kind of surveillance? You certainly seem to have the technology.'

'We've known you for a few years now, Artemis. You made first contact, and we've been keeping an eye on you ever since.'

Artemis was slightly startled. '*I* made first contact?'

'Yes. December, two years ago. You kidnapped me.'

'Is this your revenge? That explosive device? My ribs?' A horrible thought struck the Irish boy. 'And what about Butler? Is he dead?'

Holly did her best to answer all these questions. 'It is revenge, but not mine. And Butler is alive. I just had to get you out of there before another attempt was made on your life.'

'So we're friends now?'

Holly shrugged. 'Maybe. We'll see.'

All this was slightly confusing. Even for a genius. Artemis crossed his legs in the lotus position, resting his temples against pointed fingers.

'You had better tell me everything,' he said, closing his eyes. 'From the beginning. And leave nothing out.'

So Holly did. She told Artemis how he had kidnapped her, then released her at the last moment. She told him how they had journeyed to the Arctic to rescue his father, and how they had foiled a goblin rebellion bankrolled by Opal Koboi. She recounted in great detail their mission to Chicago to steal back the C Cube, a supercomputer constructed by Artemis from pirated fairy technology. Finally, in a small, quiet voice, she told of Commander Root's death and Opal Koboi's mysterious plot to bring the fairy and human worlds together.

Artemis sat perfectly still, absorbing hundreds of incredible facts. His brow was slightly creased, as if the information were difficult to digest. Finally, when his brain had organized the data, he opened his eyes.

'Very well,' he said. 'I don't remember any of this, but I believe you. I accept that we humans have fairy neighbours below the planet's surface.'

'Just like that?'

Artemis's lip curled. 'Hardly. I have taken your story and cross-referenced it with the facts as I know them. The only other scenario which could explain everything that has happened, up to and including your own bizarre appearance, is a convoluted conspiracy theory involving the Russian Mafiya and a crack team of plastic surgeons. Hardly likely. But your fairy story fits, right down to something that you could not know about, Captain Short.'

'Which is?'

'After my alleged mind wipe, I discovered mirrored contact lenses in my own eyes and in Butler's. Investigation revealed that I myself had ordered the lenses, though I had no memory of the fact. I suspect that I ordered them to cheat your *mesmer*.'

Holly nodded. It made sense. Fairies had the power to mesmerize humans, but eye contact was part of the trick, coupled with a mesmeric voice. Mirrored contact lenses would leave the subject completely in control, while still pretending to be under the *mesmer*.

'The only reason for this would be if I had planted a trigger somewhere. Something that would cause my fairy memories to come rushing back. But what?'

'I have no idea,' said Holly. 'I was hoping that just seeing me would trigger recall.'

Artemis smiled in a very annoying way. As one would to a small child who had just suggested that the moon was made of cheese.

'No, Captain. I would guess that your Mister Foaly's mind-wiping technology is an advanced version of the memory-suppressant drugs being experimented with by various governments. The brain, you see, is a complex instrument; if it can be convinced that something did not happen, it will invent all kinds of scenarios to maintain that illusion. Nothing can change its mind, so to speak. Even if the conscious accepts something, the mind wipe will have convinced the subconscious otherwise. So, no matter how convincing you are, you cannot convert my altered subconscious. My subconscious probably believes that you are a hallucination or a miniature spy. No, the only way my memories could be returned to me would be if my subconscious could not present a reasonable argument – say if the one person whom I trust completely presented me with irrefutable evidence.'

Holly felt herself growing annoyed. Artemis could get under her skin like nobody else. A child who treated everyone else like children.

'And who is this one person whom you trust?'

Artemis smiled genuinely for the first time since Munich. 'Why, myself, of course.'

Munich

Butler woke to find blood dripping from the tip of his nose. It was falling on to the white hat of the hotel chef.

The chef stood with a group of hotel kitchen staff in the middle of a destroyed storage shed. The man gripped a cleaver in his hairy fist, just in case this giant on the tattered mattress that was wedged into the rafters was a madman.

'Excuse me,' said the chef politely, which is unusual for a chef, 'are you alive?'

Butler considered the question. Apparently, unlikely as it seemed, he was alive. The mattress had saved him from the strange missile. Artemis had survived too. He remembered feeling his charge's heartbeat just before he passed out. It wasn't there now.

'I am alive,' he grunted, a paste of tile dust and blood spilling from his lips. 'Where is the boy who was with me?'

The crowd assembled in the ruined shed looked at one another.

'There was no boy,' said the chef finally. 'You fell into the roof all on your own.'

Doubtless, this group would like an explanation, or they would inform the police.

'Of course there was no boy. Forgive me, the mind tends to wander after a three-storey fall.'

The group nodded as one. Who could blame the giant for being a touch rattled?

'I was leaning against the railing, sunning myself, when the railing gave way. Luckily for me, I managed to grab the mattress on the way down.'

)8• ⰔⰑⰀⰃ)8Ⰴ• ⰄⰔⰀⰍⰑ• ⰒⰑⰃⰄ⬥•

This explanation was met with the mass scepticism it thoroughly deserved. The chef voiced the group's doubts.

'You managed to grab a mattress?'

Butler had to think quickly, which is not easy when all the blood in your body is concentrated in your forehead.

'Yes. It was on the balcony. I had been resting in the sun.'

This entire sun business was extremely unlikely. Especially considering that it was the middle of winter. Butler realized that there was only one way to dispel the crowd. It was drastic, but it should work.

He reached inside his jacket, pulling out a small spiral pad.

'Of course I intend to sue the hotel for damages. Trauma alone should be worth a few million euro. Not to mention injuries. I presume I can count on you good people to be witnesses.'

The chef paled, as did the others. Giving evidence against one's employers was the first step to un-employment.

'I . . . I don't know, sir,' he stammered. 'I didn't actually see anything.' He paused to sniff the air. 'I think I smell my pavlova burning. Dessert will be ruined.'

The chef hopped over the chunks of shattered tile and disappeared back into the hotel. The remaining staff followed his lead, and within seconds Butler was on his own again. He smiled, though the action sent a flare of pain down his neck. The threat of a lawsuit generally scattered witnesses as effectively as any gunfire.

The giant Eurasian disentangled himself from the remains of the rafters. He really had been amazingly lucky not to be impaled on the beams. The mattress had absorbed most of the impact, while the timbers were rotten and had splintered harmlessly.

Butler dropped to the floor, brushing dust from his suit. His priority now was to find Artemis. It seemed likely that whoever had made the attempt on his life had taken the boy. But why would someone try to kill him, and then take him prisoner? Unless it was their unknown enemy who had taken advantage of the situation and decided to look for a ransom.

Butler returned to the hotel room, where everything was as they had left it. There was absolutely no sign that anything had exploded in here. The only unusual things revealed by Butler's investigations were small clusters of dead insects and spiders. Curious. It was as though the blue flash of light affected only living things, leaving the buildings unaffected.

A blue rinse, said his subconscious, but his conscious self took no notice.

Butler quickly packed Artemis's box of tricks and, of course, his own. The weapons and surveillance equipment would be held in a deposit box at the airport. He left the Kronski Hotel without checking out. An early checkout would arouse suspicion, and with any luck this entire matter could be resolved before the school group returned home.

The bodyguard collected the Hummer in the hotel car park, and set off for the airport. If Artemis had been kidnapped, then the kidnappers would contact Fowl Manor with their ransom demand. If Artemis had simply removed himself from danger, he had always been told to head for home. Either way, the trail led to Fowl Manor, so that was where Butler intended to go.

TEMPLE BAR, DUBLIN, IRELAND

Artemis had recovered sufficiently for his natural curiosity to surface. He walked around the cramped room, touching the spongy surface of the walls.

'What is this place? Some form of surveillance hide?'

'Exactly,' said Holly. 'I was on stakeout here a few months ago. A group of rogue dwarfs was meeting their jewellery fences here. From the outside, this is just another patch of sky on top of a building. It's a cham pod.'

'Cam, camouflage?'

'No, cham, chameleon. This suit is cam, camouflage.'

'You do know, I suppose, that chameleons don't actually change colour to suit their surroundings. They change according to mood and temperature.'

· ⚘⯑⯑⟨◯◉⯑· ⯑⟨⟨◯⯑⯑· ⯑⯑◯⯑◯⊕

Holly looked out over Temple Bar. Below them, thousands of tourists, musicians and residents were winding their way through the small artisans' streets.

'You'd have to tell Foaly about that. He names all this stuff.'

'Ah, yes,' said Artemis. 'Foaly. He is a centaur, is he not?'

'That's right.' Holly turned to face Artemis. 'You're taking this very calmly. Most humans completely freak out when they find out about us. Some go into shock.'

Artemis smiled. 'I am not most humans.'

Holly turned back to the view. She was not going to argue with that statement.

'So tell me, Captain Short. If all I am to the fairy People is a threat, why did you heal me?'

Holly rested her forehead against the cham pod's translucent face.

'It's our nature,' she replied. 'And of course I need you to help me find Opal Koboi. We've done it before, we can do it again.'

Artemis stood beside her at the window. 'So first you mind-wipe me, and now you need me?'

'Yes, Artemis. Gloat all you like. The mighty LEP needs your help.'

'Of course there is the matter of my fee,' said Artemis, buttoning his jacket across the bloodstain on his shirt.

Holly rounded on him. 'Your fee? Are you serious?

After all the fairy People have done for you? Can't you just do something good for once in your life?'

'Obviously you elves are an emotional race. Humans are slightly more business-minded. Here are the facts: you are a fugitive from justice, on the run from a murdering pixie genius. You have no funds and few resources. I am the only one who can help you track down this Opal Koboi. I think that's worth a few bars of anybody's gold.'

Holly glowered at him. 'Like you said, Mud Boy. I don't have any resources.'

Artemis spread his hands magnanimously. 'I'm prepared to accept your word. If you can guarantee me one metric tonne of gold from your hostage fund, I will devise a plan to defeat this Opal Koboi.'

Holly was in a hole and she knew it. There was no doubt that Artemis could give her the edge over Opal, but it galled her to pay someone who used to be a friend. 'And what if Koboi defeats us?'

'If Koboi defeats and presumably murders us both, then you can consider the debt null and void.'

'Great,' growled Holly. 'It would be almost worth it.'

She left the window and began raiding the pod's medical chest. 'You know something, Artemis. You're exactly how you were when we first met: a greedy Mud Boy who doesn't care about anyone except himself. Is that really how you want to be for the rest of your life?'

Artemis's features remained static, but below the

surface his emotions were in turmoil. Of course he was right to ask for a fee; it would be stupid not to. But even asking had made him feel guilty. It was this idiotic new-found conscience. His mother seemed able to activate it at will, and this fairy creature could do it too. He would have to keep a tighter check on his emotions.

Holly finished raiding the cabinet. 'Well, Mister Consultant. What's our first move?'

Artemis did not hesitate. 'There are only two of us, and we are not very tall. We need reinforcements. As we speak, Butler will be making for Fowl Manor. He may even be there already.'

Artemis turned on his mobile, speed dialling Butler's phone. A recorded message told him that the customer he was trying to reach was not available. He declined the offer to try again, instead dialling Fowl Manor. An answering machine cut in after the third ring. Obviously his parents had already left for the spa in Westmeath.

'Butler,' said Artemis to the recorder. 'You are well, I hope. I myself am fine. Listen very carefully to what I have to tell you, and believe me, every word is true . . .' Artemis proceeded to summarize the day's events into the phone. 'We will arrive at the manor shortly. I suggest we stock up on essentials and proceed to a safe house . . .'

Holly tapped him on the shoulder.

'We should get out of here. Koboi is no fool. I

wouldn't be surprised if she had some back-up plan in case we survived.'

Artemis covered the mouthpiece with his palm.

'I agree. That is what I would do. This Koboi person is probably on her way right now.'

As if on cue, one of the pod walls fizzled and dissolved. Opal Koboi was standing in the hole, flanked by Merv and Scant Brill. The pixie twins were armed with transparent plastic handguns. Merv's gun barrel glowed gently in the aftermath of his wall-melting shot.

'Murderer!' shouted Holly, reaching for her gun. Merv casually put a blast close enough to her head to singe her eyebrows. Holly froze, raising her hands in submission.

'Opal Koboi, I presume?' said Artemis, although if Holly had not told him the whole story he never would have guessed that the female before him was anything but a human child. Her black hair was braided down her back, and she wore a checked pinafore of the type worn by a million schoolgirls around the world. Her ears were, of course, rounded.

'Artemis Fowl, how nice to see you again. I do believe that in different circumstances we could have been allies.'

'Circumstances change,' said Artemis. 'Perhaps we can still be allies.'

Holly chose to give Artemis the benefit of the doubt. Maybe he was acting like a traitor to save their skins. Maybe.

Opal fluttered her long, curved eyelashes. 'Tempting, but no. I feel the world is only large enough for one child genius. And now that I'm pretending to be a child, that genius would be me. Meet Belinda Zito, a girl with big plans.'

Holly reached out a hand towards her weapon but stopped when Merv levelled his transparent handgun at her.

'I know you,' she said to the Brill brothers. 'The pixie twins. You were on TV.'

Scant couldn't hold back a grin. 'Yes, on *Canto*. It was the season's highest-rated show. We're thinking of writing a book, aren't we, Merv? All about how we . . .'

'Finish each other's sentences,' completed Merv, though he knew it would cost him.

'Shut up, you utter imbecile,' snapped Opal, shooting Merv a poisonous glare. 'Keep your weapon up and your mouth closed. This is not about you, it is about me. Remember that, and I may not have to liquidize the pair of you.'

'Yes, of course, Miss Koboi. It's all about you.'

Opal almost purred. 'That's right. It's always about me. I am the only important one here.'

Artemis casually slipped one hand into his pocket. The one holding the mobile phone that was still connected to Fowl Manor.

'If I may, Miss Koboi. This delusion of self-importance

is common among those recently awakened from comas. It is known as the Narcissus Syndrome. I wrote a paper on this precise subject for the *Psychologists' Yearbook*, under the pseudonym of Sir E. Brum. You have spent so much time in your own company, so to speak, that everyone else has become unreal . . .'

Opal nodded at Merv. 'For heaven's sake, shut him up.'

Merv was glad to oblige, sinking a blue power slug into Artemis's chest. The Irish boy dropped in mid-lecture.

'What have you done?' shouted Holly, dropping to Artemis's side. She was relieved to find a steady heartbeat under the bloodied shirt.

'Oh no,' said Opal. 'Not dead, merely painfully stunned. He is having quite a day, young Artemis.'

Holly glared at the small pixie, her pretty features distorted by grief and outrage. 'What do you want from us? What else can you do?'

Opal's face was the picture of innocence. 'Don't blame me. You have brought this on yourself. All I wanted to do was bring down fairy society as we know it, but oh no, you wouldn't have it. Then I planned a couple of relatively simple assassinations, but you insisted on surviving. Kudos to you for evading the bio-bomb, by the way. I was watching the whole thing from twenty metres up in my stealth shuttle. Containing the solinium with an LEP helmet – good thinking. But now, because you have caused me so much trouble and exasperation, I think I will indulge myself a little.'

Holly swallowed the fear that was crawling up her throat.

'Indulge yourself?'

'Oh yes. I had a nasty little scenario planned for Foaly, something theatrical involving the Eleven Wonders. But now I have decided that you are worthy of it.'

Holly tensed herself. She should go for her gun, there was no other option. But she had to ask; it was fairy nature.

'How nasty?'

Opal smiled, and evil was the only word for that expression.

'Troll nasty,' she said. 'And one more thing. I am telling you this because you are about to die, and I want you to hate me as much as I hate you at the moment of your death.' Opal paused, allowing the tension to build. 'Do you remember the sweet spot on the bomb I strapped to Julius?'

Holly felt as though her heart was expanding to fill her chest. 'I remember.'

Opal's eyes flared. 'Well, there wasn't one.'

Holly went for her gun, and Merv hit her in the chest with a blue charge. She was asleep before she hit the ground.

CHAPTER 6: TROLL NASTY

 THREE thousand metres below the surface of the Atlantic, an LEP sub-shuttle was speeding through a minor volcanic trench towards the mouth of a subterranean river. The river led to an LEP shuttle port, where the sub-shuttle's passengers could transfer to a regular craft.

Three passengers and a pilot were aboard it. The passengers were a dwarf felon and the two Atlantis marshals who were escorting him. Mulch Diggums, the felon in question, was in high spirits for someone in prison clothes, the reason being, his appeal had finally come through, and his lawyer was optimistic that all charges against his client were about to be quashed on a technicality.

Mulch Diggums was a tunnel dwarf who had abandoned the mines in favour of a life of crime. He removed items of value from Mud People's houses and sold them on the black market. In the past few years his destiny had become intertwined with those of Artemis Fowl and Holly Short, and he had played a key part in their adventures. Inevitably, this rollercoaster lifestyle had come crashing down around him as the long arm of the LEP closed in.

Before he had been led away to serve the remainder of his sentence, Mulch Diggums was permitted to say goodbye to his human friend. Artemis had given him two things. One was a note advising him to check the dates on the original search warrant for his cave. The other was a gold medallion, to be returned to Artemis in two years. Apparently Artemis had wished to resurrect their partnership at that time. Mulch had studied the medallion a thousand times, searching for its secrets, until his constant rubbing wore down the gold plating, to reveal a computer disk beneath. Obviously, Artemis had recorded a message to himself. A way to return the memories that the LEP had taken from him.

As soon as he had been transported to the Deeps maximum-security prison outside Atlantis, Mulch had put in a request for a counsel call. When his state-appointed attorney had grudgingly turned up, Mulch advised him to check the dates on the search warrant leading to his original arrest. Somehow, amazingly, the dates were wrong. According to the LEP computer, Julius Root had searched his cave before obtaining a search warrant. This nullified both this and all later arrests. All that remained was a lengthy processing period and one last interview with the arresting officer, and Mulch would be a free dwarf.

Finally, the day had come. Mulch was being shuttled to Police Plaza for his meeting with Julius Root. Fairy law allowed Root one thirty-minute interview to squeeze some kind of confession from Mulch. All the dwarf had to do was stay quiet, and he would be eating vole curry in his favourite dwarf chop house by dinnertime.

Mulch closed his fist round the medallion. He had no doubt who was pulling the strings here. Somehow Artemis had hacked into the LEP computer and changed his records. The Mud Boy was setting him free.

One of the marshals, a slight elf with Atlantean gills, sucked a slobbery breath in through his neck, letting it out through his mouth.

'Hey, Mulch,' he wheezed. 'What are you going to do when your appeal is turned down? Are you gonna crack up like a little girl? Or are you gonna take it real stoic, like a dwarf should?'

Mulch smiled, exposing his unfeasibly large number of teeth. 'Don't worry about me, fishboy. I'll be eating one of your cousins by tonight.'

Generally the sight of Mulch's tombstone teeth was enough to freeze any smart alec comments, but the marshal was not used to backchat from an inmate.

'Keep at it with the big mouth, dwarf. I have plenty of rocks for you to chew, back in the Deeps.'

'In your dreams, fishboy,' retorted Mulch, enjoying the banter after months of kowtowing.

The officer rose to his feet. 'It's Vishby, the name is Vishby.'

'Yes, fishboy, that's what I said.'

The second officer, a water sprite with batlike wings folded behind his back, chuckled. 'Leave him alone, Vishby. Don't you know who you're talking to? This here is Mulch Diggums. The most famous thief under the world.'

Mulch smiled, though fame is not a good thing when you're a thief.

'This guy has a whole list of genius moves to his credit.'

Mulch's smile faded as he realized that he was about to be the butt of more jokes.

'Yeah, so first he steals the Jules Rimet trophy from the humans and tries to sell it to an undercover LEP fairy.'

Vishby sat, rubbing his hands in glee. 'You don't say? What a brain! How does it fit inside that itty-bitty head?'

The sprite strutted along the shuttle's aisle, delivering his lines like an actor. 'So then he lifts some of the Artemis Fowl gold, and he lies low in Los Angeles. And do you want to know how he lies low?'

Mulch groaned.

'Tell me,' wheezed Vishby, his gills unable to suck in air fast enough.

'He buys hisself a penthouse apartment, and starts building a collection of stolen Academy Awards.'

Vishby laughed until his gills flapped.

Mulch could take it no longer. He shouldn't have to put up with this, he was virtually a free fairy, for goodness' sake. 'Hisself? Hisself? I think you've spent a bit too long underwater. The pressure is squashing your brain.'

'*My* brain is squashed?' said the sprite. 'I'm not the one who spent a couple of centuries in prison. I'm not the one wearing manacles and a mouth ring.'

It was true. Mulch's criminal career had not exactly been an unqualified success. He had been caught more often than he'd escaped. The LEP were just too techno-logically advanced to evade. Maybe it was time to go straight, while he still had his looks.

Mulch shook the manacles that shackled him to a rail in the holding area. 'I won't be wearing these for long.'

Vishby opened his mouth to respond, then he paused. A plasma screen was flashing red on a wall panel. Red was urgent. There was an important message coming through. Vishby hooked an earphone over his ear, turning the screen away from Mulch. As the message was delivered, his face lost every trace of levity.

Several moments later he tossed the headphones on to

the console. 'It looks like you'll be wearing those chains for a bit longer than you thought.'

Mulch's jaw strained against the steel mouth ring. 'Why? What's happened?'

Vishby scratched a strip of gill-rot on his neck. 'I shouldn't be telling you this, convict, but Commander Root has been murdered.'

Mulch couldn't have been more shocked if they had connected him to the underworld grid.

'Murdered? How?'

'Explosion,' said Vishby. 'Another LEP officer is the prime suspect. Captain Holly Short. She's missing, presumed dead, on the surface, but that hasn't been confirmed.'

'I'm not a bit surprised,' said the water sprite. 'Females are too temperamental for police work. They couldn't even handle a simple transport job like this.'

Mulch was in shock. He felt as though his brain had snapped its moorings and was spinning inside his head. Holly murdered Julius? How could that be possible? It wasn't possible, simple as that. There must be a mistake. And now Holly was missing, presumed dead. How could this be happening?

'Anyways,' continued Vishby, 'we gotta turn this crate round and head back to Atlantis. Obviously your little hearing is being postponed indefinitely, until this entire mess gets sorted out.'

The water sprite slapped Mulch playfully on the cheek. 'Tough break, dwarf. Maybe they'll get the red tape untangled in a couple of years.'

Mulch barely felt the slap, though the words penetrated. A couple of years. Could he take a couple of years in the Deeps? Already his soul was crying out for the tunnels. He needed to feel soft earth between his fingers. His insides needed real roughage to clear them out. And, of course, there was a chance that Holly was still alive and needed help. A friend. He had no option but to escape.

Julius dead. It couldn't be true.

Mulch mentally leafed through his dwarf abilities to select the best tool for this escape. He had long since forfeited his magic by breaking most of the fairy Book's commandments, but dwarfs had extraordinary gifts granted them by evolution. Some of these were common knowledge among the People, but dwarfs were a notoriously secretive race who believed that their survival depended on concealing these talents. It was well known that dwarfs excavated tunnels by ingesting the earth through their unhinged jaws, then ejecting the recycled dirt and air through the other end. Most fairies were aware that dwarfs could drink through their pores, and if they stopped drinking for a while then these pores were transformed into mini suction cups. Fewer People knew that dwarf spit was luminous and hardened when layered.

And no one knew that a by-product of dwarf flatulence was a methane-producing bacterium called methanobrevibacter smithii that prevented decompression sickness in deep-sea divers. In fairness, dwarfs didn't know this either. All they knew was that on the rare occasions when they found themselves accidentally burrowing into the open sea, the bends did not seem to affect them.

Mulch thought about it for a moment and realized that there was a way to combine all of his talents and get out of here. He had to put his 'on the hoof' plan into effect immediately before they went into the deep Atlantic trenches. Once the sub-shuttle went too deep, he would never make it.

The craft swung in a long arc until it was heading back the way it had come. The pilot would punch the engines as soon as they were outside Irish fishing waters. Mulch began to lick his palms, smoothing the spittle through his halo of wild hair.

Vishby laughed. 'What are you doing, Diggums? Cleaning up for your cellmate?'

Mulch would have dearly loved to unhinge his jaw and take a bite out of Vishby, but the mouth ring prevented him from opening his mouth far enough to unhinge. He had to content himself with an insult.

'I may be a prisoner, fishboy, but in ten years I'll be free. You, on the other hand, will be an ugly bottom-feeder for the rest of your life.'

Vishby scratched his gill-rot furiously. 'You just bought yourself six weeks in solitary, mister.'

Mulch slathered his fingers with spittle, spreading it around the crown of his head, reaching as far back as the manacles would allow. He could feel it hardening, clamping on to his head like a helmet. Exactly like a helmet. As he licked, Mulch drew great breaths of air through his nose, storing the air in his intestines. Each breath sucked air out of the pressurized space faster than the pumps could push it back in.

The marshals did not notice this unusual behaviour, and even if they had, the pair would doubtless have put it down to nerves. Deep breathing and grooming: classic nervous traits. Who could blame Mulch for being nervous – after all, he was heading back to the very place criminals had nightmares about.

Mulch licked and breathed, his chest blowing up like a bellows. He felt the pressure fluttering down below, anxious to be released.

Hold on, he told himself. *You will need every bubble of that air.*

The shell on his head crackled audibly now, and if the lights were dimmed, it would glow brightly. The air was growing thin, and Vishby's gills noticed even if he didn't. They rippled and flapped, boosting their oxygen intake. Mulch sucked again, a huge gulp of air. A bow plate clanged as the pressure differential grew.

The sprite noticed the change first. 'Hey, fishboy.'

Vishby's pained expression spoke of years enduring this nickname. 'How many times do I have to tell you?'

'OK, Vishby, keep your scales on. Is it getting hard to breathe in here? I can't keep my wings up.'

Vishby touched his gills; they were flapping like bunting in the wind. 'Wow. My gills are going crazy. What's happening here?' He pressed the cabin intercom panel. 'Everything all right? Maybe we could boost the air pumps?'

The voice that came back was calm and professional, but with an anxious undertone that was unmistakable. 'We're losing pressure in the holding area. I'm trying to nail down the leak now.'

'Leak?' squeaked Vishby. 'If we depressurize at this depth, the shuttle will crumple like a paper cup.'

Mulch took another huge breath.

'Get everyone into the cockpit. Come through the airlock, right now.'

'I don't know,' said Vishby. 'We're not supposed to untie the prisoner. He's a slippery one.'

The slippery one took another breath. And this time a stern plate actually buckled with a crack like thunder.

'OK, OK. We're coming.'

Mulch held out his hands. 'Hurry up, fishboy. We don't all have gills.'

Vishby swiped his security card along the magnetic strip

on Mulch's manacles. The manacles popped open. Mulch was free . . . as free as you can be in a prison sub with three thousand crushing metres of water overhead. He stood, taking one last gulp of air. Vishby noticed the act.

'Hey, convict, what are you doing?' he asked. 'Are you sucking in all the air?'

Mulch burped. 'Who, me? That's ridiculous.'

The sprite was equally suspicious. 'He's up to something. Look, his hair is all shiny. I bet this is one of those secret dwarf arts.'

Mulch tried to look sceptical. 'What? Air sucking and shiny hair? I'm not surprised we kept it a secret.'

Vishby squinted at him. The marshal's eyes were red-rimmed, and his speech was slurred from oxygen deprivation. 'You're up to something. Put out your hands.'

Getting shackled again now was not part of the plan. Mulch feigned weakness. 'I can't breathe,' he said, leaning against the wall. 'I hope I don't die in your custody.'

This statement caused enough distraction for Mulch to heave one more mighty breath. The stern plate creased inwardly, a silver stress-line cracking through the paint. All over the compartment red pressure lights flared on.

The pilot's voice blared through the speaker. 'Get in here!' he shouted, all traces of composure gone. 'She's gonna fold.'

Vishby grabbed Mulch by the lapels. 'What did you do, dwarf?'

154

Mulch sank to his knees, flicking open the bum-flap at the rear of his prison overalls. He gathered his legs together under him, ready to move.

'Listen, Vishby,' he said. 'You're a moron, but not a bad guy, so do like the pilot says and get in there.'

Vishby's gills flapped weakly, searching for air. 'You'll be killed, Diggums.'

Mulch winked at him. 'I've been dead before.'

Mulch could hold on to the gas no longer. His digestive tract was stretched like a magician's animal balloon. He folded his arms across his chest, aimed the coated tip of his head at the weakened plate and let the gas loose.

The resultant emission shook the sub-shuttle to its very rivets, sending Mulch rocketing across the hold. He slammed into the stern plate, smack in the centre of the fault line, punching straight through. His speed popped him out into the ocean, perhaps half a second before the sudden change in pressure flooded the sub's chamber. Half a second later, the rear chamber was crushed like a ball of used tinfoil. Vishby and his partner had escaped to the pilot's cockpit just in time.

Mulch sped towards the surface, a stream of released gas bubbles clipping him along at a rate of several knots. His dwarf lungs fed on the trapped air in his digestive tract, and the luminous helmet of spittle sent out a corona of greenish light to illuminate his way.

Of course they came after him. Vishby and the water

sprite were both amphibious Atlantis dwellers. As soon as they jettisoned the wreckage of the rear compartment, the marshals cleared the airlock, finning after their fugitive. But they never had a prayer. Mulch was gas-powered; they merely had wings and fins. Whatever pursuit equipment they'd had was at the bottom of the ocean, along with the rear compartment, and the cockpit's back-up engines could barely outrun a crab.

The Atlantis marshals could only watch as their captive jetted towards the surface, mocking them with every bubble from his behind.

Butler's mobile phone had been reduced to so many plastic chips and bits of wiring by the jump from the hotel window. This meant that Artemis could not call him if he needed immediate assistance. The bodyguard double-parked the Hummer outside the first Phonetix store he saw, and purchased a tri-band car-phone kit. Butler activated the phone on the way to the airport and punched in Artemis's number. No good; the phone was switched off. Butler hung up and tried Fowl Manor. Nobody home, and no messages.

Butler breathed deeply, stayed calm and floored the accelerator. The drive to the airport took less than ten minutes. The giant bodyguard did not waste time returning the Hummer to the rental-agency car park, preferring to abandon it in the set-down area. It would be towed, and he would be fined, but he didn't have time to worry about it now.

The next plane to Ireland was fully booked, so Butler paid a Polish businessman two thousand euro for his first-class ticket, and in forty-five minutes he was on the Aer Lingus shuttle to Dublin Airport. He kept trying Artemis's number until they started the engines, and switched his phone on again as soon as the wheels touched down.

It was dark by the time he left the Arrivals terminal. Less than half a day had passed since they had broken into the safety deposit box in Munich's International Bank. It was incredible that so much could happen in such a short time. Still, when you worked for Artemis Fowl II, the incredible was almost a daily occurrence. Butler had been with Artemis since the day of his birth, just over fourteen years ago, and in that time he had been dragged into more fantastic situations than the average presidential bodyguard.

The Fowl Bentley was parked in the prestige level of the short-stay car park. Butler slotted his new phone into the car kit and tried Artemis again. No luck. But when he remote accessed the mailbox at Fowl Manor, there was one message. From Artemis. Butler's grip tightened on the leather steering wheel. Alive. The boy was alive at least.

The message started well enough, then took a decidedly strange turn. Artemis claimed to be unhurt, but perhaps was suffering from concussion or post-traumatic stress, because Butler's young charge also claimed that fairies were responsible for the strange missile. A pixie, to be precise. And now he was in the company of an elf, which was apparently a completely different animal from a pixie. Not only that, but the elf was an old friend who they had forgotten. And the pixie was an old enemy who they couldn't remember. It was all very strange. Butler could only conclude that Artemis was trying to tell him something, and that hidden inside these crazed meanderings was a message. He would have to analyse the tape as soon as he returned to Fowl Manor.

Then the recording became an unfolding drama. More players came within range of Artemis's microphone. The alleged pixie, Opal, and her bodyguards joined the group. Threats were exchanged and Artemis tried to talk his way out. It didn't work. If Artemis had a fault, it was that he tended to be very patronizing, even in crisis situations. The pixie, Opal, or whoever it really was, certainly didn't take kindly to being spoken down to. It appeared that she considered herself every bit Artemis's equal, if not his superior. She ordered Artemis silenced in mid-lecture, and her command was obeyed instantly. Butler experienced a moment of dread, until the pixie stated that Artemis was not dead, merely stunned. Artemis's new ally was similarly stunned, but not before she learned of their planned theatrical demise. Something to do with the Eleven Wonders, and trolls.

'You cannot be serious,' muttered Butler, pulling off the motorway at the exit for Fowl Manor.

To the average passer-by it would seem as though several rooms in the manor at the end of the avenue were occupied, but Butler knew that the bulbs in these rooms were all on timers and would switch on and off at irregular intervals. There was even a stereo system wired to each room that would pump talk radio into various areas of the house. All measures designed to put off a casual burglar. None of which, Butler knew, would put off a professional thief.

The bodyguard opened the electronic gates and sped up the pebbled driveway. He drew up directly in front of the main door, not bothering to park it in the shelter of the double garage. He pulled out his handgun and clip holster from a magnetic strip under the driver's seat. It was possible that the kidnappers had sent a representative who could already be inside the manor.

Butler knew as soon as he opened the main door that something was wrong. The alarm's thirty-second warning should have begun its countdown immediately, but it did not. This was because the entire box was covered in a case of some shiny, crackling, fibreglass-like substance. Butler poked it gingerly. The stuff glowed and seemed almost organic.

Butler proceeded along the lobby, sticking to the walls. He glanced towards the ceilings. Green lights winked in the shadows. At least the CCTV cameras were still working. Even if the manor's visitors had left, he should get a look at them on the security tapes.

The bodyguard's foot brushed against something. He glanced down. A large crystal bowl lay on the rug, the remains of a sherry trifle slopping in its base. Beside it lay a wad of gravy-encrusted tinfoil. A hungry kidnapper? A little way on, he found an empty champagne bottle and a stripped chicken carcass. Just how many intruders had been here?

The remnants of food formed a trail that led towards the study. Butler followed it upstairs, stepping over a half-eaten T-bone steak, two chunks of fruit cake and a pavlova shell. A light shone from the study doorway, casting a small shadow into the hall. There was someone in the study. A not very tall someone. Artemis?

Butler's spirits rose for a second when he heard his employer's voice, but they sank just as quickly. He recognized those words: he had listened to them himself in the car. The intruder was playing the taped message on the answering machine.

Butler crept into the study, stepping so lightly that his footfalls would not have alerted a deer. Even from the back, this intruder was a strange fellow. He was barely a metre tall, with a stocky torso and thick, muscled limbs. His entire body appeared to be covered with wild wiry hair that seemed to move independently. His head was

⊕⚘⚘⊕⬩ ⚘⚘⊕⬩ ⚘⚘⊕⬩ ⚘⚘⬩

encased in a helmet of the same glowing substance that had incapacitated the alarm box. The intruder was wearing a blue jumpsuit with a flap in the seat. The flap was half unbuttoned, giving Butler a view of a hairy rear end that seemed unsettlingly familiar.

The taped message was coming to an end.

Artemis's abductor was describing what lay in store for the Irish boy. 'Oh yes,' she said. 'I had a nasty little scenario planned for Foaly, something theatrical involving the Eleven Wonders. But now I have decided that you are worthy of it.'

'How nasty?' asked Artemis's new ally, Holly.

'Troll nasty,' responded Opal.

The Fowl Manor intruder made a loud sucking noise, then discarded the remains of an entire rack of lamb.

'Not good,' he said. 'This is really bad.'

Butler cocked his weapon, aiming it squarely at the intruder.

'It's about to get worse,' he said.

Butler sat the intruder in one of the study's leather armchairs, then pulled a second chair round to face him. From the front, this little creature looked even stranger. His face was basically a mass of wire-like hair surrounding eyes and teeth. The eyes occasionally glowed red like a fox's, and the teeth looked like two rows of picket fencing. This was no hairy child, this was an adult creature of some sort.

'Don't tell me,' sighed Butler. 'You're an elf.'

The creature sat up straight. 'How dare you!' he cried. 'I am a dwarf, as you very well know.'

Butler thought back to Artemis's confusing message.

'Let me guess. I used to know you, but somehow I forgot. Oh yes, the fairy police wiped my mind.'

Mulch burped. 'Correct. You're not as slow as you look.'

Butler raised the gun. 'This is still cocked, so less of the lip, little man.'

'Pardon me, I didn't realize we were enemies now.'

Butler leaned forward in his chair. 'We were friends?'

Mulch thought about it. 'Not at first, no. But I think you grew to love me for my charm and noble character.'

Butler sniffed. 'And personal hygiene?'

'That's not fair,' objected Mulch. 'Do you have any idea what I had to do to get here? I escaped from a sub-shuttle and swam a couple of miles in freezing cold water. Then I had to break into a blacksmith's in the west of Ireland – about the only place they still have blacksmiths – and snip off my mouth ring. Don't ask. *Then* I burrowed across the entire country to find out the truth about this entire affair. And when I get here, one of the few Mud Men that I don't feel like taking a bite out of is pointing a gun at me.'

'Hold on a minute,' said Butler. 'I need to get a tissue to wipe my eyes.'

'You don't believe any of this, do you?'

'Do I believe in fairy police and pixie conspiracies and tunnelling dwarfs? No, I don't.'

Mulch reached slowly inside his jumpsuit, pulling out the gold-plated computer disk.

'Maybe this will open your mind.'

Butler turned on one of Artemis's Powerbooks, making sure the laptop was not connected to any other computer by wire or infrared. If this disk did contain a virus, then they would lose only one hard drive. He cleaned the disk off with a cleaner spray and cloth, sliding it into the multi-drive.

The computer asked for a password.

'This disk is locked,' said Butler. 'What's the password?'

Mulch shrugged, a French stick in each hand. 'Hey, I don't know. It's Artemis's disk.'

Butler frowned. If this really was Artemis's disk, then Artemis's password would open it. He typed in three words. *Aurum potestas est.* Gold is power. The family motto. Seconds later the locked disk icon was replaced by a window containing two folders. One was labelled 'Artemis', the other 'Butler'. Before the bodyguard opened either, he ran a virus check just in case. The check came up clean.

Feeling strangely nervous, Butler opened the folder

with his name on it. There were over a hundred files on it. Mostly text files, but some video too. The largest file was labelled 'view me first'. Butler double-clicked that file.

A small Quicktime player opened on the screen. In the picture, Artemis was seated at the very desk which the laptop rested on. Bizarre. Butler clicked the 'play' triangle.

'Hello, Butler,' said Artemis's voice. Either that or a very sophisticated fake. 'If you are watching this, then our good friend Mister Diggums has come good.'

'You hear that?' spat Mulch through a mouthful of bread. '*Good friend* Mister Diggums.'

'Quiet!'

'Everything you think you know about this planet is about to change,' continued Artemis. 'Humans are not the only sentient beings on Earth; in fact we are not even the most technologically advanced. Below the surface are several species of fairy. Most are possibly primates, but I have not had an opportunity to conduct medical examinations as yet.'

Butler could not hide his impatience. 'Please, Artemis. Get to the point.'

'But more of that at another time,' said Artemis, as if he had heard. 'There is a possibility that you are watching this at a time of peril, so I must arm you with all the knowledge that we have gathered during our adventures with the Lower Elements Police.'

Lower Elements Police? thought Butler. *This is all a fake. Somehow it's fake.*

Again the video-Artemis seemed to read his thoughts. 'In order to verify the fantastical facts that I am about to reveal, I will say one word. Just one. A word that I could not possibly know unless you had told me. Something you said as you lay dying, before Holly Short cured you with her magic. What would you tell me if you lay dying, old friend? What would be the single word you would say?'

I would tell you my first name, thought Butler. Something only two other people in the world know. Something completely forbidden by bodyguard etiquette, unless it is too late to matter.

Artemis leaned in to the camera. 'Your name, my old friend, is Domovoi.'

Butler was reeling mentally. *Oh my God,* he thought. *It's true, it's all true.*

Something began to happen in his brain then. Disjointed images flashed through his subconscious, releasing repressed memories. The false past was swept away by blinding truth. An electric join-the-dots jolted through his cranium, making everything clear. It all made sense now. He felt old, because the healing had aged him. Sometimes he found it difficult to breathe, because Kevlar strands had been woven into the skin over his chest wound. He remembered Holly's kidnapping, and the B'wa Kell goblin revolution. He remembered Holly and Julius, the centaur Foaly and, of course, Mulch Diggums. There was no need to read the other files; one word had been enough. He remembered everything.

Butler studied the dwarf with fresh eyes. Everything was so familiar now: the vibrating frizz of hair, the bow-legged stance, the smell. He sprang from his chair, striding across to Mulch, who was busy raiding the study's mini-fridge.

'Mulch, you old reprobate. Good to see you.'

'Now he remembers,' said the dwarf without turning round. 'Do you have anything to say?'

Butler glanced at the open bum-flap. 'Yes. Don't point that thing at me. I've seen the damage it can do.'

The bodyguard's smile froze on his face as he remembered one detail of Artemis's phone message.

'Julius? I heard something about a bomb.'

Mulch turned from the fridge, his beard laced with a cocktail of dairy products.

'Yes. Julius is gone. I can't believe it. He's been chasing me for so many years.'

Butler felt a terrific weariness weighing on his shoulders. He had lost too many comrades over the years.

'And what's more,' continued Mulch, 'Holly is accused of murdering him.'

𝕒⚬𝕒ᘐ • ⨾ᘐ • ⋃ᕧᘇᘄᕲᘕᕊ • ✶᛭ᘕᘐ • ✦᛭ᘉ •

'That's just not possible. We have to find them.'

'Now you're talking,' said the dwarf, slamming the fridge door. 'Do you have a plan?'

'Yes. Find Holly and Artemis.'

Mulch rolled his eyes. 'Pure genius. It's a wonder you need Artemis at all.'

Now that the dwarf had eaten his fill, the two reacquainted friends sat round the conference table and brought each other up to speed.

Butler cleaned his gun as he spoke. He often did this in times of stress. It was a comfort thing.

'So, Opal Koboi somehow gets out of prison and hatches this complicated plot to avenge herself on everyone who put her in there. Not only that, but she sets Holly up to take the blame.'

'Remind you of anyone?' asked the dwarf.

Butler polished the Sig Sauer's slide. 'Artemis may be a criminal, but he is not evil.'

'Who said anything about Artemis?'

'Well, what about you, Mulch? Why didn't Opal try to kill you?'

'Ah well,' sighed the dwarf, ever the martyr. 'The LEP didn't advertise my involvement. It wouldn't do to have the proud officers of our police force tarnished by association with a known criminal.'

Butler nodded. 'It makes sense. So, you're safe for

now, and Artemis and Holly are alive. But Opal has something planned for them. Something to do with trolls and the Eleven Wonders. Any ideas?'

'We both know about trolls, right?'

Butler nodded again. He had fought a troll not so long ago – without a doubt the toughest battle he had ever been involved in. He couldn't believe the LEP had managed to wipe it from his mind.

'But what about the Eleven Wonders?'

'The Eleven Wonders is a theme park in Haven's Old Town district. Fairies are obsessed with Mud Men, so one bright-spark billionaire thought it would be a great idea to build smaller models of the human wonders of the world and put them all in one place. It did OK for a few years, but I think looking at these buildings made the People remember just how much they missed the surface.'

Butler ran through a list in his head. 'But there are only seven wonders in the world.'

'There used to be eleven,' said Mulch. 'Trust me, I have photographs. Anyway, the park is closed down now. That whole area of the city has been abandoned for years – the tunnels are not safe. And the whole place is overrun by trolls.' He stopped suddenly, the horror of what he had just said hitting home. 'Oh gods. Trolls.'

Butler began to quickly reassemble his weapon. 'We need to get down there right now.'

'Impossible,' said Mulch. 'I can't even begin to think how.'

Butler dragged the dwarf to his feet, propelling him towards the door.

'Maybe not. But you know someone. People in your business always know someone.'

Mulch ground his teeth, thinking about it. 'You know, there *is* someone. A sprite who owes Holly his life. But whatever I persuade him to do for us won't be legal.'

Butler grabbed a bag of weaponry from a cabinet.

'Good,' he said. 'Illegal is always faster.'

CHAPTER 7: **THE TEMPLE OF ARTEMIS**

THE LOWER ELEMENTS

 OPAL Koboi's shuttle was a concept model that had never gone into mass production. It was years ahead of anything on the market, but its skin of stealth ore and cam foil made the cost of such a vehicle so exorbitant that even Opal Koboi couldn't have afforded one without the government grants that had helped to pay for it.

Scant secured the prisoners in the passenger bay, while Merv piloted them across to Scotland, then underground through a mountain river in the Highlands. Opal busied herself making sure that her other plan, the one involving world domination, was proceeding smoothly.

She folded up the screen on a video phone, dialling a connection to Sicily. The person at the other end picked up in the middle of the first ring.

'Belinda, my dear. Is it you?'

The man who had answered was in his late forties, with Latin good looks and grey-streaked black hair framing his tanned face. He wore a white lab coat over an open-necked, striped Versace shirt.

'Yes, Papa. It's me. Don't worry, I am safe.'

Opal's voice was layered with the hypnotic *mesmer*. The poor human was utterly in her power, as he had been for over a month.

'When are you coming home, my dear? I miss you.'

'Today, Papa, in a few hours. How is everything there?'

The man smiled dreamily. '*Molto bene*. Wonderful. The weather is fine. We can take a drive to the mountains. Perhaps I can teach you to ski.'

Opal frowned impatiently. 'Listen to me, *idiota* . . . Papa. How is everything with the probe? Are we on schedule?'

For a moment, a flash of annoyance wrinkled the Italian's brow, then he was bewitched again.

'Yes, my dear. Everything is on schedule. The explosive pods are being buried today. The probe's systems check was a resounding success.'

Opal clapped her hands, the picture of a delighted daughter. 'Excellent, Papa. You are so good to your little Belinda. I will be with you soon.'

'Hurry home, my dear,' said the man, who seemed to

be utterly lost without the creature he believed to be his daughter.

Opal ended the call. 'Fool,' she said contemptuously. But Giovanni Zito would be allowed to live — at least until the probe he was constructing to her specifications punctured the Lower Elements.

Now that she had spoken to Zito, Opal was eager to concentrate on the probe portion of her plan. Revenge was certainly sweet, but it was also a distraction. Perhaps she should just dump these two from the shuttle and let the Earth's magma core have them.

'Merv,' she barked. 'How long to the theme park?'

Merv checked the instruments on the shuttle's dashboard. 'We've just entered the main chute network, Miss Koboi. Five hours,' he called over his shoulder. 'Perhaps less.'

Five hours, mused Opal, curling in her bucket seat like a contented cat. *She could spare five hours.*

Some time later, Artemis and Holly were stirring in their seats. Scant helped them back into consciousness with a couple of jolts from a buzz baton.

'Welcome back to the land of the condemned,' said Opal. 'How do you like my shuttle?'

The craft was impressive, even if it was ferrying Artemis and Holly to their deaths. The seats were covered with illegally harvested fur and the decor was plusher than your average palace. There were small entertainment hologram cubes suspended from the ceiling, in case the passengers wanted to watch a movie.

Holly began to squirm when she noticed what she was sitting on.

'Fur! You animal!'

'No,' said Opal. '*You're* sitting on the animals. As I told you, I am human now. And that is what humans do, skin animals for their own comfort. Isn't that right, Master Fowl?'

'Some do,' said Artemis coolly. 'Not me personally.'

'Really, Artemis,' said Opal archly. 'I hardly think that qualifies you for sainthood. From what I hear, you're just as eager to exploit the People as I am.'

'Perhaps. I don't remember.'

Opal rose from her seat and fixed herself a light salad from the buffet.

'Of course, they mind-wiped you. But surely you must remember now? Not even your subconscious could deny that this is happening.'

Artemis concentrated. He could remember something. Vague, out-of-focus images. Nothing very specific.

'I do remember something.'

Opal lifted her eyes from her plate. 'Yes?'

Artemis fixed her with a cool stare. 'I remember how Foaly defeated you before with superior intellect. I am certain he will do it again.'

Of course Artemis had not truly remembered this, he was simply repeating what Holly had told him. But the statement had the desired effect.

'That ridiculous centaur!' shrieked Opal, hurling her plate against the wall. 'He was lucky, and I was hampered by that idiot, Cudgeon. Not this time. This time I am the architect of my own fate. And of yours.'

'And what is it this time?' Artemis asked mockingly. 'Another orchestrated rebellion? Or perhaps a mechanical dinosaur?'

Opal's face grew white with rage. 'Is there no end to your impudence, Mud Boy? No small-scale rebellions this time. I have a grander vision. I will lead the humans to the People. When the two worlds collide, there will be a war and my adopted people will win.'

'You're a fairy, Koboi,' interjected Holly. 'One of us. Rounded ears don't change that. Don't you think the humans will notice when you don't get any taller?'

Opal patted Holly's cheek almost affectionately. 'My poor, dear, underpaid police officer, don't you think I thought of all this while I stewed in that coma for almost a year? Don't you think I thought of everything? I have always known that humans would discover us eventually, so I have prepared.' Opal leaned over, parting her jet-black hair to reveal a magically fading seven-centimetre scar on her scalp. 'Getting my ears rounded wasn't the only surgery I had done. I also had something inserted in my skull.'

'A pituitary gland,' guessed Artemis.

'Very good, Mud Boy. A rather tiny, artificial human pituitary gland. HGH is one of seven hormones secreted by the pituitary.'

'HGH?' interrupted Holly.

'Human growth hormone,' explained Artemis.

'Exactly. As the name implies, HGH enhances the growth of various organs and tissues, especially muscle and bone. In three months, I have already grown a centimetre. Oh, maybe I'll never make the netball team, but no one will ever believe that I am a fairy.'

'You're no fairy,' said Holly bitterly. 'At heart you've always been human.'

'That's meant to be an insult, I suppose. Maybe I deserve that, considering what I am about to do to you. In an hour's time there won't be enough of you two left to fill the booty box.'

This was a term that Artemis had not heard before. 'Booty box? That sounds like a pirate expression.'

Opal opened a secret panel in the flooring, revealing a small compartment underneath. 'This is a booty box. The term was coined by vegetable smugglers, over eight thousand years ago. A secret compartment that would go unnoticed by Customs officials. Of course these days, with X-ray, infrared and motion-sensitive cameras, a booty box isn't much good.' Opal smiled slyly like a child who has put one over on her teacher. 'Unless, of course, the box is completely constructed from stealth ore, refrigerated and equipped with internal projectors to fool X-ray and infrared. The only way to detect this booty box is to put your foot into it. So even if the LEP did board my shuttle, they would not find whatever it is I am choosing to smuggle – which in this case is a jar of chocolate truffles. Hardly illegal, but the cooler is full. Chocolate truffles are my passion, you know. All that time I was away, truffles were one of two things I craved. The other was revenge.'

Artemis yawned. 'How fascinating. A secret compartment. What a genius you are. How can you fail to take over the world with a *booty box* full of truffles?'

Opal smoothed Artemis's hair back from his forehead. 'Make all the jokes you want, Mud Boy. Words are all you have now.'

Minutes later, Merv brought the stealth shuttle in to land. Artemis and Holly were handcuffed and led down the retractable gangplank. They emerged into a giant tunnel, dimly illuminated by glo-strips. Most of the lighting panels were shattered and the rest were on their last legs. This section of the chute had once been part of a thriving metropolis, but now it was completely deserted and derelict. Demolition notices were pasted across various drooping billboards.

Opal pointed to one. 'This whole place is being torn down in a month. We just made the deadline.'

'Lucky us,' muttered Holly.

Merv and Scant prodded them wordlessly along the chute with their gun barrels. The road surface beneath their feet was buckled and cracked. Swear toads clustered in damp patches, spouting obscenities. The roadside was lined with abandoned concession stands and souvenir shops. In one window, human dolls were arranged in various warlike poses.

Artemis stopped, despite the gun at his back. 'Is that how you see us?' he asked.

'Oh no,' said Opal. 'You're much worse than that, but the manufacturers don't want to scare the children.'

Several huge hemispherical structures squatted at the end of the tunnel, each one the size of a football stadium. They were constructed of hexagonal panels, welded together along the seams. Some panels were opaque, others were transparent, and each panel was roughly the size of a small house.

Before the hemispheres stood a huge arch with strips of tattered gold leaf hanging from its frame. A sign hung from the arch, emblazoned with two-metre-high Gnommish letters.

'The Eleven Wonders of the Human World,' declared Opal theatrically. 'Ten thousand years of civilization, and you only manage to produce eleven so-called wonders.'

Artemis tested his handcuffs. They were tightly fastened.

'You know of course that there are only seven wonders on the official list.'

'I know that,' said Opal testily. 'But humans are so narrow-minded. Fairy scholars studied the video footage and decided to include the Abu Simbel Temple in Egypt, the Moai Statues in Rapa Nui, the Borobudur temple in Indonesia and the Throne Hall of Persepolis in Iran.'

'If humans are so narrow-minded,' commented Holly, 'I'm surprised that you want to be one of them.'

Opal passed through the arch. 'Well, I would prefer to be a pixie – no offence, Artemis – but the fairy People are shortly to be wiped out. I shall be seeing to that personally as soon as I have dropped you off in your new home. In ten minutes we'll be on our way to the island, watching on the shuttle monitors while you two get torn apart.'

They proceeded through the theme park, past the first hemisphere, which contained a two-thirds scale-model of the Great Pyramid of Giza. Several of the hexagonal panels had been ripped out and Artemis could see the remains of the model through the gaps. It was an impressive sight, made even more so by the scores of shaggy creatures scrambling up and down the pyramid's slopes.

'Trolls,' explained Opal. 'They have taken over the exhibits. But don't worry, they are extremely territorial and won't attack unless you approach the pyramid.'

Artemis was beyond amazement at this point, but, even

so, the sight of these magnificent carnivores preying on each other was enough to speed his heart up by a few beats. He paused to study the nearest specimen. It was a terrifying creature, at least two and a half metres tall, with grimy dreadlocks swinging about its massive head. The troll's fur-matted arms swung below its knees and two curved, serrated tusks jutted from its lower jaw. The beast watched them pass, its night eyes glowing red in their sockets.

The group arrived at the second exhibit, the Temple of Artemis at Ephesus. The hologram at the entrance displayed a revolving image of the Turkish building.

Opal read the history panel. 'Interesting,' she said. 'Now why do you suppose someone would name a male child after a female goddess?'

'It's my father's name,' said Artemis wearily, having explained this a hundred times. 'It can be used for girls or boys, and it means the hunter. Rather apt, don't you think? It may interest you to know that your chosen human name, Belinda, means "beautiful snake". Also rather fitting. Half of it, at any rate.'

Opal pointed a tiny finger at Artemis's nose. 'You are a very annoying creature, Fowl. I do hope all humans are not like you.' She nodded at Scant. 'Spray them,' she ordered.

Scant took a small atomizer from his pocket, dousing Holly and Artemis liberally with the contents. The liquid was yellow and foul-smelling.

'Troll pheromones,' said Scant, almost apologetically. 'These trolls will take one whiff of this and go absolutely crazy. To them, you smell like females in heat. When they find out you're not, they'll tear you into a thousand little bits, then chew on the pieces. We've had any broken panels repaired, so there's no escape. You can jump in the river if you like – the scent should wash off in about a thousand years. And, Captain Short, I have removed the wings from your suit and shorted out the cam foil. I did leave the heating coils – after all, one deserves a sporting chance.'

A lot of use heating coils will be against trolls, thought Holly glumly.

Merv was checking the exhibit's entrance through one of the transparent panels. 'OK. We're clear.'

The pixie opened the main entrance with a remote. Distant howls resonated from inside the exhibit. Artemis could see several trolls brawling on the steps of the replica temple. He and Holly would be torn apart.

The Brill brothers propelled them into the hemisphere.

'Best of luck,' said Opal, as the door slid shut. 'Remember, you're not alone. We'll be watching you via the cameras.'

The door clanged shut ominously. Seconds later, the electronic locking panel began to fizzle as one of the Brill brothers melted it from the outside. Artemis and Holly were locked in with a bunch of amorous trolls, and they smelt like females of the species.

The Temple of Artemis exhibit was a scale model that had been constructed with painstaking accuracy, complete with animatronic humans going about their daily business as they would have been in 400 BC. Most of the models had been stripped to the wires by the trolls, but some moved jerkily along their tracks, bringing their gifts to the goddess. Any robot whose path brought them too close to a pack of trolls was pounced on and torn to shreds. It was a grim preview of Artemis and Holly's own fate.

There was only one food supply: the trolls themselves. Cubs and stragglers were picked off by the bulls and butchered with teeth, claws and tusks. The pack leader took the lion's share, then tossed the carcass to the baying pack. If the trolls were confined here much longer, they would wipe themselves out.

Holly shouldered Artemis roughly to the ground. 'Quickly,' she said. 'Roll in the mud. Cover yourself, smother the scent.'

Artemis did as he was told, scooping mud over himself with his manacled hands. Any spots he missed were quickly slathered by Holly. He did the same for her. In moments the pair were almost unrecognizable.

Artemis was feeling something he could not remember having felt before: absolute fear. His hands shook, rattling the chains. There was no room in his brain for analytical thought. *I can't*, he thought. *I can't do anything.*

Holly took charge, dragging him to his feet and propelling him to a cluster of fake merchants' tents beside a fast-flowing river. They crouched behind the ragged canvas, peering at the trolls through rents in the material made by long claws. Two animatronic merchants sat on mats outside the tents, their baskets brimming with gold-and-ivory statuettes of the goddess Artemis. Neither model had a head. One of the heads lay in the dust some distance away, its artificial brain poking out through a bite hole.

'We need to get the cuffs off,' said Holly urgently.

'What?' mumbled Artemis.

Holly shook her manacles in his face. 'We need to get these off now! The mud will protect us for a minute, then the trolls will be on our trail. We have to get in the water, and with cuffs on we'll drown in the current.'

Artemis's eyes had lost their focus. 'The current?'

'Snap out of it, Artemis,' Holly hissed into his face. 'Remember your gold? You can't collect it if you're dead. The great Artemis Fowl, collapsing at the first sign of trouble. We've been in worse scrapes than this before.' Not exactly true, but the Mud Boy couldn't remember, could he?

Artemis composed himself. There was no time for a calming meditation, he would simply have to repress the emotions he was experiencing. Very unhealthy, psychologically speaking, but better than being reduced to chunks of meat between a troll's teeth.

He studied the handcuffs. Some form of ultra-light-plastic polymer. There was a digit pad in the centre, positioned so the wearer could not reach the digits.

'How many numbers?' he said.

'What?'

'In the code for the cuffs. You are a police officer. Surely you know how many numbers in the code for handcuffs.'

'Three,' replied Holly. 'But there are so many possibilities.'

'Possibilities but not probabilities,' Artemis said, irritating even when his life was in danger. 'Statistically, however, thirty-eight per cent of humans don't bother changing the factory code on digital locks. We can only hope that fairies are equally negligent.'

Holly frowned. 'Opal is anything but negligent.'

'Perhaps. But her two little henchfairies might not be so attentive to detail.' Artemis held out his cuffs to Holly. 'Try three zeroes.'

Holly did so, using a thumb. The red light stayed red.

'Nines. Three nines.'

Again the light stayed red.

Holly quickly tried all ten digits three times. None had any effect.

Artemis sighed. 'Very well. Triple digits was a bit too obvious, I suppose. Are there any other three-digit numbers that are burned into fairy consciousness? Something all fairies would know, and wouldn't be likely to forget?'

Holly racked her brain. 'Nine five one. The Haven area code.'

'Try it.'

She did. No good.

'Nine five eight. The Atlantis code.'

Again no good.

'Those numbers are too regional,' snapped Artemis. 'What is the one number that every male, female and infant knows?'

Holly's eyes widened. 'Of course. Of course. Nine zero nine. The police emergency number. It's on the corner of every billboard under the world.'

Artemis noticed something. The howling had ceased. The trolls had stopped fighting and were sniffing the air. The pheromones were in the breeze, drawing the beasts like puppets on strings. In eerie unison, their heads turned towards Holly and Artemis's hiding place.

Artemis shook his manacles. 'Try it quickly.'

Holly did. The light winked green and the cuffs popped open.

'Good. Excellent. Now let me do yours.'

Artemis's fingers paused over the keyboard. 'I can't read the fairy language or numerals.'

'You can, in fact you are the only human who can,' said Holly. 'You just don't remember. The pad is standard layout. One to nine, left to right, and zero at the bottom.'

'Nine zero nine,' muttered Artemis, pressing the appropriate keys. Holly's cuffs popped on the first try – which was fortunate, because there was no time for a second.

The trolls were coming, loping from the Temple's steps with frightening speed and co-ordination. They used the weight of their shaggy arms to swing forward while simultaneously straightening muscular legs. This launch method could take them up to six metres in a single bound. The animals landed on their knuckles, swinging their legs underneath them for the next jump.

It was an almost petrifying sight: a score of crazed carnivores jostling their way down a shallow, sandy incline. The larger males took the easy way down, charging right through the ravine. Adolescents and older males stuck to the slopes, wary of casual bites and scything tusks. The trolls crashed through mannequins and scenery, heading straight for the tent. Dreadlocks swung with every step, and eyes glowed red in the half-light. They held their heads back so that their highest point was their nose. Noses which were leading them directly to Holly and Artemis. And what was worse, Holly and Artemis could smell the trolls too.

Holly stuck both pairs of cuffs into her belt. They had

charge packs and could be adapted for heat or even as weapons, if they lived that long.

'OK, Mud Boy. Into the water.'

Artemis did not argue or question; there was no time for that. He could only assume that, like many animals, trolls were not lovers of water. He ran towards the river, feeling the ground below his feet vibrate with a hundred feet and fists. The howling had started again too, but it had a different tone, more reckless, mindless and brutal, as if whatever control the trolls had had was now gone.

Artemis hustled to catch up to Holly. She was ahead of him, lithe and limber, bending low to scoop up one of the fake plastic logs from a campfire. Artemis did the same, tucking it under his arm. They could be in the water for a long time.

Holly dived in, gracefully arcing through the air before entering the water with barely a splash. Artemis stumbled after her. All this running for one's life was not what he was built for. His brain was big, but his limbs were slight – which was exactly the opposite of what you needed when trolls were at your heels.

The water was lukewarm, yet the mouthful Artemis inadvertently swallowed tasted remarkably sweet. No pollutants, he supposed, using that small portion of his brain that was still thinking rationally. Something tagged his ankle, slicing through sock and flesh. Then he kicked into the river, and he was clear. A trail of hot blood lingered for a moment, before being whipped away by the current.

Holly was treading water in the centre of the river. Her auburn hair stood up in slick spikes.

'Are you hurt?' she asked.

Artemis shook his head. No breath for words.

Holly noticed his ankle, which was trailing behind him. 'Blood, and I don't have a drop of magic left to heal you. That blood is almost as bad as pheromones. We have to get out of here.'

On the bank, the trolls were literally hopping mad. They head-butted the ground repeatedly, drumming their fists in complex rhythms.

'Mating ritual,' explained Holly. 'I think they like us.'

The current was strong out in the centre of the river and it drew the pair quickly downstream. The trolls followed along, some hurling small missiles into the water. One clipped Holly's plastic log, almost dislodging her.

She spat out a mouthful of water. 'We need a plan, Artemis. That's *your* department. *I* got us this far.'

'Oh yes, well done, you,' said Artemis, having apparently recovered his sense of sarcasm. He raked wet strands of hair from his face and cast his eyes around, beyond the mêlée on the waterline. The Temple was huge, throwing an elongated, multi-pronged shadow across the desert area. The interior was wide open, with no obvious shelter from the trolls. The only deserted spot was the temple roof.

'Can trolls climb?' he spluttered.

Holly followed his gaze. 'Yes, if they have to, like big monkeys. But only if they have to.'

Artemis frowned. 'If only I could remember,' he said. 'If only I knew what I know.'

Holly kicked over to him and grasped his collar. They swirled in the white water, bubbles and froth squeezing between their logs.

'"If only" is no good, Mud Boy. We need a plan before the filter.'

'The filter?'

'This is an artificial river. It's filtered through a central tank.'

A bulb went on in Artemis's brain. 'A central tank. That's our way out.'

'We'll be killed! I have no idea how long we'll be underwater.'

Artemis took one last look around, measuring, calculating. 'Given the present circumstances, there is no other option.'

Up ahead, the currents began to circle, pulling in any rubbish picked up from the banks. A small whirlpool formed in the middle of the river. The sight of it seemed to calm the trolls. They gave up on the butting and banging and settled down to watch. Some, who would later prove to be the clever ones, moved along the bank.

'We follow the current,' shouted Artemis over the hiss. 'We follow it and hope.'

'That's it? That's your brilliant plan?' Holly's suit crackled as the water wormed its way into the circuits.

'It's not so much a plan as a lifesaving strategy,' retorted Artemis. He might have said more, but the river interrupted him, snatching him away from his elfin companion into the whirlpool.

He felt about as significant as a twig in the face of such power. If he tried to resist the water, it would slap the air from his lungs like a bully slapping his victim. Artemis's chest was compressed; even when his gasping mouth was above water, he could not force adequate amounts of air into his lungs. His brain was starved of oxygen. He couldn't think straight. Everything was curved: the swirl of his body, the sweep of the water. White circles on blue ones on green ones. His feet dancing little Möbius-strip patterns below his body. Riverdance. Ha ha.

Holly was in front of him, pinioning the two logs between them. A makeshift raft. She shouted something, but it was lost. There was only water now. Water and confusion.

She held up three fingers. Three seconds. Then they were going under. Artemis breathed as deeply as his constricted chest would allow. Two fingers now. Then one.

Artemis and Holly let go of their logs and the current

sucked them under like spiders down a drain. Artemis
fought to hold on to his air, but the buffeting water
squeezed it from between his lips. Bubbles spiralled
behind them, racing for the surface.

The water was not so deep or dark. But it was fast and
would not allow many images to stand still long enough to
be identified. Holly's face flashed past him, and all Artemis
could make out were big, hazel eyes.

The whirlpool's funnel grew narrower, forcing Holly
and Artemis together. They were swept diagonally down
in a flurry of bumping torsos and flapping limbs. They
pressed their foreheads together, finding some comfort
in each other's eyes. But it was short lived. Their progress
was cut brutally short by a metal grille covering the
drainage pipe. They slammed into it, feeling the sharp
wire leave indents on their skin.

Holly slapped at the grille, then wormed her fingers
through the holes. The grille was shiny and new. Fresh
weld marks dotted its rim. This was new and everything
else was old. Koboi!

Something nudged Holly's arm. An aqua tele-pod. It
was anchored to the grille by a plastic tie. Opal's face filled
the small screen sealed inside, and her grin filled most of
her face. She was saying something again and again on a
short loop. The words were inaudible over the din of sluice
and bubble, but the meaning was clear: *I beat you again.*

Holly grabbed the tele-pod, ripping it from its tether.

The effort threw her from the slipstream into the relatively calm surrounding waters. Her strength was gone, and she had no option but to go where the river led her. Artemis dragged himself from the flat face of the grille, using the last of his oxygen to kick his legs, just twice.

He was free of the whirlpool, floating along after Holly towards a dark mound, further down the river. *Air*, he thought with keen desperation, *I need to breathe. Not soon. Now. If not now, never.*

Artemis broke the surface mouth-first. His throat was sucking down air before the water cleared. The first breath came back up, laced with fluid, but the second was clear, and the third. Artemis felt the strength flow back into his limbs like mercury in his veins.

Holly was safe. Lying on the dark island in the river. Her chest heaved like a bellows and the tele-pod lay beneath her splayed fingers.

'Uh-huh,' said Opal Koboi on-screen. 'Sooo predictable.' She said it over and over, until Artemis struggled from the shallow water, climbed on the mound and found the mute button.

'I am really starting to dislike her,' he panted. 'She may come to regret little touches like the underwater television, because it's things like that which give me the motivation to get out of here.'

Holly sat up, looking around. They were lying on a mound of rubbish. Artemis guessed that since Opal had welded the grille across the filter pipe, the current swept everything the trolls discarded to this shallow spot. A small island of junk in the river bend. There were disembodied robot heads on the heap, along with battered statues and troll remains. Troll skulls with the thick wedge of forehead bone, and rotting pelts.

At least those particular trolls could not eat them. The dangerous trolls had followed them and were working themselves up into a lather again along the banks on both sides. But there was at least six metres of fifteen-centimetre-deep water separating them from the land. They were safe, for the moment.

Artemis felt memories attempting to break through to the surface. He was on the verge of remembering everything, he was certain of it. He sat completely still, willing it to happen. Unconnected images flashed behind his eyes: a mountain of gold; green, scaly creatures snorting fireballs; Butler packed in ice. But the images slid from his consciousness like drops of water off a windshield.

Holly sat up. 'Anything?'

'Maybe,' said Artemis. 'Something. I'm not sure. Everything is happening so fast. I need time to meditate.'

'We're out of time,' said Holly, climbing to the top of the junk pile. Skulls cracked beneath her feet. 'Look.'

Artemis turned towards the left bank. One of the trolls had picked up a large rock and raised it above his head.

Artemis tried to make himself small. If that rock hit, they would both be gravely injured, at the very least.

The troll grunted like a tennis pro serving, spinning the rock into the river. It barely missed the pile, landing with a huge splash in the shallow waters.

'A poor shot,' said Holly.

Artemis frowned. 'I doubt it.'

A second troll grabbed a missile, and a third. Soon all the brutes were hurling rocks, robot parts, sticks or whatever they could get their hands on towards the rubbish heap. Not one hit the shivering pair huddled on the pile.

'They keep missing,' said Holly. 'Every one of them.'

Artemis's bones ached from cold, fear and sustained tension.

'They're not trying to hit us,' he said. 'They're building a bridge.'

TARA, IRELAND, DAWN

The fairy shuttle port in Tara was the biggest in Europe. More than eight thousand tourists a year passed through its X-ray arches. Eight hundred and fifty cubic metres of terminal concealed beneath an overgrown hillock in the middle of the McGraney farm. It was a marvel of subterranean architecture.

Mulch Diggums, fugitive kleptomaniac dwarf, was

pretty marvellous himself in the subterranean area. Butler drove the Fowl Bentley north from the manor, and on Mulch's instructions slowed the luxury car down, five hundred metres from the shuttle port's camouflaged entrance. This allowed Mulch to dive through the rear door straight into the earth. He quickly disappeared, submerged below a layer of rich Irish soil. The best in the world.

Mulch knew the shuttle port layout well. He had once broken his cousin Nord out of police custody here, when the LEP had arrested him on industrial pollution charges. A vein of clay ran right up to the shuttle port wall and, if you knew where to look, there was a sheet of metal casing that had been worn thin by years of Irish damp. But on this particular occasion, Mulch was not interested in evading the LEP; quite the opposite.

He surfaced inside the holographic bush that hid the shuttle port's service entrance. He climbed out of his tunnel, shook the clay from his behind, got all the tunnel wind out of his system a bit more noisily than was absolutely necessary, and waited.

Five seconds later, the entrance hatch slid across and four grabbing hands reached out, yanking Mulch into the shuttle port's interior. Mulch did not resist, allowing himself to be bundled along a dark corridor and into an interview room. He was plonked down on an uncomfortable chair and left on his own to stew.

⚷☮⚸◗◉ • ⚐⚑ • ⚶ • ⚘⚙⚚⚛⚜⚝⚞ • ⚟⚐

Mulch did not have time to stew. Every second he spent sitting here picking insects from his beard hair was another second that Artemis and Holly had to spend running from trolls.

The dwarf rose from the chair, slapping his palms against the two-way mirror inset in the interview room wall.

'Chix Verbil,' he shouted, 'I know you're watching me. We need to talk. It's about Holly Short.'

Mulch kept right on banging on the glass until the cell door swung open and Chix Verbil entered the room. Chix was the LEP's fairy on the surface. Chix had been the first LEP casualty in the B'wa Kell goblin revolution, a year previously, and, had it not been for Holly Short, he would have been its first fatality. As it turned out, he got a medal from the Committee, a series of high-profile interviews on network television and a cushy surface job in E1.

Chix entered suspiciously, his sprite wings folded behind him. The strap was off his Neutrino holster.

'Mulch Diggums, isn't it? Are you surrendering?'

Mulch snorted. 'What do you think? I go to all the trouble of breaking out, just to surrender to a sprite. I think not, lame brain.'

Chix bristled, his wings fanning out behind him. 'Hey, listen, dwarf. You're in no position to be making cracks. You're in my custody, in case you hadn't noticed. There are six security fairies surrounding this room.'

'Security fairies. Don't make me laugh. They couldn't secure an apple in an orchard. I escaped from a sub-shuttle under a couple of miles of water. I can see at least six ways out of here without breaking a sweat.'

Chix hovered nervously. 'I'd like to see you try. I'd have two charges in your behind before you could unhinge that jaw of yours.'

Mulch winced. Dwarfs don't like 'behind' jokes.

'OK, easy there, Mister Gung-ho. Let's talk about your wing. How's it healing up?'

'How do you know about that?'

'It was big news. You were all over the TV for a while, even on pirate satellite. I was watching your ugly face in Chicago not so long ago.'

Chix preened. 'Chicago?'

'That's right. You were saying, if I remember rightly, how Holly Short saved your life, and how sprites never forget a debt, and whenever she needed you, you were there, whatever it took.'

Chix coughed nervously. 'A lot of that was scripted. And, anyway, that was before . . .'

'Before one of the most decorated officers in the LEP suddenly decided to go crazy and shoot her own commander?'

'Yes. Before that.'

Mulch looked Verbil straight in his green face. 'You don't believe that, do you?'

· ⚇⚇⚇ · ⚇⚇⚇ · ⚇ · ⚇⚇⚇ · ⚇⚇⚇ ⚇

Chix hovered even higher for a long moment, his wings whipping the air into currents. Then he settled back down to earth, sitting in the room's second chair. 'No. I don't believe it. Not for a second. Julius Root was like a father to Holly, to all of us.'

Chix covered his face with his hands, afraid to hear the answer to his next question.

'So, Diggums. Why are you here?'

Mulch leaned in close. 'Is this being recorded?'

'Of course. Standard operating procedure.'

'Can you switch off the mike?'

'I suppose. Why should I?'

'Because I'm going to tell you something important to the People's survival. But I'll only tell you if the mikes are off.'

Chix's wings began to flap once more. 'This better be really good. I better really like this, dwarf.'

Mulch shrugged. 'Oh, you're not going to like it. But it is really good.'

Chix's green fingers tapped a code into a keyboard on the table. 'OK, Diggums. We can talk freely.'

Mulch leaned forward across the desk. 'The thing is, Opal Koboi is back.'

Chix did not respond verbally, but the colour drained from his face. Instead of its usual robust emerald, the sprite's complexion was now pasty lime-green.

'Opal has escaped, somehow, and she has set this big

revenge thing in motion. First General Scalene, then Commander Root, and now Holly and Artemis Fowl.'

'O-Opal?' stammered Chix, his wounded wing suddenly throbbing.

'She's taking out anyone who had a hand in her imprisonment. Which, if memory serves me correctly, includes you.'

'I didn't do anything,' squeaked Verbil, as though protesting his innocence to Mulch could help him.

Mulch sat back. 'Hey, there's no point telling me. *I'm* not out to get you. If I remember correctly, you were on all the chat shows, spouting how you *personally* were the first member of the LEP to come into contact with the goblin smugglers.'

'Maybe she didn't see that,' said Chix hopefully. 'She was in a coma.'

'I'm sure someone taped it for her.'

Verbil thought about it, absently grooming his wings.

'So what do you want from me?'

'I need you to get a message to Foaly. Tell him what I said about Opal.' Mulch covered his mouth with a hand to fox any lip-readers who might review the tape. 'And I want the LEP shuttle. I know where it's parked. I just need the starter chip and the ignition code.'

'What? Ridiculous! I'd go to jail.'

Mulch shook his head. 'No, no. Without sound, all Police Plaza are going to see is another ingenious Mulch

Diggums escape. I knock you out, steal your chip and tunnel out through the pipe behind that water dispenser.'

Chix frowned. 'Go back to the "knock me out" part again.'

Mulch slammed one palm down on the table. 'Listen, Verbil, Holly is in mortal danger right now. She may already be dead.'

'That's what I heard,' interjected Chix.

'Well, she will definitely be dead if I don't get down there right now.'

'Why don't I just call this in?'

Mulch sighed dramatically. 'Because, moron, by the time Police Plaza Retrieval team get here, it will be too late. You know the rules: no LEP officer can act on the information of a convicted felon, unless that information has been verified by another source.'

'No one pays any attention to that rule, and calling me "moron" isn't helping.'

Mulch rose to his feet. 'You are a sprite, for heaven's sake. You are supposed to have this ancient code of chivalry. A female saved your life, and now hers is in danger. You are honour bound, as a sprite, to do whatever it takes.'

Chix held Mulch's gaze. 'Is all of this true? Tell me, Mulch, because this will have repercussions. This isn't some little jewellery heist?'

'It's true,' said Mulch. 'You have my word.'

Chix almost laughed. 'Oh, whoopee. Mulch Diggums's word. I can take that to the bank.' He took several deep breaths and closed his eyes. 'The chip is in my pocket. The code is written on the tab. Try not to break anything.'

'Don't worry, I'm an excellent driver.'

Chix winced in anticipation. 'I don't mean the shuttle, stupid. I mean my face. The ladies like me the way I am.'

Mulch drew back one gnarled fist.

'Well, I'd hate to disappoint the ladies,' he said and knocked Chix Verbil from his chair.

Mulch expertly rifled Chix's pockets. The sprite was not actually unconscious, but he was pretending. A wise move. In seconds Mulch had removed the starter chip and stuffed it into his beard. A clump of beard hair wrapped itself tightly around the chip, forming a waterproof cocoon. He also relieved Verbil of his Neutrino, though this was not part of the deal. Mulch crossed the room in two strides, jamming a chair under the door handle. That should buy him a couple of seconds. He wrapped one arm around the water dispenser, simultaneously unbuttoning his bum-flap. Speed was vital now because whoever had been watching the interview through the two-way mirror was already hammering on the door. Mulch saw a black dot appear on the door; they were burning their way in.

He ripped the dispenser from the wall, allowing several gallons of cooled water to flood the interview room.

'Oh, for heaven's sake,' moaned Chix from the floor. 'It takes forever to dry these wings.'

'Shut up. You're supposed to be unconscious.'

As soon as the water had drained from the supply pipe, Mulch dived in. He followed it to the first joint, then kicked it loose. Clumps of clay fell through, blocking the pipe. Mulch unhinged his jaw. He was back in the earth. No one could catch him now.

The shuttle bay was on the lower level, closest to the chute itself. Mulch angled himself downwards, guided by his infallible dwarf's internal compass. He had been in this terminal before, and the layout was burned into his memory, as was the layout of every building he'd ever been in. Sixty seconds of chewing earth, stripping it of minerals and ejecting waste at the other end brought Mulch face to face with an air duct. This particular duct led straight to the shuttle bay; the dwarf could even feel the vibration of the engines through his beard hair.

Generally, he would burn through the duct's metal panelling with a few drops of dwarf rock polish, but prison guards tended to confiscate items like that, so instead Mulch blasted a panel with a concentrated burst from the stolen handgun. The panel melted like a sheet of ice in front of a bar heater. He gave the molten metal a minute to solidify and cool, then slithered into the duct. Two left turns later, his face was pressed to the grille overlooking the shuttle bay itself. Red alarm lights were revolving over every door, and a harsh klaxon made sure that everyone knew there was some sort of emergency. The shuttle-bay workers were gathered in front of the intranet screen, waiting for news.

Mulch dropped to the ground with more grace than his frame suggested was possible, creeping across to the LEP shuttle. The shuttle was suspended nose up over a vertical supply tunnel. Mulch crept aboard, opening the passenger door with Chix Verbil's chip. The controls were hugely complicated, but Mulch had a theory about vehicle controls: *Ignore everything except the wheel and the pedals, and you'll be fine.* So far in his career he had stolen over fifty types of transportation, and his theory hadn't let him down yet.

The dwarf thrust the starter chip into its socket, ignoring the computer's advice that he run a systems check, and hit the release button. Eight tonnes of LEP shuttle dropped like a stone into the chute, spinning like an ice skater. The Earth's gravity grabbed hold of it, reeling it in towards the Earth's core.

Mulch's foot jabbed the thruster pedal, just enough to halt the drop. The radio on the dash started talking to him.

'You in the shuttle. You better come back here right now. I'm not kidding! In twenty seconds I personally am going to press the self-destruct.'

Mulch spat a wad of dwarf spittle on to the speaker, muffling the irate voice. He gargled up another wad in his throat, then deposited it on a circuit box below the radio. The circuits sparked and fizzled. So much for the self-destruct.

The controls were a bit heavier than Mulch was used to. Nevertheless he managed to tame the machine after a few scrapes along the chute wall. If the LEP ever recovered the craft, it would need a fresh coat of paint, and perhaps a new starboard fender.

A bolt of sizzling laser energy flashed past the porthole. That was his warning shot. One across the bows before they let the computer do the aiming. Time to be gone. Mulch kicked off his boots, wrapped his double-jointed toes around the pedals and sped down the chute towards the rendezvous point.

Butler parked the Bentley fifteen miles north-east of Tara, near a cluster of rocks shaped like a clenched fist. The rock forming the index finger was hollow, just as Mulch had told him it would be. The dwarf had, however, neglected to mention that the opening would be cluttered with crisp bags and chewing gum patties left over from a thousand teenagers' picnics. Butler picked his way through the rubbish, to discover two boys huddled at the rear, smoking secret cigarettes. A Labrador pup was asleep at their feet. Obviously, these two had volunteered to walk the dog so that they could sneak some cigarettes. Butler did not like smoking.

The boys looked up at the enormous figure looming over them, jaded teenage expressions freezing on their faces.

Butler pointed at the cigarettes. 'Those things will seriously damage your health,' he growled. 'And if they don't, I might.'

The teenagers stubbed out their cigarettes and scurried from the cave, which was exactly what Butler wanted them to do. He pushed aside a wizened scrub cluster at the rear of the cave to discover a mud wall.

'Punch right through the mud,' Mulch had told him. 'Generally, I eat through and patch it up afterwards, but you might not want to do that.'

Butler jabbed four rigid fingers at the centre of the mud wall where cracks were beginning to spread and, sure enough, the wall was only a few centimetres thick and crumbled easily under the pressure. The bodyguard pulled away chunks until there was sufficient space to squeeze through to the tunnel beyond.

To say there was *sufficient* space is perhaps a slight exaggeration; *barely enough* is probably more accurate. Butler's bulky frame was compressed on all sides by uneven walls of black clay. Occasionally a jagged rock poked through, tearing a gash in his designer suit. That was two suits ruined in as many days, one in Munich and now the second, below ground in Ireland. Still, suits were the least of his worries. If Mulch were right, then Artemis was running around the Lower Elements right now with a group of bloodthirsty trolls on his trail. Butler had fought a troll once, and the battle had very nearly killed him. He couldn't even imagine fighting an entire group.

Butler dug his fingers into the earth, pulling himself forward through the tunnel. This particular tunnel, Mulch had informed him, was one of many illicit back doors into the Lower Elements chute system, chewed out by fugitive dwarfs over the centuries. Mulch himself had excavated this one almost three hundred years ago, when he had needed to sneak back to Haven for his cousin's birthday bash. Butler tried not to think about the dwarf's recycling process as he went.

After several metres, the tunnel widened into a bulb-shaped chamber. The walls glowed a gentle green. Mulch had explained that too. The walls were coated with dwarf spittle, which hardened on prolonged contact with air and also glowed. Amazing. Drinking pores, living hairs and now luminous saliva. What next? Explosive phlegm? He wouldn't be a bit surprised. Who knew what secrets the dwarfs were hiding up their sleeves? Or in other places.

Butler kicked aside a pile of rabbit bones, the remains of previous dwarf snacks, and sat down to wait.

He checked the luminous face of his Omega wristwatch. He had dropped Mulch at Tara almost thirty minutes ago; the little man should be here by now. The bodyguard would have paced the chamber, but there was barely enough room for him to stand up, never mind pace. Butler crossed his legs, settling down for a power nap. He hadn't slept since the missile attack in Germany, and he wasn't as young as he used to be. His heartbeat and breathing slowed until eventually his chest barely moved at all.

Eight minutes later, the small chamber began to shake violently. Chunks of brittle spittle cracked from the wall, shattering on the floor. The ground beneath his feet glowed red, and a stream of insects and worms flowed away from the hot spot. Butler stood to one side, calmly brushing himself down. Moments later, a cylindrical section of earth dropped cleanly out of the floor, leaving a steaming hole.

Mulch's voice drifted through the hole, borne on the waves of the stolen shuttle's amplification system. 'Let's go, Mud Man. Move yourself. We have people to save, and the LEP is on my tail.'

On Mulch Diggums's tail, thought Butler, shuddering. *Not a nice place to be.*

Nevertheless, the bodyguard lowered himself into the hole and through the open roof hatch of the hovering LEP shuttle. Police shuttles were cramped, even for fairies, but Butler could not even sit up straight in a chair, even if there had been one wide enough for him. He had to content himself with kneeling behind the command seat.

'All set?' he enquired.

Mulch picked a beetle from Butler's shoulder. He

shoved it into his beard, where the unfortunate insect was immediately cocooned by hair.

'For later,' he explained. 'Unless you want it?'

Butler smiled, but it was an effort. 'Thanks. I already ate.'

'Oh, really? Well, whatever you ate, hold on to it, because we are in a hurry, so I may have to break a few speed limits.'

The dwarf cracked every joint in his fingers and toes, then sent the craft into a steep, spiralling dive. Butler slid to the rear of the craft and had to hook three seat belts together to prevent further jostling.

'Is this really necessary?' he grunted through rippling cheeks.

'Look behind you,' replied Mulch.

Butler struggled to his knees, directing his gaze through the rear window. They were being pursued by a trio of what looked like fireflies, but which were actually smaller shuttles. The craft matched their every spiral and jink exactly. One fired a small, sparking torpedo, which sent a shock wave through the hull. Butler felt the pores in his shaven head tingle.

'LEP uni-pods,' explained Mulch. 'They just took out our communications mast, in case we have accomplices in the chutes somewhere. Those pods have got a lock on our navigation system. Their own computers will follow us forever, unless.'

'Unless what?'

'Unless we can outrun them. Get out of their range.'

Butler tightened the belts across his torso. 'And can we?'

Mulch flexed his fingers and toes. 'Let's find out,' he said, flicking the throttle wide.

THE ELEVEN WONDERS, TEMPLE OF ARTEMIS EXHIBIT, THE LOWER ELEMENTS

Holly and Artemis huddled together on the small island of rotting carcasses, waiting for the trolls to finish building their bridge. The creatures were frantic now, hurling rock after rock into the shallow water. Some even braved placing a toe in the currents, but quickly drew them out again with horrified howls.

Holly wiped water from her eyes.

'OK,' she said. 'I have a plan. I stay here and fight them. You go back in the river.'

Artemis shook his head curtly. 'I appreciate it. But no. It would be suicide for both of us. The trolls would devour you in a second, then simply wait for the current to sweep me straight back here. There must be another way.'

Holly threw a troll skull at the nearest creature. The brute caught it deftly in his talons, crushing it to shards. 'I'm listening, Artemis.'

Artemis rubbed a knuckle against his forehead, willing the memory blocks to dissolve. 'If only I could remember. Then maybe . . .'

'Don't you remember anything?'

'Images. Something. Nothing coherent. Just nightmare pictures. This could all be a hallucination. That is the most likely explanation. Perhaps I should just relax and wait to wake up.'

'Think of it as a challenge. If this were a role-playing game, how would the character escape?'

'If this were a war game, I would need to know the other side's weaknesses. Water is one . . .'

'And light,' blurted Holly. 'Trolls hate light. It burns their retinas.'

The creatures were venturing on to their make-shift bridge now, testing each step carefully. The stink of their unwashed fur and fetid breath drifted across to the little island.

'Light,' repeated Artemis. 'That's why they like it here. Hardly any light.'

'Yes. The glow strips are on emergency power, and the fake sun is on minimum.'

Artemis glanced upwards. Holographic clouds scudded across an imitation sky, and right in the centre, poised dramatically above the Temple's roof, was a crystal sun, with barely a flicker of power in its belly.

An idea blossomed in his mind.

'There is scaffolding on the nearest corner of the Temple. If we could climb up and get to the sun, could you use the power cells from our handcuffs to light up the sun?'

Holly frowned. 'Yes, I suppose so. But how do we get past the trolls?'

Artemis picked up the waterproof pod that had been playing Opal's video message.

'We distract them with a little television.'

Holly fiddled with the tele-pod's on-screen controls until she found brightness. She flicked the setting to maximum. Opal's image was whited out by a block of glaring light.

'Hurry,' advised Artemis, tugging Holly's sleeve. The first troll was halfway across the bridge, followed by the rest of the precariously balanced bunch. The world's shaggiest conga line.

Holly wrapped her arms around the tele-pod. 'This is probably not going to work,' she said.

Artemis moved behind her. 'I know, but there is no other option.'

'OK. But if we don't make it, I'm sorry you don't remember. It's good to be with a friend at a time like this.'

Artemis squeezed her shoulder. 'If we make it through this, we will be friends. Bonded by trauma.'

Their little island was shaking now. Skulls were

dislodged from their perches and rolled into the water. The trolls were almost upon them, picking their way across the precarious walkway, squealing at every drop of water that landed on their fur. Any animals still on the shoreline were hammering the earth with their knuckles, long ropes of drool swinging from their jaws.

Holly waited until the last moment for maximum effect. The tele-pod's screen was pressed into the rubbish heap, so the approaching animals would not have a clue what was coming.

'Holly?' said Artemis urgently.

'Wait,' whispered Holly. 'Just a few seconds more.'

The first troll in the line reached their island. This was obviously the pack leader. He reared up to a height of almost three metres, shaking his shaggy head and howling at the artificial sky. Then he appeared to notice that Artemis and Holly were not in fact female trolls, and a savage rage took hold of his tiny brain. Dribbles of venom dropped from his tusks, and he inverted his talons for an upward slash. Trolls' preferred kill strike was under the ribs; this popped the heart quickly and did not give the meat time to toughen.

More trolls crowded on to the tiny island, eager for a share in the kill or a shot at a new mate. Holly chose that moment to act. She swung the tele-pod upwards, pointing the buzzing screen directly at the nearest troll. The creature reared back, clawing at the hated light as if it were a solid enemy. The light blasted the troll's retinas, sending him staggering backwards into his companions. A bunch of the animals tumbled into the river. Panic spread back along the line like a virus. The creatures reacted to water as though it were acid dappling their fur, back-pedalling furiously towards the shore. This was no orderly retreat. Anything in the way got scythed or bitten. Gouts of venom and blood flew through the air, and the water bubbled as though it were boiling. The trolls' howls of bloodlust changed to keening screams of pain and terror.

This can't be real, thought a stunned Artemis Fowl. *I must be hallucinating. Perhaps I am in a coma following the fall from the hotel window.* And because his brain provided this possible explanation, his memories stayed under lock and key.

'Grab my belt,' Holly ordered, advancing across the makeshift bridge.

Artemis obeyed instantly. This was not the time to argue about leadership. In any case, if there was the slightest possibility that this were actually happening, then Captain Short was better qualified to handle these creatures.

Holly wielded the tele-pod like a portable laser cannon, advancing step by step across the makeshift bridge. Artemis tried to concentrate on keeping his balance on the treacherous ground. They stepped from rock to rock, wobbling like novice tightrope walkers. Holly swung the tele-pod in smooth arcs, blasting trolls from every angle.

Too many, thought Artemis. *There are too many. We can never make it.*

But there was no future in giving up. So they kept going, taking two steps forward and one step back.

A crafty bull ducked low, avoiding Holly's first sweep. He reached out one taloned hand, cracking the pod's waterproof casing. Holly stumbled backwards, knocking over Artemis. The pair keeled over into the river, landing with a solid thump in the shallow water.

Artemis felt the air shoot from his lungs, and took an instinctive breath. Unfortunately, he took in water rather than air. Holly kept her elbows locked, so the ruptured casing stayed out of the river. Some water drops crept into the crack and sparks began to play across the screen.

Holly struggled to her feet, simultaneously aiming the screen at the bull troll. Artemis came up behind her, coughing water from his lungs.

'The screen's damaged,' panted Holly. 'I don't know how much time we have.'

Artemis wiped his hair from his eyes. 'Go,' he spluttered. 'Go.'

They trudged through the water, stepping around thrashing trolls. Holly chose a clear spot on the bank to climb ashore. It was a relief to be on dry land again, but at least the water had been on their side, as it were. Now they were truly in troll territory.

The remaining animals encircled them at a safe distance. Whenever one came too close, Holly swung the tele-pod in its direction, and the creature skipped back as though stung.

Artemis fought the cold and the fatigue and the shock in his system. His ankle felt scalded where the troll had snagged him.

'We need to go straight for the temple,' he said through chattering teeth. 'Up the scaffolding.'

'OK. Hold on.'

Holly took several deep breaths, building up her strength. Her arms were sore from holding the tele-pod but she would not let the fatigue show in her face, nor the fear. She looked those trolls straight in their red eyes and let them know they were dealing with a formidable enemy.

'Ready?'

'Ready,' replied Artemis, although he was no such thing.

Holly took one final breath, then charged. The trolls were not expecting this tactic. After all, what kind of creature would attack a troll? They broke ranks in the face of the arc of white light, and their disconcertedness lasted just long enough for Artemis and Holly to charge through the hole in the line.

They hurried up the incline towards the temple. Holly made no attempt to avoid the trolls, running straight at them. When they lashed out in temporary blindness, they only caused more confusion among themselves. A dozen vicious squabbles erupted in Holly and Artemis's wake as animals accidentally sliced each other with razor-sharp talons. Some of the cannier trolls used the opportunity to settle old scores. The squabbles chain-reacted across the plain until the entire area was a mass of dust and writhing animals.

Artemis grunted and puffed his way up the ravine, his fingers wrapped round Holly's belt. Captain Short's breathing had settled into a steady rhythm of quick bursts.

I am not physically fit, thought Artemis. *And it may cost me dearly. I need to exercise more than my brain in future. If I have a future.*

The temple loomed above them, a scale model but still over fifteen metres high. Dozens of identical columns rising into the holographic clouds supported a triangular roof decorated with intricate plaster mouldings. The columns' lower regions were scarred by a thousand claw marks where younger trolls had scampered out of harm's way. Artemis and Holly clambered up the twenty or so steps to the columns themselves.

Fortunately, there were no trolls on the scaffolding. All the animals were busy trying to kill each other or avoid being killed, but it would be only a matter of seconds before they remembered that there were intruders in their midst. Fresh meat. Not many of the trolls had tasted elf meat, but those who had were eager to try it again. Only one of the present gathering had tasted human meat, and the memory of its sweetness still haunted his dull brain at night.

It was this particular troll who hauled himself from the river, carrying ten extra kilos of moisture weight. He casually cuffed a cub who had come too close, and sniffed the air. There was a new scent here. A scent he could remember from his short time under the moon. The scent of man. The mere recognition of the smell brought saliva flowing from the glands in his throat. He set off at a pitched run towards the Temple. Soon a rough group of flesh-hungry beasts was hurtling towards the scaffolding.

'We're back on the menu,' noted Holly when she reached the scaffolding.

Artemis unhooked his fingers from the LEP captain's belt. He would have answered, but his lungs demanded oxygen. He whooped in gulps of air, resting his knuckles on his knees.

Holly took his elbow. 'No time for that, Artemis. You have to climb.'

'After you,' Artemis managed to gasp. He knew his father would never allow a lady to remain in distress while he himself fled.

'No time for discussion,' said Holly, steering Artemis by the elbow. 'Climb for the sun. I'll buy us a few seconds with the tele-pod. Go.'

216

Artemis looked into Holly's eyes to say thank you. They were round and hazel and . . . familiar? Memories fought to be free of their bonds, pounding against cell walls.

'Holly?' he said.

Holly spun him round to the bars, and the moment was gone. 'Up. You're wasting time.'

Artemis marshalled his exhausted limbs, trying to co-ordinate his movements. Step, grab, pull. It should be easy enough. He'd climbed ladders before. One ladder at least. Surely.

The scaffold bars were coated with gripped rubber, especially for climbers, and were spaced precisely forty centimetres apart, the comfortable reach distance of the average fairy. Also, coincidentally, the comfortable reach of a fourteen-year-old human. Artemis started to climb, feeling the strain in his arms before he had risen six steps. It was too early to be tired yet. There was too far to go.

'Come on, Captain,' he gasped over his shoulder. 'Climb.'

'Not just yet,' said Holly. She had her back to the scaffold and was trying to find some pattern in the approaching bunches of trolls.

There had been an in-service course on troll attacks in Police Plaza. But that had been on the basis of a one-on-one situation. To Holly's eternal embarrassment, the lecturer had used video footage of her own tangle with a troll in Italy over two years previously. 'Here,' the lecturer had said, freezing Holly's image in the big screen and rapping it with a telescopic pointer, 'is a classic example of how not to do it.'

This was a completely different scenario. They had never received instruction on what to do when attacked by an entire pack of trolls in their own habitat. No one, the instructors reasoned, would be that stupid.

There were two converging groups coming straight towards her, the one from the river led by a veritable monster with anaesthetic venom dripping from both tusks. Holly knew that if one drop of that venom got under her skin, she would fall into a happy stupor. And even if she escaped the troll's claws, the slow poison would eventually paralyse her.

The second group approached from the western ridge, composed mainly of latecomers and cubs. There were a few females in the centre of the temple itself, but they were using the distraction to pick meat from abandoned carcasses.

Holly flicked the tele-pod's setting to low. She would have to time this exactly right for maximum effect. It was the last chance she would get, because once she started to climb, she could no longer aim.

The trolls sped up the Temple steps, jostling for first place. The two groups were approaching at right angles, both heading directly for Holly. Their leaders launched themselves from a distance, determined to get the first bite of the intruder. Their lips were peeled back to reveal rows of carnivorous teeth, and their eyes were focused solely on the target. And that was when Holly acted. She flicked the brightness setting to high and scorched the retinas of the two beasts while they were still in the air. With piercing howls they swatted at the hated light, crashing to the ground in a mêlée of arms, claws, tusks and teeth. Each troll assumed he was being attacked by a rival group, and in seconds the scaffold's base was a chaos of primeval violence.

Holly took full advantage of the confusion, skipping lithely up the first three rungs of the metal structure. She clipped the tele-pod to her belt so that it pointed downwards like a rear gun. Not much protection, but better than nothing.

In moments, she had caught up with Artemis. The human boy's breath was ragged and his progress was slow. Blood dripped from the wound on his ankle. Holly could easily have passed him, but instead she hooked an arm through the scaffold bars and checked on the troll situation. Just as well. One relatively little guy was scaling the bars with the agility of a mountain gorilla. His immature tusks barely jutted beyond his lips, but those tusks were sharp and venom gathered in beads along the tips. Holly turned the screen on him, and he released his grip to shield his scorched eyes. An elf would have been smart enough to hang on with one hand and use the other forearm to shield the eyes, but trolls are not much further up the IQ scale than stinkworms, and they act almost completely on instinct.

The little troll tumbled back to earth, landing on the shaggy, writhing carpet below. He was instantly dragged into the brawl. Holly returned to the climb, feeling the tele-pod knock against her back. Artemis's progress was painfully slow, and in less than a minute she was at Artemis's shoulder.

'Are you all right?'

Artemis nodded, tight-lipped. But his eyes were wide, on the verge of panic. Holly had seen that look before, on the faces of battle-stressed LEP officers. She needed to get the Mud Boy to safety before he lost his reason.

'Come on now, Artemis. Just a few more steps. We're going to make it.'

Artemis closed his eyes for five seconds, breathing deeply through his nose. When he opened them again, they shone with a new resolve. 'Very well, Captain. I'm ready.'

Artemis reached above him for the next bar, hauling himself forty centimetres closer to salvation. Holly followed, urging him on like a drill sergeant.

It took a further minute to reach the roof itself. By this time the trolls had remembered what they were chasing and began to scale the scaffolding. Holly dragged Artemis on to the slanted roof, and they scampered on all fours towards its highest point. The plaster was white and unmarked; in the low light it seemed as though they were walking across a field of snow.

Artemis paused. The sight had awoken a vague memory.

'Snow,' he said uncertainly. 'I remember something . . .'

Holly caught his shoulder, dragging him forward. 'Yes, Artemis. The Arctic, remember? Later, we'll discuss it at great length, when there are no trolls trying to eat us.'

Artemis snapped back to the present. 'Very well. Good tactics.'

The temple roof sloped upwards at a forty-degree angle towards the crystal orb that was the fake sun. The pair crawled as quickly as Artemis's exhausted limbs would allow. A ragged trail of blood marked their path across the white plaster. The scaffold shook and banged against the roof as the trolls climbed ever closer.

Holly straddled the roof's apex, reaching up to the crystal sun. The surface was smooth beneath her fingers.

'D'Arvit!' she swore. 'I can't find the power port. There should be an external socket.'

Artemis crawled round to the other side. He was not particularly afraid of heights, but even so he tried not to look down. One did not have to suffer from vertigo to be worried by a fifteen-metre drop and a pack of ravenous trolls. He stretched upwards, probing the globe with the fingers of one hand. His index finger found a small indent.

'I've got something,' he announced.

Holly scooted round to his side, examining the hole.

'Good,' she said. 'An external power port. Power cells have uniform connection points, so the cuffs' cells should clip right on.'

She fumbled the cuffs from her pocket, popping the cell covers. The cells themselves were about the size of credit cards, and glowed bright blue along their length.

Holly stood up on the razor-edge rooftop, balancing nimbly on her toes. The trolls were swarming over the lip of the roof now. Advancing like the hounds of hell. The white roof plaster was blanketed by the black, brown and ginger of troll fur. Their howls and stink preceded them as they closed in on Holly and Artemis.

Holly waited until they were all over the lip, then she slid the power cells into the globe's socket. The globe buzzed, vibrated into life, then flashed once: a blinding wall of light. For a moment, the entire exhibit glowed brilliant white, then the globe faded again with a high-pitched whine.

The trolls rolled like balls on a tilted pool table. Some tumbled over the edge of the roof, but most collected on the lip, where they lay, whining and scratching their faces.

Artemis closed his eyes to accelerate the return of his night vision. 'I had hoped the cell would power the sun for longer. It seems like a lot of effort for such a brief reprieve.'

Holly pulled out the dead cells, tossing them aside. 'I suppose a globe like this needs a lot of juice.'

Artemis blinked then sat comfortably on the roof, clasping his knees.

'Still. We have some time. It can take nocturnal creatures up to fifteen minutes to recover their orientation following exposure to bright light.'

Holly sat beside him. 'Fascinating. You're very calm all of a sudden.'

'I have no choice,' said Artemis simply. 'I have analysed the situation and concluded that there is no way for us to escape. We are on top of a ridiculous model of the Temple of Artemis, surrounded by temporarily blinded trolls. As soon as they recover, they will lope up here and devour us. We have perhaps a quarter of an hour to live, and I have no intention of spending it in hysterics for Opal Koboi's amusement.'

Holly looked up, searching the hemisphere for cameras. At least a dozen tell-tale red lights winked in the darkness. Opal would be able to watch her revenge from every angle.

Artemis was right. Opal would be tickled pink if they fell to pieces for the cameras. She would probably replay the video to cheer herself up when being princess of the world got to be too stressful.

Holly drew back her arm, sending the spent power cells skidding across the roof. It seemed then that this was it. She felt more frustrated than scared. Julius's final order had been to save Artemis, and she hadn't managed to accomplish even that.

'I'm sorry you don't remember Julius,' she said. 'You two argued a lot, but behind it all he admired you. It was Butler he really liked, though. Those two were on the same wavelength. Two old soldiers.'

Below them, the trolls were gathering themselves. Blinking away the stars in their eyes.

Artemis slapped some of the dust from his trousers.

'I do remember, Holly. I remember it all. Especially you. It's a real comfort to have you here.'

Holly was surprised — shocked even. More by Artemis's tone than by what he had actually said, though that was surprising too. She had never heard Artemis sound so warm, so sincere. Usually emotional displays were difficult for the boy, and he stumbled through them awkwardly. This wasn't like him at all.

'That's very nice, Artemis,' she said after a moment's consideration. 'But you don't have to pretend for me.'

Artemis was puzzled. 'How did you know? I thought I portrayed the emotions perfectly.'

Holly looked down at the massing trolls. They were advancing warily up the slope, heads down in case of a second flash.

⊗♦⟨♦⟩⊗ · ♦⟨⟩)⟨⊗ · ⊘⟨⊓⟩⟨ℝ · ⟨♦⟨ℝ ·

'Nobody's that perfect. That's how I knew.'

The trolls were hurrying now, swinging hairy forearms forward to increase their momentum. As their confidence returned, so did their voices. Howls rose to the roof, bouncing back off the metal structure. Artemis drew his knees closer to his chin. The end. All over. Inconceivable that he should die in this way, when there was so much still to be done.

The howling made it hard to concentrate. The smell didn't help either.

Holly gripped his shoulder. 'Close your eyes, Artemis. You won't feel a thing.'

But Artemis did not close his eyes. Instead he cast his gaze upwards. Above ground, where his parents were waiting to hear from him. Parents who never had the chance to be truly proud of him.

He opened his mouth to whisper a goodbye, but what he saw over his head choked the words in his throat.

'That proves it,' he said. 'This must be a hallucination.'

Holly looked upwards. A section of the hemisphere's panel had been removed, and a rope was being lowered towards the temple roof. Swinging from the rope was what appeared to be a naked and extremely hairy rear end.

'I don't believe it!' Holly exclaimed, jumping to her feet. 'You took your sweet time getting here!'

She seemed to be conversing with a posterior. And

then, even more amazingly, the posterior appeared to answer.

'I love you too, Holly. Now close anything that's open, because I'm about to overload these trolls' senses.'

For a moment, Holly's face was blank, then realization widened her eyes and sucked the blood from her cheeks. She grabbed Artemis by the shoulders.

'Lie flat, with your hands over your ears. Shut your eyes and mouth. And whatever you do, don't breathe in.'

Artemis lay on the roof. 'Tell me there's a creature on the other end of that posterior.'

'There is,' confirmed Holly. 'But it's the posterior we have to worry about.'

The trolls were metres away by this point. Close enough to see the red in their eyes and the years of dirt caked in every dreadlock.

Overhead, Mulch Diggums (for, of course, it was he) released a gentle squib of wind from his backside. Just enough to propel him in a gentle circle on the end of his rope. The circular motion was necessary to ensure an even spread of the gas he intended to release. Once he had completed three revolutions, he bore down internally and let fly with every bubble of gas in his bloated stomach.

Because trolls are by nature tunnel-dwelling creatures, they are guided as much by their sense of smell as by their night vision. A blinded troll can often survive for years, navigating his way to food and water supplies by smell alone.

Mulch's sudden gaseous recyclings sent a million conflicting scent messages to each troll's brain. The smell was bad enough, and the wind was sufficient to blow back the trolls' dreadlocks, but the combination of scents inside the dwarf gas – including clay, vegetation, insect life and anything else Mulch had eaten over the past few days – was enough to short out the trolls' entire nervous systems. They collapsed to their knees, clasping their poor, aching heads in taloned hands. One was so close to Artemis and Holly that one shaggy forearm rested across the LEP Captain's back.

Holly wriggled out from under the limb. 'Let's go,' she said, pulling Artemis to his feet. 'The gas won't put the trolls out for any longer than the light.'

Overhead, Mulch's revolutions were slowing.

'I thank you,' he said, with a theatrical bow, which is not easy on a rope. The dwarf scampered up the rope, gripping with fingers and toes, then lowered it to Artemis and Holly.

'Jump on,' he said. 'Quickly.'

Artemis tested the rope sceptically. 'Surely that strange creature is too small to haul both of us all the way up there.'

Holly put her foot in a loop at the rope's end. 'True, but he's not alone.'

⊗) ◊ ᛒ · ⚛ ᛒ · ⱥ · ᛞ ᚦ ⌀ ⊡ ⊗ · ᚹ ᛞ ⊖ ⊗ ᚢ ▢ ·

Artemis squinted at the hemisphere's missing panel. Another figure had appeared in the gap. The figure's features were in deep shadow, but the silhouette was unmistakable. 'Butler!' he said through his smile. 'You're here.'

And suddenly, in spite of everything, Artemis felt completely safe.

'Hurry up, Artemis,' called his bodyguard. 'We don't have a second to waste.'

Artemis stepped on to the rope beside Holly, and Butler quickly pulled them both out of danger.

'Well,' said Holly, her face inches from his own, 'we survived. Does that mean we're friends now? Bonded by trauma?'

Artemis frowned. Friends? Did he have room in his life for a friend? Then again, maybe he had no choice in the matter.

'Yes,' he replied. 'Though I've had little experience in this area, so I may have to read up on it.'

Holly rolled her eyes. 'Friendship is not a science, Mud Boy. Forget about your massive brain for one minute. Just do what you feel is right.'

Artemis couldn't believe what he was about to say. Perhaps the thrill of survival was affecting his judgement. 'I feel that I shouldn't be paid to help a friend. Keep your fairy gold. Opal Koboi has to be stopped.'

Holly smiled with genuine warmth for the first time

since the commander's death, but there was a hint of steel in there too.

'With the four of us on her tail, she doesn't stand a chance.'

CHAPTER 8: SOME INTELLIGENT CONVERSATION

 MULCH had left the stolen LEP shuttle at the theme-park gate. It had been a simple matter for Butler to disable the park's cameras and remove a half-rotted section from the hemisphere's roof in order to effect the rescue.

When they got back to the shuttle, Holly powered up the engines and ran a systems check.

'What on earth were you doing, Mulch?' she asked, amazed by the readings the computer was displaying. 'The computer says you came all the way down here in first gear.'

'There are gears?' said the dwarf. 'I thought this crate was automatic.'

'Some jockeys prefer gears. Old-fashioned, I know, but more control around the bends. And another thing, you didn't have to do that gas thing on the rope. There are plenty of stun grenades in the weapons locker.'

'This thing has a locker too? Gears and lockers. Well I never.'

Butler was giving Artemis a field physical.

'You seem all right,' he said, placing a massive palm over Artemis's chest. 'Holly fixed up your ribs, I see.'

Artemis was in a bit of a daze. Now that he was out of immediate danger, the day's events were catching up on him. How many times could one person cheat death in twenty-four hours? Surely his odds were getting short.

'Tell me, Butler,' he whispered so the others wouldn't hear, 'is it all true? Or is it a hallucination?' Even as the words left his lips, Artemis realized that it was an impossible question. If this was all a hallucination, then his bodyguard was a dream too.

'I turned down gold, Butler,' continued Artemis, still unable to accept his own grand gesture. 'Me. I turned down gold.'

Butler smiled, much more the smile of a friend than of a bodyguard. 'That doesn't surprise me one bit. You were becoming quite charitable before the mind wipe.'

Artemis frowned. 'Of course you would say that, if you were part of the hallucination.'

Mulch was eavesdropping on the conversation and couldn't resist a comment. 'Didn't you smell what I shot those trolls with? You think you could hallucinate that, Mud Boy?'

Holly started the engines.

'Hold on, back there,' she called over her shoulder. 'It's time to go. The sensors have picked up some shuttles sweeping local chutes. The authorities are looking for us. I need to get us somewhere off the charts.'

Holly teased the throttle, lifting them smoothly from the ground. If the shuttle had not had portholes, the passengers might not have noticed the take-off.

Butler elbowed Mulch. 'Did you see that? That's a take-off. I hope you learned something.'

The dwarf was highly offended. 'What do I have to do to get a bit of respect around here? You are all alive because of me, and all I get is abuse.'

Butler laughed. 'OK, little friend. I apologize. We owe you our lives, and I for one will never forget it.'

Artemis followed this interaction curiously. 'I would deduce that you remember everything, Butler. If, for a moment, I accept this situation as reality, then your memory must have been stimulated. Did I, perhaps, leave something behind?'

Butler pulled the laser disk from his pocket.

'Oh yes, Artemis. There was a message on this disk for me. You left yourself a message too.'

Artemis took the disk. 'At last,' he said. 'Some intelligent conversation.'

Artemis found a small bathroom at the rear of the shuttle. The indoor toilet was only to be used in an emergency and the seat was made from a spongy material that, Mulch had assured him, would break down any waste as it passed through. Artemis decided he would test the filter at another time, and he sat on a small ledge by the porthole.

There was a plasma screen on the wall, presumably for in-restroom entertainment. All he had to do was slip the computer disk into the drive below the screen, and his fairy memories would be returned to him. A whole new world. An old one.

Artemis spun the disk between his thumb and fore-finger. Psychologically speaking, if he loaded this disk, it meant that some part of him accepted the truth of all this. Putting the disk in the slot could plunge him deeper into some kind of psychotic episode. Not putting it in could condemn the world to a war between species. The fairy and human worlds would collide.

What would Father do? Artemis asked himself.

He loaded the disk.

Two files appeared on the desktop, marked with animated 3D gifs, something the fairy system had obviously added on. Both were tagged with the file names in English and the fairy language. Artemis selected his own file by touching the plasma screen's transparent covering. The file glowed orange, then expanded to fill the screen. Artemis saw himself in Fowl Manor, sitting at his desk in the study.

'Greetings,' said the screen Artemis. 'How nice for

you to see me. Doubtless this will be the first intelligent conversation you have had for some time.'

The real Artemis smiled. 'Correct,' he replied.

'I paused for a second there,' continued the screen Artemis, 'to give you a chance to respond, thus qualifying this as a conversation. There will be no more pausing, as time is limited. Captain Holly Short is downstairs, being distracted by Juliet, but doubtless she will check on me soon. We depart for Chicago presently to deal with Mister Jon Spiro, who has stolen something from me. The price of fairy assistance in this matter is a mind wipe. All memories of the People will be erased forever, unless I can leave a message for my future self, thus prompting recall. This is that message. The following video footage contains specific details of my involvement with the fairy People. Hopefully, this information will get those brain-cell pathways sparking again.'

Artemis rubbed his forehead. The vague, mysterious flashes persisted. It seemed as though his brain was ready to rebuild those pathways. All he needed was the right stimulus.

'In conclusion,' said the screen Artemis, 'I would like to wish you, myself, the best of luck. And welcome back.'

The next hour passed in a blur. Images flashed from the screen, adhering to empty spaces in Artemis's brain. Each memory felt right, the instant Artemis processed it.

Of course, he thought. *This explains everything. I had the*

234

mirrored contact lenses made so I could lie to the fairies and hide the existence of this journal. I fixed Mulch Diggums's search warrant so that he could return the disk to me. Butler looks older because he is older; the fairy healing in London saved his life, but cost him fifteen years.

The memories were not all proud ones. *I kidnapped Captain Short. I imprisoned Holly. How could I have done that?*

He could not deny it any longer. This was all true. Everything that his eyes had seen was real. The fairies existed and his life had been intertwined with theirs for more than two years. A million images sprouted in his consciousness, rebuilding electric bridges in his brain. They strobed behind his eyes in a confusing display of colour and wonder. A lesser mind than Artemis's might have been utterly exhausted, but the Irish boy was exhilarated.

I know it all now, he thought. *I beat Koboi before, and I will do it again.* This determination was fuelled by sadness. *Commander Root is gone. She took him from his People.*

Artemis had known this earlier, but now it meant something.

There was one other thought, more persistent than the rest. It crashed into his mind like a tsunami.

I have friends? thought Artemis Fowl II. *I have friends.*

Artemis emerged from the bathroom a different person. Physically, he was still battered, bruised and exhausted, but emotionally he felt prepared for everything that lay ahead. If a body-language analyst had studied him at that moment, they would have observed his relaxed shoulders and open palms and would have concluded that this was (psychologically speaking) a more welcoming and trust-worthy individual than the one who had entered the bathroom an hour earlier.

The shuttle was parked in a secondary chute, off the beaten track, and its occupants were at the mess table. A selection of LEP field ration packs had been torn open and devoured. The biggest pile of foil packs was stacked in front of Mulch Diggums.

Mulch glanced at Artemis and noticed the change immediately. 'About time you got your head in order,' grunted Mulch, struggling from his chair. 'I need to get into that bathroom urgently.'

'Nice to see you too, Mulch,' said Artemis, stepping aside to allow the dwarf past.

Holly froze, a sachet of juice halfway to her mouth. 'You remember him?'

Artemis smiled. 'Of course, Holly. We have known each other for over two years.'

Holly jumped from her chair and clasped Artemis by the shoulders.

'Artemis. It's great to see you. The real you. The gods know we need Artemis Fowl right now.'

'Well, he's here and ready for duty, Captain.'

'Do you remember everything?'

'Yes, I do. And first of all, let me apologize for that "consultant" business. That was very rude. Please forgive me.'

'But what made you remember?' wondered the elf. 'Don't tell me a visit to the bathroom jogged your memory.'

'Not exactly.' Artemis held up the computer disk. 'I gave this to Mulch. It is my video diary. He was supposed to return it to me on his release from prison.'

Holly shook her head. 'That's not possible. Mulch was searched by experts. The only thing you gave to him was the gold medallion.'

Artemis angled the disk so that it caught the light.

'Of course,' groaned Holly, slapping her forehead. 'You passed off that disk as the gold medallion. Very clever.'

Artemis shrugged. 'Genius, actually. It seems merely clever in hindsight, but the original idea was pure genius.'

Holly cocked her head. 'Genius. Of course. Believe it or not, I actually missed that smug grin.'

Artemis took a breath. 'I am so sorry about Julius. I know our relationship was a rocky one, but I had nothing but respect and admiration for the commander.'

Holly wiped her eyes with the heels of her hands. She said nothing, just nodding. If Artemis needed another reason to go after Opal Koboi, the sight of the elfin captain so disturbed was it.

Butler ate the contents of a field ration pack in one

mouthful. 'Now that we're all reacquainted, we should try to track Opal Koboi down. It's a big world.'

Artemis waved his fingers dismissively. 'No need. I know exactly where our would-be murderer is. Like all megalomaniacs, she has a tendency to show off.'

He crossed to a plastic computer keyboard on the wall, calling up a map of Europe.

'I see your Gnommish has come back to you,' sniffed Holly.

'Of course,' said Artemis, enlarging part of the map. 'Opal revealed a little bit more of her plans than she knew. She let two words slip, though one would have been sufficient. She said that her human name was to be Belinda Zito. Now, if you wished to lead the humans to the fairy People, who better to have adopt you than the renowned billionaire environmentalist Giovanni Zito?'

Holly crossed the shuttle deck to the screen. 'And where would we find Mister Zito?'

Artemis tapped a few keys, zooming in on Sicily.

'At his world-famous Earth Ranch. Right here in Messina Province,' he said.

Mulch stuck his head out of the bathroom. The rest of him was mercifully hidden behind the door. 'Did I hear you talking about a Mud Man named Zito?'

Holly turned towards the dwarf, then kept right on turning. 'Yes. So what? And for heaven's sake close the door.'

Mulch pulled the door so only a crack remained. 'I was just watching a bit of human television in here, as you do. Well, there's a Zito on CNN. Do you think it's the same person?'

Holly grabbed a remote control from the table.

'I really hope not,' she said. 'But I'd bet my life it is.'

A group of humans appeared on the screen. They were gathered in what looked like a prefabricated laboratory, and each wore a white coat. One stood out from the rest. He was in his mid-forties, with tanned skin, strong, handsome features and long, dark hair curling over his collar. He wore rimless glasses and a lab coat. A striped Versace shirt protruded from under his white lapels.

'Giovanni Zito,' said Artemis.

'It is incredible, really,' Zito was telling a reporter in slightly accented English. 'We have sent crafts to other planets, and yet we have no idea what lies beneath our feet. Scientists can tell us the chemical make-up of Saturn's rings, but we don't honestly know what lies at the centre of our own planet.'

'But probes have been sent down before,' said the reporter, trying to pretend he hadn't just picked up this knowledge from his earpiece.

'Yes,' agreed Zito. 'But only to a depth of about nine miles. We need to get through to the outer core itself, over one thousand eight hundred miles down.

Imagine if the currents of liquid metal in the outer core could be harnessed. There's enough free energy in that metal to power mankind's machines forever.'

The reporter was sceptical – at least, the real scientist speaking in his earpiece told him to be sceptical. 'But this is all speculation, Doctor Zito. Surely a voyage to the centre of the Earth is nothing but a fantasy? Possible only in the pages of science fiction.'

A brief flash of annoyance clouded Giovanni Zito's features. 'This is no fantasy, sir, I assure you. This is no fantastical voyage. We are sending an unmanned probe, bristling with sensors. Whatever is down there, we will find it.'

The reporter's eyes widened in panic as a particularly technical question came through his earpiece. He listened for several seconds, mouthing the words as he heard them.

'Doctor Zito, eh . . . This probe you are sending down, I believe it will be encased in one hundred million tonnes of molten iron at about five and a half thousand degrees Celsius. Is that correct?'

'Absolutely,' confirmed Zito.

The reporter looked relieved. 'Yes. I knew that. Anyway, my point is, it will take several years to gather so much iron. So why did you ask us here today?'

Zito clapped his hands excitedly. 'This is the wonderful part. As you know, the core probe was a long-term project. I had planned to accumulate the iron over the next ten years. But now, laser drilling has revealed a deep orebody of haematite, iron ore, on the bottom edge of the crust, right here in Sicily. It's incredibly rich, perhaps eighty-five per cent iron. All we need to do is detonate several charges inside that deposit and we will have our molten iron. I have already secured the mining permits from the government.'

The reporter asked the next question all on his own. 'So, Doctor Zito, when do you detonate?'

Giovanni Zito removed two thick cigars from his lab coat pocket.

'We detonate today,' he said, passing a cigar to the reporter. 'Ten years early. This is a historic moment.' Zito drew the office curtains, revealing a fenced-off area of scrubland outside the window. A metallic section of piping protruded from the earth in the centre of the half-mile-square enclosure. As they watched, a crew of workmen clambered out of the piping, moving hurriedly away from the opening. Wisps of gaseous coolant spiralled from the pipe. The men climbed into a golf trolley and exited the compound. They took shelter in a concrete bunker at the perimeter.

'There are several megatons of TNT buried at strategic points inside the orebody,' explained Zito. 'If this was detonated on the surface, it would cause an earthquake measuring seven on the Richter scale.'

The reporter swallowed nervously. 'Really?'

Zito laughed. 'Don't worry. The charges are shaped. The blast is focused down and in. The iron will be liquefied and begin its descent to the Earth's core, carrying the probe with it. We will feel nothing.'

'Down and in? You're sure about that?'

'Positive,' said Zito. 'We are perfectly safe here.'

On the wall behind the Italian doctor a speaker squawked three times. 'Dottore Zito,' said a gruff voice. 'All clear. All clear.'

Zito picked up a black remote detonator from the desk.

'The time has come,' he said dreamily. He looked straight into the camera. 'My darling Belinda, this is for you.'

Zito pressed the button and waited, wide-eyed. The room's other occupants, the dozen or so scientists and technicians, turned anxiously to various readout panels and monitors.

'We have detonation,' announced one.

Nine miles below ground, forty-two shaped charges exploded simultaneously, liquefying one hundred and eighteen million tonnes of iron. The rock content was pulverized and absorbed by the metal. A pillar of smoke blew out of the cylindrical opening, but there was no detectable vibration.

'The probe is functioning at one hundred per cent,' said a technician.

Zito breathed out. 'That was our big worry. Even though the probe is designed for exactly these conditions, the world has never seen this kind of explosion before.' He turned to another lab worker. 'Any movement?'

The man hesitated before answering. 'Yes, Doctor Zito. We have vertical movement. Five metres per second. Exactly as you hypothesized.'

Below the Earth's crust, a behemoth of iron and rock began its painstaking descent towards the Earth's core. It chugged and churned, bubbling and hissing, prising apart the mantle below it. Inside the molten mass, a grapefruit-sized probe continued to broadcast data.

Spontaneous euphoria erupted in the laboratory. Men and women hugged each other. Cigars were lit and champagne corks popped. Someone even pulled out a violin.

'We are on our way,' shouted a jubilant Zito, lighting the reporter's cigar. 'Man is going to the centre of the Earth. Look out below!'

In the stolen LEP shuttle, Holly froze the picture. Zito's triumphant features were spread across the screen.

'Look out below,' she repeated glumly. 'Man is coming to the centre of the Earth.'

The moods in the shuttle ranged from glum to desolate. Holly was taking it especially hard. The entire fairy civilization was under threat yet again, and this time Commander Root wasn't around to meet the challenge. Not only that, but, since the LEP pursuit pods had blown out their communications, there was no way to warn Foaly about the probe.

'I have no doubt he already knows,' said Artemis. 'That centaur monitors all the human news channels.'

'But he doesn't know that Opal Koboi is giving Zito the benefit of her fairy knowledge.' Holly pointed at Giovanni's image on the screen. 'Look at his eyes. The poor man has been mesmerized so many times, his pupils are actually ragged.'

Artemis stroked his chin thoughtfully. 'If I know Foaly, he's been monitoring this project since its initiation. He probably already has a contingency plan.'

'I'm sure he has. A contingency plan for a crackpot scheme in ten years' time that will probably never work.'

'Of course,' agreed Artemis. 'As opposed to a scientifically viable scheme, right now, that has every chance of succeeding.'

Holly headed for the cockpit. 'I have to turn myself in, even if I am a murder suspect. There is more at stake here than my future.'

'Steady on,' objected Mulch. 'I broke out of prison for you. I have no desire to be shoved back in again.'

Artemis stepped in front of her. 'Wait a minute, Holly. Think about what will happen if you do turn yourself in.'

'Artemis is right,' added Butler. 'You should think about this. If the LEP is anything like human police forces, fugitives are not exactly welcomed with open arms. Open cell doors maybe.'

Holly forced herself to stop and think, but it was difficult. Every second she waited was another second for the giant iron slug to eat its way through the mantle.

'If I give myself up to Internal Affairs, I will be taken into custody. As an LEP officer, I can be held for seventy-two hours without counsel. As a murder suspect, I can be held for up to a week. Even if someone did believe that I was completely innocent and that Opal Koboi was behind all this, it would still take at least eight hours to get clearance for an operation. But in all likelihood my claims would be dismissed as the standard protests of the guilty. Especially with you three backing up my story. No offence.'

'None taken,' said Mulch.

Holly sat down, cradling her head in her hands. 'My world is utterly gone. I keep thinking there will be a way back, but things just spin further and further out of control.'

Artemis placed a hand on her shoulder. 'Courage, Captain. Ask yourself, what would the commander do?'

Holly took three deep breaths, then sprang from her seat, her back stiff with determination.

'Don't you try to manipulate me, Artemis Fowl. I make my own decisions. Even so, Julius would take care of Opal Koboi himself. So that's what we're going to do.'

245

'Excellent,' said Artemis. 'In that case we will need a strategy.'

'Right. I'll fly the shuttle. You put that brain of yours to work and come up with a plan.'

'Each to his own,' said the boy. He sat in one of the shuttle's chairs, gently massaged his temples with his fingertips and began to think.

CHAPTER 9: DADDY'S GİRL

OPAL'S plan to bring the human and fairy worlds together was one of simplicity in its execution, but genius in its conception. She simply made it easier for a human to do what he was already thinking of doing. Almost every major energy company in the world had a 'Core Probe' file, but they were all hypothetical as regards the amount of explosives needed to blast through the crust and the iron necessary to get the probe through the mantle.

Opal had picked Giovanni Zito from her list of prospective puppets because of two things: Zito had a large fortune and he had land directly above a huge, high-grade haematite orebody.

Giovanni Zito was a Sicilian engineer and a pioneer in the field of alternative power sources. A committed environmentalist, Zito developed ways of generating electricity without stripping the land or destroying the environment. The invention that had made his fortune was the Zito solar-mill, a windmill with solar panels for blades, making it many times more efficient than conventional mills.

Six weeks earlier, Zito had returned from an environmental summit in Geneva, where he had delivered the keynote address to ministers of the European Union. By the time he reached his villa overlooking the Strait of Messina, the sunset was dropping orange blobs in the water, and Zito was exhausted. Talking to politicians was difficult. Even the ones who were genuinely interested in the environment were hamstrung by those in the pay of big business. The 'polluticians', as the media had nicknamed them.

Zito ran himself a bath. The water was heated by solar panels on his roof. In fact, the entire villa was self-sufficient when it came to power. There was enough juice in the solar batteries to keep the house hot and lit for six months. All with zero emissions.

After his bath, Zito wrapped himself in a towelling dressing gown and poured a glass of Bordeaux, settling into his favourite armchair.

Zito took a long draught of wine, willing the day's tension to evaporate. He cast his eyes over the familiar row of framed photographs on the wall. Most were magazine covers celebrating his technological innovations, but his favourite one, the one that had made him famous, was the *Time* magazine cover that showed a younger Giovanni Zito astride a humpback whale, with a whaling ship looming over them both. The unfortunate creature had strayed into shallow waters and could not dive, so Zito had leaped from a conservationists' dinghy on to the creature's back, thus shielding it from the whalers' harpoons. Someone on the dinghy had snapped a photo, and that photo had become one of the most famous media images of the last century.

Zito smiled. Heady days. He was about to close his eyes for a quick nap before dinner when something moved in the shadows in the corner of the room. Something small, barely the height of the table.

Zito sat straight up in his chair. 'What's that? Is somebody there?'

A lamp flicked on to reveal a small girl perched on a log stool. She held the lamp cord in her hand and seemed not in the least afraid or upset in any way. In fact, the girl was calm and composed, regarding Zito as if *he* were the intruder.

Giovanni stood.

'Who are you, little one? Why are you here?'

The girl fixed him with the most incredible eyes. Deep brown eyes. Deep as a vat of chocolate.

'I am here for you, Giovanni,' she said in a voice as

beautiful as her eyes. In fact, everything about the girl was beautiful: her porcelain features . . . and those eyes. They would not let him go.

Zito fought her spell. 'For me? What do you mean? Is your mother nearby?'

The girl smiled. 'Not nearby, no. You are my family now.'

Giovanni tried to make sense of this simple sentence, but he could not. Was it really important? Those eyes, and that voice. So melodic. Layers of crystal tinkling.

Humans react differently to the fairy *mesmer*. Most immediately fall under its hypnotic spell, but there are those with strong minds who need to be pushed a little. And the more they are pushed, the greater the risk of brain damage.

'I am your family now?' said Zito slowly, as though he were searching each word for its meaning.

'Yes, human,' snapped Opal impatiently, pushing harder. 'My family. I am your daughter, Belinda. You adopted me last month, secretly. The papers are in your bureau.'

Zito's eyes lost their focus. 'Adopted? Bureau?'

Opal drummed her tiny fingers on the base of the lamp. She had forgotten how dull some humans could be, especially under the *mesmer*. And this one was supposed to be a genius.

'Yes. Adopted. Bureau. You love me more than life,

remember? You would do absolutely anything for your darling Belinda.'

A tear pooled on Zito's eyelid. 'Belinda. My little girl. I'd do anything for you, dear, anything.'

'Yes, yes, yes,' said Opal impatiently. 'Of course. I said that. Just because you're mesmerized doesn't mean you have to repeat everything I say. That is so tiresome.'

Zito noticed two small creatures in the corner. Creatures with pointed ears. This fact penetrated the *mesmer*'s fugue.

'I see. Over there. Are they human?'

Opal glowered at the Brill brothers. They were supposed to stay out of sight. Mesmerizing a strong mind such as Zito's was a delicate enough operation without distractions.

She added another layer to her voice. 'You cannot see those figures. You will never see them.'

Zito was relieved. 'Of course. Good. Nothing at all. Mind playing tricks.'

Opal scowled. What was it about humans and grammar? At the first sign of stress it went out of the window. Mind playing tricks. Really.

'Now, Giovanni, Daddy. I think we need to talk about your next project.'

'The water-powered car?'

'No, idiot. Not the water-powered car. The core

probe. I know you have designed one. Quite a good design for a human, though I will be making changes.'

'The core probe. Impossible. Can't get through crust. Don't have enough iron.'

'*We* can't get through *the* crust. *We* don't have enough iron. Speak properly, for heaven's sake. It's trying enough speaking Mud Man without listening to your gibberish. Honestly, you human geniuses are not all you're cracked up to be.'

Zito's beleaguered brain made the effort. 'I am sorry, dearest Belinda. I simply mean that the core probe project is long term. It will have to wait until we can find a practical way to gather the iron, and cut through the Earth's crust.'

Opal looked at the dazed Sicilian. 'Poor, dear, stupid Daddy. You developed a super laser to cut through the crust. Don't you remember?'

A dewdrop of sweat rolled down Zito's cheek. 'A super laser? Now that you mention it . . .'

'And can you guess what you'll find when you do cut through?'

Zito could guess. Part of his intellect was still his own. 'A haematite orebody? It would have to be massive. Of very high grade.'

Opal led him to the window. In the distance the wind farm's blades flashed in the starlight.

'And where do you think we should dig?'

'I think we should dig under the wind farm,' said Zito, resting his forehead against the cool glass.

'Very good, Daddy. If you dig there, I will be ever so happy.'

Zito patted the pixie's hair. 'Ever so happy,' he said sleepily. 'Belinda, my little girl. Papers are in bureau.'

'*The* papers are in *the* bureau,' Opal corrected him. 'If you persist with this baby talk I will have to punish you.'

She wasn't joking.

E7, BELOW THE MEDITERRANEAN

Holly had to stay out of the major chutes on her way to the surface. Foaly had sensors monitoring all traffic through commercial and LEP routes. This meant navigating unlit, meandering secondary chutes, but the alternative was being picked up by the centaur's bugs and hauled back to Police Plaza before the job was done.

Holly negotiated stalactites the size of skyscrapers and skirted vast craters teeming with bioluminescent insect life. But instinct was doing the driving. Holly's thoughts were a thousand miles away, reflecting on the events of the last twenty-four hours. It seemed as though her heart were finally catching up with her body.

All her previous adventures with Artemis were

comic-book escapades compared to their current situation. It had always been '. . . happy ever after' before. There had been a few close calls but everyone had made it out alive. Holly studied her trigger finger. A faint scar circled the base, where it had been severed during the Arctic incident. She could have healed the scar or covered it with a ring, but she preferred to keep it where she could see it. The scar was part of her. The commander had been a part of her too. Her superior, her friend.

Sadness emptied her out, then filled her up again. For a while, thoughts of revenge had fuelled her. But now, even the thought of dumping Opal Koboi into a cold cell could not light a spark of vengeful joy in her heart. She would keep going, to ensure the People were safe from humans. Maybe when that task was done, it would be time to take a look at her life. Maybe there were a few things that needed changing.

Artemis summoned everyone to the passenger area as soon as he had finished work on the computer. His 'new old' memories were giving him immense pleasure. As his fingers skimmed across the Gnommish keyboards, he marvelled at the ease with which he navigated the fairy platform. He marvelled too at the technology itself, even though he was no stranger to it any more. The Irish boy felt the same thrill of rediscovery that a small child feels when he has chanced upon a lost favourite toy.

For the past hour, rediscovery had been a major theme in his life. Having a major theme for an hour doesn't seem like much, but Artemis had a catalogue of memories all clamouring to be acknowledged. The memories themselves were startling enough: boarding a radioactive train near Murmansk, or flying across the ocean, concealed beneath LEP cam foil. But it was the cumulative effect of these memories that interested Artemis. He could literally feel himself becoming a different person. Not exactly the way he used to be, but closer to that individual. Before the fairies had mind-wiped him as part of the Jon Spiro deal, his personality had been undergoing what could be seen as positive change. So much so that he had decided to go completely legitimate and donate ninety per cent of Spiro's massive fortune to Amnesty International. Since his mind wipe, he had reverted to his old ways, indulging his passion for criminal acts. Now he was somewhere in the middle. He had no desire to hurt or steal from the innocent, but he was having difficulty giving up his criminal ways. Some people just needed to be stolen from.

Perhaps the biggest surprise was the desire he felt to help his fairy friends, and the real sadness he felt at the loss of Julius Root. Artemis was no stranger to loss; at one time or another he had lost and found everyone close to him. Julius's death cut him just as deeply as any of these. His drive to avenge the commander and stop Opal Koboi was more powerful than any criminal urge he had ever felt.

Artemis smiled to himself. It seemed as though good was a more powerful motivation than bad. Who would have thought it?

The rest of the group gathered round the central holographic projector. Holly had parked the shuttle on the floor of a secondary chute, close to the surface.

Butler was forced to squat on his hunkers in the fairy-sized ship.

'Well, Artemis, what did you find out?' asked the bodyguard, trying to fold his massive arms without knocking someone smaller over.

Artemis activated a holographic animation, which rotated slowly in the middle of the chamber. The animation showed a cutaway of the Earth from crust to core. Artemis switched on a laser pointer and began his briefing.

'As you can see, there is a distance of approximately one thousand eight hundred miles from the Earth's surface to the outer core.'

The projection's liquid outer core swirled and bubbled with molten magma.

'However, humankind has never managed to penetrate more than nine miles through the crust. To go any deeper would necessitate the use of nuclear warheads, or huge amounts of dynamite. An explosion of this magnitude could generate huge shifts in the Earth's tectonic plates, causing earthquakes and tidal waves around the globe.'

Mulch was, as usual, eating something. Nobody knew

what, as he had emptied the food locker over an hour ago. Nobody really wanted to ask either. 'That doesn't sound like a good thing.'

'No, it isn't,' agreed Artemis. 'Which is why the ironclad probe theory has never been put into practice, until now. The original idea belongs to a New Zealander, Professor David Stevenson. It is quite brilliant actually, if impractical. Encase a reinforced probe in a hundred million tonnes of molten iron. The iron will sink through the crack generated by the explosive, even closing the crack behind it. Within a week the probe will reach the core. The iron will be consumed by the outer core, and the probe will gradually disintegrate. The entire process is even environmentally sound.'

The projection put Artemis's words into pictures.

'How come the iron doesn't un-melt?' asked Mulch.

Artemis raised a long thin eyebrow. 'Un-melt? The orebody's sheer size stops it from solidifying.'

Holly stood and stepped into the projection itself, studying the orebody. 'Foaly must know all about this. Humans couldn't keep something so big a secret.'

'Indeed,' said Artemis, opening a second holographic projection. 'I ran a search on the on-board database and found this: Foaly ran several computer simulations, more than eighty years ago. He concluded that the best way to deal with the threat was simply to broadcast misinformation to whichever probe was being sent down. As far as the humans were concerned, their probe would simply sink through a few hundred miles of various low-grade ores, and then the orebody would solidify. A resounding and very expensive failure.'

The computer simulation showed the information being broadcast from Haven to the metal-encased probe. Above ground, cartoon human scientists scratched their heads and tore up their notes.

'Most amusing,' said Artemis.

Butler was studying the hologram. 'I've been on enough campaigns to know that there is a big hole in that strategy, Artemis,' he said.

'Yes?'

Butler struggled to his knees, tracing the probe's path with a finger. 'Well, what if the probe's journey brought it into contact with one of the People's chutes? Once that metal punctures a chute, it's on an express ride to Haven.'

Artemis was delighted at his bodyguard's astuteness. 'Yes, of course. Which is why there is a supersonic attack shuttle on standby twenty-four hours a day, to divert the molten mass if the need should arise. All human probe projects are monitored, and if any are judged to pose a threat they are quietly sabotaged. If that doesn't work, the LEP geological unit drill in under the molten mass and divert it with some shaped charges. The orebody follows the new path blown for it, and Haven is safe. Of course, the mining shuttle has never been used.'

'There's another problem,' added Holly. 'We have to factor in Opal's involvement. She has obviously helped Giovanni Zito drill through the crust, possibly with a fairy laser. We can presume that she has upgraded the probe itself, so that Foaly's false signals will not be accepted. So her plan must be to bring that probe into contact with the People. But how?'

Artemis launched a third holographic animation, shutting down the first two. This three-dimensional rendering portrayed Zito's Earth Farm and the underlying crust and mantle.

'This is what I think,' he said. 'Zito, with Opal's help, liquefies his orebody here. It begins to sink at a rate of five metres per second towards the Earth's core, taking accurate readings, thanks to Koboi's upgrades. Meanwhile, Foaly thinks his plan is working perfectly. Now, at a depth of one hundred and six miles, the metal mass comes within three miles of this major chute, E7, which emerges in southern Italy. They run parallel for a hundred and eighty-six miles, then diverge again. If Opal were to blow a crack between these two tunnels, then the iron would follow the path of least resistance and flow into the chute.'

Holly felt the strength leave her limbs. 'Into the chute, and straight down to Haven.'

'Exactly,' said Artemis. 'This particular chute runs in a jagged westerly diagonal for twelve hundred miles, coming within five hundred metres of the city itself. With the speed the orebody will build up in freefall, it will slice off a good half of the city. Everything that's left will be broadcasting signals for the world to hear.'

'But we have blast walls,' objected Holly.

Artemis shrugged. 'Holly, there isn't a force on Earth or under it powerful enough to stop a hundred million tonnes of molten haematite in freefall. Anything that gets in the way will be obliterated. Most of the iron will curve round and follow the tunnel, but enough will continue straight down to cut right through the blast walls.'

The shuttle's occupants watched Artemis's computer simulation in which the molten orebody smashed through Haven City's defences, allowing all the fairy electronic signals to be picked up by the probe.

'We are looking at a fifty-eight per cent casualty rate,' said Artemis. 'Possibly more.'

'How can Opal do this without Foaly's sensors picking her up?'

'Simple,' replied Artemis. 'She simply plants a shaped charge in E7 at a depth of one hundred and six miles, detonating it at the last minute. That way, by the time Foaly detects the explosion it will be too late to either disarm it or do anything about it.'

'So we need to remove that charge.'

Artemis smiled. If only it were that simple. 'Opal will not take any chances with the charge. If she left it on the chute wall for any amount of time, a tremor could shake it free or one of Foaly's sensors could pick it up. I'm sure the device is well shielded, but one leak in the plating could have it broadcasting like a satellite. No, Opal will not position the charge until the last minute.'

Holly nodded. 'OK. So we wait until she plants it, then we disarm it.'

'No. If we wait in the chute, then Foaly will pick us up. If that happens, Opal will not even venture down the chute.'

'That's good, isn't it?'

'Not really. We may delay her for a few hours, but remember Opal has a hundred and eighty-six mile window to plant the charge. She can wait for the LEP to arrest us and still have ample time to complete her mission.'

Holly knuckled her eyes. 'I don't understand this. Surely everyone must know by now that Opal has escaped. Surely Foaly can put this all together.'

Artemis closed his fist. 'There's the rub. That single point is the essence of this entire situation. Foaly obviously doesn't know that Opal has escaped. She would be the first person checked after the goblin general's escape.'

'She was checked. I was there. When Scalene escaped, Opal was still catatonic. There's no way she could have planned it.'

'And yet she did,' mused Artemis. 'Could that Opal have been a double?'

'Not possible. They run DNA checks every day.'

'So the Opal under surveillance had Koboi's DNA, but little or no brain activity.'

'Exactly. She's been that way for a year.'

Artemis thought silently for over a minute. 'I wonder how far cloning technology has developed underground?'

He crossed briskly to the main computer terminal, calling up LEP files on the subject.

'The mature clone is identical to the original in every way, except that its brain functions are limited to life support,' he read. 'In greenhouse conditions, it takes one to two years to grow a clone to adulthood.' Artemis stepped away from the computer, clapping his hands. 'That's it. That's how she did it. She induced that coma so that her replacement would not be noticed. This is impressive stuff.'

Holly pounded a fist into her palm. 'So even if we did survive the attempts on our lives, all talk of Opal's escape would be seen as the ravings of the guilty.'

'I told Chix Verbil that Opal was back,' said Mulch. 'That's OK, though, because he already thinks I'm raving.'

'With Opal on the loose,' continued the Irish youth, 'the entire LEP would be on the lookout for a plot of some kind. But with Opal still deep in her coma . . .'

'There is no cause for alarm. And this probe is simply a surprise, not an emergency.'

⊕□◊•□⬡♜⤳•ᗷ∞◊•⚛ᗷ•♜•◊ᒋ⊃ᔕ♜⊕

Artemis shut down the holographic projection. 'So, we're on our own. We need to steal that final charge and detonate it harmlessly above the parallel stretch. Not only that, but we need to expose Opal so she cannot simply put her plan into action all over again. Obviously, to do this we need to find Opal's shuttle.'

Mulch was suddenly uncomfortable. 'You're going after Koboi? Again? Well, best of luck. You can just drop me off at the next corner.'

Holly ignored him. 'How long do we have?'

There was a calculator on the plasma screen, but Artemis didn't need it. 'The orebody is sinking at a rate of five metres per second. That's eleven miles per hour. At that speed it would take approximately nine and a half hours to reach the parallel stretch.'

'Nine hours from now?'

'No,' Artemis corrected her. 'Nine hours from detonation, which was almost two hours ago.'

Holly walked rapidly into the cockpit, strapping herself into the pilot's chair. 'Seven and a half hours to save the world. Isn't there some law that says we get at least twenty-four?'

Artemis strapped himself into the co-pilot's chair. 'I don't think Opal bothers with laws,' he said. 'Now. Can you talk while you fly? There are a few things I need to know about shuttles and charges.'

CHAPTER 10: HORSE SENSE

POLICE PLAZA, HAVEN CITY,
THE LOWER ELEMENTS

 EVERYBODY in Police Plaza was all talk about the Zito probe. In truth, it was a bit of a distraction from recent events. The LEP didn't lose many officers in the field. And now two in the same shift. Foaly was taking it hard, especially the loss of Holly Short. It was one thing to lose a friend in the line of duty, but for that friend to be falsely accused of murder was unbearable. Foaly could not stand the idea that the People would forever remember Holly as a cold-blooded killer. Captain Short was innocent. What's more, she was a decorated hero, and she deserved to be remembered as such.

A com screen flickered into life on his wall; it was one of his technical assistants in the outer office. The elf's pointed ears were quivering with excitement.

'The probe is down to sixty-two miles. I can't believe the humans have gotten this far.'

Foaly couldn't believe it either. In theory, it should have been decades before humans developed a laser sophisticated enough to puncture the crust without frying half a continent. Obviously, Giovanni Zito had gone right ahead and developed the laser without worrying about Foaly's projections for his species.

Foaly almost regretted having to shut Zito's project down. The Sicilian was one of the brightest hopes for the human race. His plan to harness the power of the outer core was a good one, but the cost was fairy exposure, and that was too high a price to pay.

'Keep a close eye on it,' he said, trying to sound interested. 'Especially when it runs parallel to E7. I don't anticipate any trouble, but eyes peeled, just in case.'

'Yes, sir. Oh, and we have Captain Verbil on line two, from the surface.'

A tiny spark of interest lit the centaur's eyes. Verbil? The sprite had allowed Mulch Diggums to steal an LEP shuttle. Mulch escaped on the very day his friends on the force had been killed. Coincidence? Perhaps. Perhaps not.

Foaly opened a window to the surface. In it he could see Verbil's chest.

Foaly sighed. 'Chix! You're hovering. Come down where I can see you.'

'Sorry,' said Chix, alighting on the floor. 'I'm a bit

emotional. Commander Kelp gave me a real grilling.'

'What do you want, Chix? A hug and a kiss? I have things on my mind here.'

Verbil's wings flared up behind him. It was a real effort to stay on the ground. 'I have a message for you, from Mulch Diggums.'

Foaly fought the urge to whinny. No doubt Mulch would have some choice words for him.

'Go on, then. Tell me what our foul-mouthed friend thinks of me.'

'This is between us, right? I don't want to be pensioned off on the grounds that I'm unstable.'

'Yes, Chix, it's between us. Everyone has a right to be temporarily unstable. Today of all days.'

'It's ridiculous, really. I don't believe it for a minute.' Chix attempted a confident chuckle.

Foaly snapped. 'What's ridiculous? What don't you believe? Tell me, Chix, or I'll reach down this com link and drag it out of you.'

'Are we secure?'

'Yes!' the centaur screeched. 'We're secure. Tell me. Give me Mulch's message.'

Chix took a deep breath, saying the words as he let it out. 'Opal Koboi is back.'

Foaly's laughter started somewhere around his hooves and grew in volume and intensity until it burst out of his mouth. 'Opal is back! Koboi is back! I get it now. Mulch conned you into letting him steal the shuttle. He played on your fear of Opal waking up, and you bought it. Opal is back, don't make me laugh.'

'That's what he said,' said Chix sulkily. 'There's no need to laugh so hard. You're spitting on the screen. I have feelings, you know.'

Foaly's laughter petered out. It wasn't real laughter anyway, it was just an outburst of emotion. Mostly sadness, with some frustration mixed in.

'OK, Chix. I don't blame you. Mulch has fooled smarter sprites than you.'

It took Chix a moment to realize that he was being insulted.

'It could be true,' he said, miffed. 'You could be wrong. It *is* possible, you know. Maybe Opal Koboi conned you.'

Foaly opened another window on his wall. 'No, Verbil, it is not possible. Opal could not be back because I'm looking at her right now.'

Live feed from the Argon Clinic confirmed that Opal was indeed still suspended in her coma harness. She'd had her DNA swab minutes beforehand.

Chix's petulance crumbled. 'I can't believe it,' he muttered. 'Mulch seemed so sincere. I actually thought Holly was in danger.'

Foaly's tail twitched. 'What? Mulch said Holly was in danger? But Holly is gone. She died.'

'Yes,' said Chix morosely. 'Mulch was shovelling more horse dung, I suppose. No offence.'

Of course. Opal would set Holly up to take the blame for Julius. That cruel little touch would be just like Opal. If she wasn't right there, in her harness. DNA never lies.

Chix rapped the screen surround at his end, to get Foaly's attention.

'Listen, Foaly, remember what you promised. This is between us. No need for anyone else to know I got duped by a dwarf. I'll end up scraping vole curry off the sidewalk after crunchball matches.'

Foaly absently shut the window. 'Yes, whatever. Between us. Right.'

Opal was still secure. No doubt about it. Surely she couldn't have escaped. If she had, then maybe this probe was more sinister than it seemed. She couldn't have escaped. It wasn't possible.

But Foaly's paranoid streak couldn't let it go. Just to be sure, there were a few little tests he could perform. He really should get authorization, but, if he were wrong, nobody had to know. And if he were right, nobody would care about a few hours of computer time.

The centaur ran a quick search on the surveillance database and selected the footage from the chute access tunnel where Julius had died. There was something he wanted to check.

Uncharted chute, three miles below southern Italy

The stolen shuttle made good time to the surface. Holly flew as fast as she could without burning the gearbox or smashing them into a chute wall. Time may have been of the essence, but the motley crew would be of little use to anyone if they had to be scraped off the wall like so much crunchy pâté.

'These old rigs are mainly for watch changes,' explained Holly. 'The LEP got this one second-hand at a criminal assets auction. It's souped up to avoid Customs ships. It used to belong to a curry smuggler.'

Artemis sniffed. A faint yellow odour still lingered in the cockpit.

'Why would anyone smuggle curry?'

'Extra-hot curry is illegal in Haven. Living underground, we have to be careful of emissions, if you catch my drift.'

Artemis caught her drift and decided not to pursue the subject.

'We need to locate Opal's shuttle before we venture above ground and give our position away.'

Holly pulled over, next to a small lake of black oil, the shuttle's downdraught rippling the surface.

'Artemis, I think I mentioned that it's a stealth shuttle.

Nothing can detect her. We don't have sensors sophisticated enough to spot her. Opal and her pixie sidekicks could be sitting in their craft just round the next bend, and our computers wouldn't pick them up.'

Artemis leaned in over the dashboard readouts. 'You're approaching this the wrong way, Holly. We need to find out where the shuttle is not.'

Artemis launched various scans, searching for traces of certain gases within a hundred-mile radius. 'I think we may assume that the stealth shuttle is very close to E7. Perhaps right at the mouth, but that still leaves us with a lot of ground to cover, especially if all we have to rely on are our eyes.'

'That's what I've been saying. But do go on, I'm sure you have a point.'

'So, I'm using this shuttle's limited sensor dishes to scan from here right up the chute to the surface and down about thirty miles.'

'Scanning for what?' said Holly in exasperation. 'A hole in the air?'

Artemis grinned. 'Exactly. You see, normal space is made up of various gases: oxygen, hydrogen and so on; but the stealth shuttle would prevent any of these from being detected inside the ship's hull. So if we find a small patch of space without the usual ambient gases . . .'

'Then we've found the stealth shuttle,' said Holly.

'Exactly.'

The computer completed its scan quickly, building an on-screen model of the surrounding area. The gases were displayed in various whirling hues.

Artemis instructed the computer to search for anomalies. It found three, one with an abnormally high saturation of carbon monoxide.

'That's probably an airport. A lot of exhaust fumes.'

The second anomaly was a large area with only trace elements of any gas.

'A vacuum, probably a computer plant,' surmised Artemis.

The third anomaly was a small area, just outside the lip of E7, that appeared to contain no gas of any kind.

'That's her. The volume is exactly right. She's on the north side of the chute entrance.'

'Well done,' said Holly, punching him lightly on the shoulder. 'Let's get up there.'

'You know, of course, that as soon as we put our nose into the main chute system, Foaly will pick us up.'

Holly gave the engines a few seconds to warm up. 'It's too late to worry about that. Haven is more than six hundred miles away. By the time anyone gets here, we'll be either heroes or outlaws.'

'We're already outlaws,' said Artemis.

'True,' agreed Holly. 'But soon we could be outlaws with no one chasing us.'

POLICE PLAZA, THE LOWER ELEMENTS

Opal Koboi was back. Could it be possible? The thought niggled at Foaly's ordered mind, unravelling any chain of thought that he tried to compose. He would not find any peace until he found out for certain one way or the other.

The first place to check was the video footage from E37. If one began with the assumption that Koboi was indeed alive, then a number of details could be explained. First, the strange haze that had appeared on all the tapes was manufactured to hide something and was not simply interference. The loss of audio signal too could have been orchestrated by Koboi to cover whatever had passed between Holly and Julius in the tunnel. And the calamitous explosion could have been Koboi's doing and not Holly's. The possibility brought tremendous peace to Foaly, but he contained it. He hadn't proved anything yet.

Foaly ran the tape through a few filters without result. The strange blurred section refused to be sharpened, cloned or shifted. That in itself was unusual. If the blurred spot was just computer glitchery, Foaly should have been able to do something about it. But the indistinct patch stood its ground, repelling everything Foaly threw at it.

You may have the high-tech ground covered, thought the centaur. *But what about good old low-tech?*

Foaly zoomed the footage on to moments before the explosion. The blurred patch had transferred itself to Julius's chest, and indeed at times the commander appeared to be looking at it. Was there an explosive device under there? If so, then it must have been remotely detonated. The jammer signal was probably sent from the same remote. The detonation command would override all other signals, including the jammer. This meant that for perhaps a thousandth of a second before detonation, whatever was on Julius's chest would become visible. Not long enough for the fairy eye to capture, but a camera would see it just fine.

Foaly fast forwarded to the explosion and then began to work his way backwards, frame by frame. It was agonizing, watching his friend being reassembled by the reversed film. The centaur tried to ignore it, concentrating on the tape. The flames shrank from orange plumes to white shards, eventually containing themselves inside an orange mini-sun. Then, for a single frame, something appeared. Foaly flicked past it, then returned. There! On Julius's chest, right where the blur used to be. A device of some kind.

Foaly's fingers jabbed the enlarge tool. A thirty-centimetre-square metal panel was secured to Julius's chest with octo-bonds. It had been picked up by the camera for a single frame. Less than one-thousandth of a second, which was why it had been missed by the investigators. On the face of the panel was a plasma screen. Someone had been communicating with the commander before he died. That someone had not wanted to be overheard, hence the audio jammer. Unfortunately, the screen was now blank, as the detonation signal that disrupted the jammer would also have disrupted the video.

I know who it is, thought Foaly. *It's Opal Koboi, back from limbo.* But he needed proof. The centaur's word was worth about as much to Ark Sool as a dwarf's denial that he had passed wind.

Foaly glared at the live feed from the Argon Clinic. There she was. Opal Koboi, still deep in her coma. Apparently.

How did you do it? How could you swap places with another fairy?

Plastic surgery wouldn't do it. Surgery couldn't change DNA. Foaly opened a drawer in his desk, pulling out a piece of equipment that resembled two miniature kitchen plungers.

There was only one way to find out what was going on here. He would have to ask Opal directly.

When Foaly arrived at the clinic, Doctor Argon was reluctant to allow him into Opal's room.

'Miss Koboi is in a deep state of catatonia,' said the gnome peevishly. 'Who knows what effect your devices will have on her psyche? It's difficult, well-nigh impossible, to explain to a lay fairy what damage intrusive stimuli may have on the recovering mind.'

Foaly whinnied. 'You had no trouble letting the TV networks in. I suppose they pay better than the LEP. I do hope you are not beginning to view Opal as your personal possession, Doctor. She is a state prisoner, and I can have her moved to a state facility any time I like.'

'Maybe just five minutes,' said Jerbal Argon, tapping in the door's security code.

Foaly clopped past him, plonking his briefcase on the table. Opal swung gently in the draught from the doorway. And it did seem to be Opal. Even this close, with every feature in focus, Foaly could have sworn that this was his old adversary. The same Opal who had competed with him for every prize at college. The same Opal who had very nearly succeeded in having him blamed for the goblin uprising.

'Get her down from there,' he ordered.

Argon positioned a bunk below the harness, complaining at every step. 'I shouldn't be doing physical labour,' he moaned. 'It's my hip. No one knows the pain I'm in. No one. The warlocks can't do a thing for me.'

'Don't you have staff to do this sort of thing?'

'Normally, yes,' said Argon, lowering the harness. 'But my janitors are on leave. Both at the same time. Normally I wouldn't allow it, but good pixie workers are hard to find.'

Foaly's ears pricked up. 'Pixies? Your janitors are pixies?'

'Yes. We're quite proud of them around here – minor celebrities, you know. The pixie twins. And, of course, they have the highest respect for me.'

Foaly's hands shook as he unpacked his equipment. It all seemed to be coming together. First Chix, then the strange device on Julius's chest, now pixie janitors who were on leave. He just needed one more piece of the puzzle.

'What is it you have there?' asked Argon anxiously. 'Nothing that could cause any damage?'

Foaly tilted the unconscious pixie's head backwards. 'Don't worry, Argon. It's just a Retimager. I'm not going in any further than the eyeballs.'

He held the pixie's eyes open, one at a time, sealing the plunger-like cups around the sockets. 'Every image is recorded on the retinas. This leaves a trail of micro-scratches that can be enhanced and read.'

'I know what a Retimager is,' snapped Argon. 'I do read science journals occasionally, you know. So you can tell what the last thing Opal saw was. What good will that do?'

Foaly connected the eyepieces to a wall computer. 'We shall see,' he said, endeavouring to sound cryptic rather than desperate.

He opened the Retimager's program on the plasma screen, and two dark images appeared.

'Left and right eyes,' explained Foaly, toggling a key until the two images overlapped. The image was obviously a head from a side angle, but it was too dark to identify.

'Ooh, such brilliance,' gushed Argon sarcastically. 'Shall I call the networks? Or should I just faint in awe?'

Foaly ignored him. 'Lighten and enhance,' he said to the computer.

A computer-generated paintbrush swabbed the screen, leaving a brighter and sharper picture behind it.

'It's a pixie,' muttered Foaly. 'But still not enough detail.' He scratched his chin. 'Computer, match this picture with patient Koboi, Opal.'

A picture of Opal flashed up on a separate window. It resized itself and revolved until the new picture was at the same angle as the original. Red arrows flashed between the pictures, connecting identical points. After a few moments the space between the two pictures was completely blitzed with red lines.

'Are these two pictures of the same person?' asked Foaly.

'Affirmative,' said the computer. 'Though there is a point zero five per cent possibility of error.'

Foaly jabbed the print button. 'I'll take those odds.'

Argon stepped closer to the screen, as though in a daze. His face was pale, and growing paler as he realized the implications of the picture.

⊗⚲·☖☖⚳☖☖⚲·✥◗⚱☎☖☖⌖·�◗·

'She saw herself from the side,' he whispered. 'That means . . .'

'There were two Opal Kobois,' completed Foaly. 'The real one, that you let escape. And this shell here, which can only be . . .'

'A clone.'

'Precisely,' said Foaly, plucking the hard copy from the printer. 'She had herself cloned, and then your janitors waltzed her right out of here under your nose.'

'Oh dear.'

'"Oh dear" hardly covers it. Maybe now would be a good time to call the networks, or faint in awe.'

Argon took the second option, collapsing to the floor in a limp heap. The sudden evaporation of his dreams of fame and fortune were too much to handle all at once.

Foaly stepped over him and then galloped all the way to Police Plaza.

E7, southern Italy

Opal Koboi was having a hard time being patient. She had used up every last drop of her patience in the Argon Clinic. And now she wanted things to happen on her command. Unfortunately, a hundred million tonnes of haematite will only sink through the Earth at five metres per second and there isn't a lot anybody can do about it.

⊕▯⚙ℬ• ⊕⚙ℬ⊕⚙• ℐⵣℬⵔⵕ• ⵔℬⵔ

Opal decided to pass the time by watching Holly Short die. That cretinous captain. Who did she think she was, with her crew cut and cute bow lips? Opal glanced at herself in a reflective surface. Now there was real beauty. There was a face that deserved its own currency, and it was quite possible that she would soon have it.

'Mervall,' she snapped. 'Bring me the Eleven Wonders disk. I need something to cheer me up.'

'Right away, Miss Koboi,' said Merv. 'Would you like me to finish preparing the meal first, or bring you the disk directly?'

Opal rolled her eyes at her reflection. 'What did I just say?'

'You said to bring you the disk.'

'So what do you think you should do, my dearest Mervall?'

'I think I should bring you the disk,' said Merv.

'Genius, Mervall. Pure genius.'

Merv left the shuttle's kitchenette, ejecting a disk from the recorder. The computer would have the film on its hard drive, but Miss Koboi liked to have her personal favourites on disk so she could be cheered up, wherever she happened to be. Highlights from the past included her father's nervous breakdown, the attack on Police Plaza and Foaly bawling his eyes out in the LEP operations booth.

Merv handed the disk to Opal.

'And?' said the tiny pixie.

Merv was stumped for a moment, then he remembered. One of Opal's new commandments was that the Brill brothers should bow when they approached their leader. He swallowed his pride and bowed low from the waist.

'Better. Now, weren't you supposed to be preparing dinner?'

Merv retreated, still bowing. There had been a lot of pride-swallowing going on around here in the last few hours. Opal was unhappy with the level of service and respect provided by the Brill brothers, and so she had drawn up a list of rules. These directives included the aforementioned bowing, never looking Opal in the eyes, going outside the shuttle to pass wind and not thinking too loudly within three metres of their employer.

'Because I know what you are thinking,' Opal had said in a low, tremulous voice. 'I can see your thoughts swirling around your head. Right now, you're marvelling at how beautiful I am.'

'Uncanny,' gasped Merv, while traitorously wondering if there was a cuckoo flitting about his head at that very moment. Opal was going seriously off the rails with all this changing her species and world domination. He and Scant would have deserted her by now if she hadn't promised that they could have Barbados when she was queen of the Earth. That and the fact that, if they deserted her now, Opal would add the Brill brothers to her vengeance list.

Merv retreated to the kitchen and continued with his efforts to prepare Miss Koboi's food without actually touching it. Another new rule. Meanwhile, Scant was in the cargo bay, checking the detonator relays on the last two shaped charges. One for the job, and one back-up. The charges were about the size of melons but they would make a much bigger mess if they exploded. He checked that the magnetic relay pods were secure on the casings. The relays were standard mining sparker units that would accept the signal from the remote detonator and send a neutron charge into the bellies of the charges.

Scant winked at his brother through the kitchen doorway.

Merv pursed his lips in silent imitation of a cuckoo. Scant nodded wearily. They were both getting tired of Opal's outrageous behaviour. Only the prospect of drinking pina coladas on the beach in Barbados kept them going.

Opal, oblivious to all the discontent in her camp, popped the video disk into the multi-drive. To watch one's enemies die in glorious colour and surround-sound was surely one of the greatest assets of technology. Several video windows opened on the screen. Each one represented the view from one of the hemisphere's cameras.

Opal watched delightedly as Holly and Artemis were driven into the river by a pack of slobbering trolls. She

꘎꘎꘎꘎꘎꘎꘎꘎꘎꘎

'Oohed' and 'Aahed' as they took refuge on the tiny island of corpses. Her tiny heart beat faster as they scaled the Temple scaffolding. She was about to instruct Mervall to fetch her some chocolate truffles from the booty box to go with the movie, when the cameras blacked out.

'Mervall,' she squealed, wringing her delicate fingers. 'Descant! Get in here.'

The Brill brothers rushed into the lounge, handguns drawn.

'Yes, Miss Koboi?' said Scant, laying the shaped charges down on a fur-covered lounger.

Opal covered her face. 'Don't look at me!' she ordered.

Scant lowered his eyes. 'Sorry. No eye contact. I forgot.'

'And stop thinking that.'

'Yes, Miss Koboi. Sorry, Miss Koboi.' Scant had no idea what he was supposed to be thinking, so he tried to blank out everything.

Opal crossed her arms, tapping her fingers on her forearms, until both brothers were bowing before her.

'Something has gone wrong,' she said, her voice trembling slightly. 'Our Temple of Artemis cameras seem to have malfunctioned.'

Merv rewound the footage up to the last image. In it, the trolls were advancing on Artemis and Holly across the Temple roof.

'It looks like they were done for anyway, Miss Koboi.'

'Yep,' agreed Scant. 'No way out of that one.'

Opal cleared her throat. 'Firstly, *yep* is not a word, and I will not be spoken to in slang. New rule. Secondly, I assumed that Artemis Fowl was dead once before, and I spent a year in a coma as a result. We must proceed as though Fowl and Short have survived and are on our trail.'

'With respect, Miss Koboi,' said Merv, directing the words at his own toes, 'this is a stealth shuttle. We didn't leave a trail.'

'Moron,' said Opal casually. 'Our trail is on every television screen above ground, and doubtless below it. Even if Artemis Fowl were not a genius, he would guess that I am behind the Zito probe. We need to plant the final charge now. How deep is the probe?'

Scant consulted a computer readout. 'Eighty-eight point two miles. We have another ninety minutes to go to the optimum blast point.'

Opal paced the deck for a few moments. 'We have not picked up any communication with Police Plaza, so if they are alive, they are alone. Best not to risk it. We will plant the charge now and guard it. Descant, check the casings again. Mervall, run a systems check on the shuttle – I don't want a single ion escaping through the hull.'

The pixie twins stepped backwards, bowing as they went. They would do as they were told, but surely the boss was being a bit paranoid.

'I heard that thought,' screeched Opal. 'I am not paranoid!'

Merv stepped behind a steel partition to shield his brain-waves. Had Miss Koboi really intercepted the thought? Or was it just the paranoia again? After all, paranoid people usually believe that everyone thinks they are paranoid. Merv poked his head out from behind the partition and beamed a thought at Opal, just to be sure.

Holly Short is prettier than you, he thought, as loudly as he could. A treasonous thought to be sure, one Opal could hardly fail to pick up on if she could indeed read minds.

Opal stared at him. 'Mervall?'

'Yes, Miss Koboi?'

'You're looking directly at me. That's very bad for my skin.'

'Sorry, Miss Koboi,' said Merv, averting his eyes, which happened to glance through the cockpit windscreen, towards the mouth of the chute. He was just in time to see an LEP shuttle rise through the holographic rock outcrop that covered the shuttle-bay door. 'Erm, Miss Koboi, we have a problem.' He pointed out through the windscreen.

The shuttle had risen to ten metres and was hovering above the Italian landscape, obviously searching for something.

'They've found us,' said Opal in a horrified whisper. Then she quelled her panic and quickly analysed the situation. 'That is a transport shuttle, not a pursuit vehicle,' she noted, walking quickly into the cockpit, closely followed by the twins. 'We must assume that Artemis Fowl and Captain Short are aboard. They have no weapons and basic scanners. In this poor light, we are virtually invisible to the naked eye. They are blind.'

'Should we blast them from the skies?' asked the younger Brill brother eagerly. At last, some of the aggression he had been promised.

'No,' replied Opal. 'A plasma burst would give away our position to human and fairy police satellites. We go silent. Turn off everything. Even life support. I don't know how they got this close, but the only way they're going to discover our exact location is to run into us. And if that happens, their sad little shuttle will crumple like cardboard.'

The Brills obeyed promptly, switching off all the shuttle's systems.

'Good,' whispered Opal, placing a slim finger over her lips. They watched the shuttle for several minutes, until Opal decided to break the silence.

'Whoever is passing wind, please stop it, or I will devise a fitting punishment.'

'It wasn't me,' mouthed the Brill brothers simultaneously. Neither was anxious to find out what the fitting punishment for passing wind was.

E7, Ten Minutes Earlier

Holly eased the LEP shuttle through a particularly tricky secondary shaft and into E7. Almost immediately, two red lights began pulsing on the console.

'The clock is ticking,' she announced. 'We just triggered two of Foaly's sensors. They're going to put the shuttle together with the probe and come running.'

'How long?' asked Artemis.

Holly calculated in her head. 'If they come supersonic in the attack shuttle, less than half an hour.'

'Perfect,' said Artemis, pleased.

'I'm glad you think so,' moaned Mulch. 'Supersonic LEP officers are never a welcome sight among burglars. As a general rule, we prefer our police officers subsonic.'

Holly clamped the shuttle to a rocky outcrop on the chute wall. 'Are you backing out, Mulch? Or is this just the usual moaning?'

The dwarf rotated his jaws, warming them up for the work ahead. 'I think I'm entitled to a little moan. Why do these plans always involve me putting myself in harm's way while you three get to wait it out in the shuttle?'

Artemis handed him a cooler sack from the galley. 'Because you are the only one who can do this, Mulch. You alone can foil Koboi's plan.'

Mulch was not impressed. 'I'm not impressed,' he said.

'I better get a medal for this. Real gold too. No more gold-plated computer disks.'

Holly hustled him to the starboard hatch. 'Mulch, if they don't lock me in prison for the rest of my life, I will start the campaign to give you the biggest medal in the LEP cabinet.'

'And amnesty for any past and future crimes?'

Holly opened the hatch. 'Past, maybe. Future, not a chance. But no guarantees. I'm not exactly flavour of the month at Police Plaza.'

Mulch tucked the sack inside his shirt. 'OK. Possible big medal and probable amnesty. I'll take it.' He put one foot outside on to the flat surface of the rock. Tunnel wind sucked at his leg, threatening to tumble him into the abyss. 'We meet back here in twenty minutes.'

Artemis handed the dwarf a small walkie-talkie from the LEP locker. 'Remember the plan,' Artemis shouted over the roar of the wind. 'Don't forget to leave the communicator. Only steal what you are supposed to. Nothing else.'

'Nothing else,' echoed Mulch, looking none too pleased. After all, who knew what valuables Opal might have lying about up there. 'Unless something really jumps out at me.'

'Nothing,' insisted Artemis. 'Now, are you sure you can get in?'

Mulch's grin revealed rows of rectangular teeth. 'I can

get in. You just make sure their power is off and they're looking the other way.'

Butler hefted the bag of tricks he had brought with him from Fowl Manor. 'Don't worry, Mulch. They'll be looking the other way. I guarantee it.'

POLICE PLAZA, THE LOWER ELEMENTS

All the brass were in the operations room, watching live television updates on the probe's progress when Foaly burst in.

'We need to talk,' blurted the centaur to the general assembly.

'Quiet,' hissed Council Chairman Cahartez. 'Have a bowl of curry.'

Chairman Cahartez ran a fleet of curry vans in Haven City. Vole curry was his speciality. Obviously, he was doing the catering for this little viewing session.

Foaly ignored the buffet table. He snatched a remote control from a chair armrest, muting the master volume.

'We have big trouble, ladies and gentlemen. Opal Koboi is loose and I think she's behind the Zito probe.'

A high-backed swivel chair swung round. Ark Sool was lounging in it.

'Opal Koboi? Amazing. And she's doing all this psychically, I suppose.'

'No. What are you doing in that chair? That's the commander's chair. The real commander, not Internal Affairs.'

Sool tapped the golden acorns on his lapel. 'I've been promoted.'

Foaly blanched. 'You're the new Recon commander.'

Sool's smile could have illuminated a dark room. 'Yes. The Council felt that Recon has been getting a bit out of hand lately. They felt – and I must say I agree – that Recon needs a firm hand. Of course, I will stay on at Internal Affairs until a suitable replacement can be found.'

Foaly scowled. There was no time for this. Not now. He had to get clearance for a supersonic launch immediately.

'OK, Sool, Commander. I can lodge my objection later. Right now we have an emergency on our hands.'

Everyone was listening now. But none with much enthusiasm except Wing Commander Vinyáya, who had always been a staunch supporter of Julius Root and would certainly have not voted for Sool. Vinyáya was all ears. 'What's the emergency, Foaly?' she asked.

Foaly slipped a computer disk into the room's multidrive. 'That thing in the Argon Clinic is not Opal Koboi, it's a clone.'

'Evidence?' demanded Sool.

Foaly highlighted a window on the screen. 'I scanned her retinas and found that the last image the clone saw was Opal Koboi herself. Obviously during her escape.'

Sool was not convinced. 'I've never trusted your gadgets, Foaly. Your Retimager is not accepted as actual evidence in a courtroom.'

'We're not in a courtroom, Sool,' said Foaly through clenched teeth. 'If we accept that Opal could be loose, then the events of the past twenty-four hours take on a whole new significance. A pattern begins to emerge. Scalene is dead, pixies are missing from the clinic, Julius is murdered and Holly blamed. Then, within hours of this, a probe is sent down, decades ahead of schedule. Koboi is behind all of this. That probe is on its way here and we're sitting around watching it on PPTV . . . Eating stinking vole curry!'

'I object to the disparaging curry remark,' said Cahartez, wounded. 'But otherwise I take your point.'

Sool jumped from his chair. 'What point? Foaly is joining dots that don't exist. All he is trying to do is exonerate his late friend, Captain Short.'

'Holly may be alive!' snapped Foaly. 'And trying to do something about Opal Koboi.'

Sool rolled his eyes. 'But her vitals flatlined, centaur. We remote-destroyed her helmet. I was there, remember.'

A head poked into the room, one of Foaly's lab apprentices.

'I got that case, sir,' he panted. 'Quick as I could.'

'Well done, Roob,' said Foaly, snatching the case

from the apprentice's hand. He spun the case around. 'I issued Holly and Julius with new suits. Prototypes. They both have bio-sensors and trackers. They are not linked with the LEP mainframe. I never thought to check them earlier. Holly's helmet may be out of action, but her suit is still functioning.'

'What do the suit's sensors tell us, Foaly?' asked Vinyáya.

Foaly was almost afraid to look. If the suit sensors were flatlining, it would be like losing Holly again. He counted to three, then consulted the small screen in the case. There were two readouts on the screen. One was flat. Julius. But the other was active in all areas.

'Holly is alive!' shouted the centaur, kissing Commander Vinyáya soundly on the cheek. 'Alive and reasonably well, apart from elevated blood pressure and next to zero magic in her tank.'

'And where is she?' asked Vinyáya, smiling.

Foaly enlarged the locator section of the screen. 'On her way up E7, in the shuttle that was stolen by Mulch Diggums, if I'm not much mistaken.'

Sool was delighted. 'Let me get this straight. Murder suspect Holly Short is in a stolen chute next to the Zito probe.'

'That's right.'

'That would make her the prime suspect in any irregularities concerning the probe.'

Foaly was very tempted to actually trample Sool, but he held his temper in check for Holly's sake. 'All I'm asking, Sool, is that you give me a green light to send the supersonic shuttle to investigate. If I'm right, then your first act as Commander will be to avert a calamity.'

'And if you're wrong? Which you probably are.'

'If I'm wrong, then you get to bring in public enemy number one, Captain Holly Short.'

Sool stroked his goatee. It was a win–win situation. 'Very well. Send the shuttle. How long will it take to prep?'

Foaly pulled a phone from his pocket, hitting a number on the speed-dial.

'Major Kelp,' he said into the mouthpiece. 'Green light. Go.' Foaly smiled at Ark Sool. 'I briefed Major Kelp on my way over. I felt sure you'd see it my way. Commanders generally do.'

Sool scowled. 'Don't get familiar with me, pony boy. This is not the start of a beautiful relationship. I'm sending the shuttle because it is the only option. If you are somehow manipulating me, or bending the truth, I will bury you in tribunal hearings for the next five years. Then I will fire you.'

Foaly ignored him. There would be plenty of time for trading threats later. Right now he needed to concentrate on the shuttle's progress. He had gone through the shock of Holly's death once before and he did not intend to go through it again.

E7

Mulch Diggums could have been an athlete. He had the jaws and recycling equipment for sprint digging, or even cross country. Plenty of natural ability, but no dedication. He tried it for a couple of months in college, but the strict regime of training and diet did not suit him.

Mulch could still remember his college tunnelling coach giving him a pep talk after training one night. 'You got the jaws, Diggums,' the old dwarf admitted, 'and you sure got the behind. I ain't never seen no one who could pump out the bubbles like you do. But you ain't got the heart, and that's what's important.'

Maybe the old dwarf was right. Mulch never did have the heart for selfless activity. Tunnelling was a lonely job, and there wasn't much money in it either. And because it was an ethnic sport, the TV networks were not interested. No advertising meant no big pay deals for the athletes. Mulch decided his digging prowess could more profitably be utilized on the shady side of the law. Maybe if he had some gold, then female dwarfs would be more likely to return his calls.

And now here he was, breaking all his rules, preparing

to break into a craft that was bristling with fairy sensors *and* occupied by armed hostiles. Just to help someone else. Of all the vehicles on the planet or under it, Artemis just had to get into the most technologically advanced shuttle in existence. Every square centimetre of the stealth shuttle's plating would be alarmed with lasers, motion sensors, static sheets and who knew what else. Still, alarms were no good if they weren't activated, and that was what Mulch was counting on.

Mulch waved goodbye in the general direction of the shuttle, just in case anyone was still watching him, and traversed the rocky outcrop to the safety of the chute wall. Dwarfs do not like heights, and being technically below sea level was not helping his vertigo.

The dwarf sank his fingers into a vein of soft clay sprouting through the rock wall. Home. Anywhere on earth was home to a dwarf, as long as there was clay. Mulch felt calm settle over him. He was safe now – for the time being at any rate.

The dwarf unhinged his jaw with twin *cracks!* that would make any other sentient species wince. He popped the snaps on his bum-flap and launched himself into the clay. His gnashing teeth scooped bucketfuls of clay from the chute wall, creating an instant tunnel. Mulch crawled into the space, sealing the cavity behind him with recycled clay from his rear end.

After half a dozen mouthfuls, the sonar filaments in

his hair detected a shelf of rock ahead and he adjusted his course accordingly. The stealth shuttle would not be set down on rock because it was top-of-the-range and as such would have a battery rod. The rods telescoped from the belly of the ship, drilling fifteen metres below the ground, recharging the shuttle's batteries with the power of the Earth. The cleanest of energies.

The battery rod vibrated slightly as it harvested, and it was this vibration that Mulch honed in on now. It took him just over five minutes of steady munching to clear the rock shelf and reach the tip of the battery rod. The vibrations had already loosened the earth, and it was a simple matter for Mulch to clear himself a little cave. He spread saliva on the walls and waited.

Holly piloted the LEP craft through the small shuttle port, overriding the shuttle doors with her Recon access code. Police Plaza hadn't bothered to change her code because, as far as they were concerned, she was dead.

A sheet of black rain-clouds was spreading shadows across the Italian countryside as they cleared the holographic outcrop that shielded the shuttle port. A light frost coated the reddish clay and a southerly wind lifted the shuttle's tail.

'We can't stay out here for long,' said Holly, throttling back to a hover. 'This transporter doesn't have defences.'

'We won't need long,' said Artemis. 'Fly in a grid

search pattern, as though we're not certain where exactly the stealth shuttle is.'

Holly punched some co-ordinates into the flight computer. 'You're the genius.'

Artemis turned to Butler, who was sitting, cross-legged, in the aisle. 'Now, old friend, can you make certain that Opal is looking this way?'

'Can do,' said Butler, crawling to the port-side exit. He knuckled the access button and the door slid back. The shuttle bucked slightly as the cabin pressure equalized then settled.

Butler opened his bag of weaponry and selected a handful of metal spheres, roughly the size of tennis balls. He flicked back the safety cap on one, then depressed the button below it with his thumb. The button began to rise to its original position.

'Ten seconds until the button is flush with the surface. Then it makes a connection.'

'Thank you for the lecture,' said Artemis dryly. 'Though now is hardly the time.'

Butler smiled, tossing the metal sphere into the air. Five seconds later, it exploded, blowing a small crater in the earth below. Scorch lines ran from the crater, giving it the appearance of a black flower.

'I bet Opal is looking now,' said Butler, priming the next grenade.

'I'm sure others will be looking soon. Explosions don't

tend to go unnoticed for long. We are relatively isolated here. The nearest village is approximately ten miles away. If we are lucky, that gives us a ten-minute window. Next grid square, please, Holly. But not too close, we don't want to scare them off.'

Fifteen metres below the ground, Mulch Diggums waited in his little DIY cave, watching the tip of the battery rod. As soon as it stopped vibrating, he began working his way upwards through the loose clay. The telescopic rod was warm to the touch, heated by the energy it conducted to the shuttle's batteries. Mulch used it to help him on his journey, pulling himself upwards, hand over hand. The clay he consumed was broken and aerated from the rod's drilling action, and Mulch was glad of that extra air. He converted it to wind, using it to boost himself upwards.

Mulch increased his pace, pumping the air and clay through his recycling passages. Opal would be distracted by the shuttle only for so long, before it occurred to her that it was a diversion. The rod thickened as he went along it, until he arrived at a rubber seal in the belly of the shuttle itself, which was raised on three retractable legs, half a metre off the ground. When the shuttle was in flight, this seal would be covered by a metal panel, but the shuttle was not in flight at the moment and the sensors were turned off.

Mulch climbed out of his tunnel and rehinged his jaw. This was precision work, and he needed fine control of his teeth. Rubber was not a recommended part of a dwarf's diet and so could not be swallowed. Half-digested rubber could seal up his insides as effectively as a barrel of glue.

It was an awkward bite. Difficult to get a grip. Mulch flattened his cheek against the battery rod, worming upwards until his incisors could get some purchase on the seal. He bore down on the heavy rubber, rotating his jaw in small circles until his upper tooth broke through. Then he ground his teeth, enlarging the rent until there was a ten-centimetre tear in the rubber. Now Mulch could get one side of his mouth into the gap. He tore off large chunks, taking care to spit them out immediately.

In less than a minute, Mulch had torn a thirty-centimetre-square hole. Just enough for him to squeeze through. Anyone unfamiliar with dwarfs would have bet money that Mulch could never squeeze his well-fed bulk through such a narrow aperture, but they would have lost their cash. Dwarfs have spent millennia escaping from cave-ins, and they have developed the ability to squeeze through tighter holes than this one.

Mulch sucked in his gut and wriggled through the torn seal, head first. He was glad to be out of the faint morning sunlight. Sun was another thing dwarfs do not like; after mere minutes in direct sunlight, a dwarf's skin will be redder than a boiled lobster's. He shinned up the battery rod into the shuttle's engine compartment. Most of the small space was taken up with flat batteries and a hydrogen generator. There was an access hatch overhead that should lead into the cargo bay. Ropes of lights ran the length of the compartment, giving off pale-green light. Any radiation leak from the generator would show up purple. The reason why the light ropes were still working without power was because the illumination was supplied by specially cultivated, decaying algae. Not that Mulch knew any of this, he just thought that the light was very similar to the luminescence from dwarf spittle, and the familiarity made him relax. He relaxed a bit too much, as it happened, allowing a small squib of tunnel gas to escape through his bum-flap. Hopefully nobody would notice that . . .

Maybe half a minute later, he heard Opal's voice from above.

'Now, whoever is passing wind, please stop it, or I will devise a fitting punishment.'

Oops, thought Mulch guiltily. In dwarf circles it is considered almost criminal to allow someone else to be blamed for your air bubbles. Through sheer force of habit, Mulch almost raised his hand and confessed, but luckily his instinct for self-preservation was stronger than his conscience.

Moments later, the signal came. It was hard to miss. The explosion rocked the entire shuttle twenty degrees off centre. It was time to make his move and trust Artemis when he said that it was almost impossible not to watch an explosion.

Mulch nudged the hatch open a crack with the crown of his head. The dwarf half expected someone to stamp on the hatch, but the cargo bay was empty. Mulch folded the hatch back and crept all the way into the small chamber. There was a lot here to interest him. Crates of ingots, perspex boxes of human currency and antique jewellery hanging from mannequins. Obviously Opal did not intend to be poor in her new role as a human. Mulch snagged a single diamond earring from a nearby bust. So Artemis had told him not to take anything? So what? One earring wouldn't slow him down.

Mulch popped the pigeon's-egg-sized diamond into his mouth and swallowed. He would pass that later, when he was on his own. Until then it could lodge in his stomach wall, and come out shinier than it went in.

Another explosion bucked the floor beneath his feet, reminding Mulch to move on. He crossed to the bay door, which was slightly ajar. The next chamber was the passenger area, and it was just as plush as Holly had described. Mulch's lip rippled at the sight of fur-covered chairs. Repulsive. Beyond the passenger area was the cockpit. Opal and her two friends were clearly visible, staring intently out of the front windscreen. They were making not a sound, and saying not a word. Just as Artemis had said.

Mulch dropped to his knees and crawled across the lounge's carpet. He was now completely exposed. If one of the pixies decided to turn around, he would be stranded in the middle of the lounge with nothing but a smile to hide behind.

Just keep going and don't think about that, Mulch told himself. *If Opal catches you, pretend you're lost or have amnesia, or just came out of a coma. Maybe she'll sympathize, give you some gold and send you on your way. Yeah, right.*

Something creaked slightly under Mulch's knee. The dwarf froze, but the pixies didn't react to the sound. Presumably that was the lid of the booty box, Opal's little hidey-hole. Mulch crawled round the box. If there was one thing he didn't need, it was more creaks.

Two shaped charges lay on a chair, level with Mulch's nose. He couldn't believe it. Right there, less than a metre away. This was the one part of the plan that relied on luck. If one of the Brill brothers had the charge tucked under his arm or if there were more charges than he could carry, then they would have to ram the shuttle and hope to disable her. But here they were, almost begging to be stolen. When he was committing a robbery, Mulch often gave voices to the objects he was about to steal. This, he knew, would sound a little crazy to the rest of the world, but he spent a lot of time on his own and he needed someone to talk to.

Come on, Mister Handsome Dwarf, said one of the charges

in a breathy falsetto. *I'm waiting. I don't like it here, you know. Please rescue me.*

Very well, Madame, thought Mulch, taking the bag from inside his shirt. *I'll take you, but we're not going very far.*

Me too, said the other charge. *I want to go too.*

Don't worry, ladies. Where you're going, there's plenty of room for both of you.

When Mulch Diggums crept out through the torn seal a minute later, the charges were no longer on the chair. In their place was a small hand-held communicator.

The three pixies sat quietly in the stealth shuttle's cockpit. One was concentrating on the transport craft that was hovering two hundred metres off their bows. The other two were concentrating on not passing wind and not thinking about not passing wind.

The transport shuttle's side entrance opened and something winked in the morning light as it tumbled earthwards. Seconds later, the something exploded, rocking the stealth shuttle on its suspension bags.

The Brill brothers gasped, and Opal cuffed them both on the ear.

Opal was not worried. They were searching. Shooting in the dark, or very close to it. Maybe in thirty minutes there would be enough light to see the ship with the naked eye, but until then they were blending very nicely into the surrounding countryside, thanks to a hull made from

᠃᠎᠐᠑᠒᠃ · ᠔᠕᠖᠗᠘᠙᠃ · ᠃᠐᠑᠃ · ᠃·

stealth ore and cam foil. Fowl must have guessed where they were because of this chute's proximity to the probe. But all he had was an approximation. Of course, it would be delightful to blast them out of the air, but plasma bursts would light up Foaly's satellite scanners and paint a bullseye on their hull.

She plucked a digi-pad and pen from the dash and scrawled a message on it.

Stay quiet and calm. Even if one of those charges hits us, it will not penetrate the hull.

Mervall took the pad. *Maybe we should leave. Mud Men will be coming.*

Opal wrote a response. *Dear Mervall, please don't start thinking — you will hurt your head. We wait until they leave. At this close range, they could actually hear our engines starting.*

Another explosion rocked the stealth shuttle. Opal felt a bead of sweat roll down her forehead. This was ridiculous, she didn't perspire — certainly not in front of the help. In five minutes, the humans would come to investigate; it was their nature. So she would wait five minutes, then try to slip past the LEP shuttle, and if she couldn't slip past, then she would blast them out of the sky and take her chances with the supersonic shuttle that would no doubt come to investigate.

More grenades dropped from the LEP craft, but they were further away now and the shockwaves barely caused a shudder in the stealth shuttle. This went on for two or three minutes without the remotest danger to Opal or the Brills, then suddenly the transport shuttle sealed its door and peeled away, back down the chute.

'Hmm,' said Opal. 'Surprising.'

'Maybe they ran out of ammunition,' offered Merv, though he knew that Opal would punish him for offering an opinion.

'Is that what you think, Mervall? They ran out of explosives and so they decided just to let us go. Do you really imagine that to be true, you imbecilic excuse for a sentient being? Don't you have any frontal lobes?'

'I was just playing devil's advocate,' mumbled Merv weakly.

Opal rose from her seat, waving a hand at each Brill brother. 'Just shut up. I need to talk to myself for a minute.' She paced the narrow cockpit. 'What's going on here? They track us to the chute, then put on a big fireworks display, then leave. Just like that. Why? Why?' She rubbed both temples with her knuckles. 'Think.' Suddenly Opal remembered something. 'Last night. A shuttle was stolen in E1. We heard about it on the police band. Who stole it?'

Scant shrugged. 'I dunno. Some dwarf. Is it important?'

'That's right. A dwarf. And wasn't there a dwarf involved in the Artemis Fowl siege? And weren't there rumours of that same dwarf helping Julius to break into Koboi labs?'

'Rumours. No actual evidence.'

Opal turned on Scant. 'Maybe that's because, unlike you, this dwarf is smart. Maybe he doesn't want to be caught.' The pixie took a moment to join the dots. 'So they have a dwarf burglar, a shuttle and explosives. Short must know that those pathetic grenades can't penetrate our hull, so why drop them? Unless . . .'

The truth hit her like a physical blow in the stomach.

'Oh no,' she gasped. 'Distraction. We sat here like fools, watching the pretty lights. And all the time . . .'

She heaved Scant aside and rushed past him to the lounge.

'The charges,' she shrieked. 'Where are they?'

Scant went straight to the chair. 'Don't worry, Miss Koboi, they're right −' He stopped, the sentence's final word stuck in his throat. 'I, ah, they were right there. In the chair.'

Opal picked up the small hand-held radio. 'They're toying with me. Tell me you put the back-up somewhere safe.'

'No,' said Scant miserably. 'They were together.'

Merv pushed past him into the cargo bay. 'The engine compartment is open.' He stuck his head through the hatch. His voice wafted up, muffled by the floor panels. 'The battery rod seal has been ripped apart. And there are footprints. Someone came in through here.'

Opal threw back her head and screamed. She held it for

a long time for such a small individual. Finally her breath ran out.

'Follow the shuttle,' she gasped, when her wind returned. 'I modified those charges myself and they cannot be disarmed. We can still detonate. At the very least we will destroy my enemies.'

'Yes, Miss Koboi,' said Merv and Scant together.

'Don't look at me,' howled Opal.

The Brill brothers fled to the cockpit, trying to simultaneously bow, look at their feet, not think anything dangerous and, above all, not pass wind.

Mulch was waiting at the rendezvous site when the LEP shuttle arrived. Butler opened the door and hauled the dwarf in by the collar.

'Did you get it?' asked Artemis anxiously.

Mulch passed him the bulging bag. 'Right here! And before you ask, I left the radio.'

'So everything went according to plan?'

'Completely,' replied Mulch, neglecting to mention the diamond nestling in his stomach wall.

'Excellent,' said Artemis, striding past the dwarf to the cockpit.

'Go,' he shouted, thumping Holly's headrest.

Holly already had the shuttle ticking over and was holding it with the brake.

'We're gone,' she said, releasing the brake and flooring

the throttle. The LEP craft bolted out of the rocky outcrop like a pebble from a catapult.

Artemis's legs were dragged from the floor, flapping behind him like windsocks. The rest of him would have followed if he hadn't held on to the headrest.

'How much time do we have?' Holly asked through lips rippled by G-force.

Artemis pulled himself into the passenger seat. 'Minutes. The orebody will hit a depth of one hundred and six miles in precisely a quarter of an hour. Opal will be after us any second.'

Holly shadowed the chute wall, spinning between two towers of rock. The lower portion of E7 was quite straight, but this stretch corkscrewed through the crust, following the cracks in the plates.

'Is this going to work, Artemis?' said Holly.

Artemis pondered the question. 'I considered eight plans, and this was the best one. Even so, we have a sixty-four per cent chance of success. The key is to keep Opal distracted so she doesn't discover the truth. That's up to you, Holly. Can you do it?'

Holly wrapped her fingers round the wheel. 'Don't worry. It's not often I get a chance to do some fancy flying. Opal will be so busy trying to catch us, she won't have time to consider anything else.'

Artemis looked out through the windscreen. They were pointing straight down, towards the centre of the

Earth. Gravity fluctuated at this depth and speed, so they were alternately pinned to their chairs and straining to be free of their seatbelts. The chute's blackness enveloped them like tar, except for the cone of light from the shuttle's headlamps. Gigantic rock formations darted in and out of the cone, heading straight for their nose. Somehow, Holly steered them through without once tapping the brake.

On the plasma dash, the icon representing the gaseous anomaly that was Opal's ship inched across the screen.

'They're on to us,' said Holly, catching the movement in the corner of one eye.

Artemis's stomach was knotted from flight nausea, anxiety, fatigue and exhilaration. 'Very well,' he said, almost to himself. 'The chase is on.'

At the mouth of E7, Merv was at the wheel of the stealth shuttle. Scant was on instruments and Opal was in charge of giving orders and general ranting.

'Do we have a signal from the charges?' she screeched from her chair.

Her voice is getting really annoying, thought Scant, but not too loudly.

'No,' he replied. 'Nothing. Which means they must be in their shuttle. Their shields must be blocking the charges' signal. We need to get closer – or I could send the detonation signal anyway. We might get lucky.'

Opal's screech grew more strident. 'No! We must not detonate before that shuttle reaches a hundred and six miles. If we do, the orebody will not change course. What about this stupid communicator? Anything from that?'

'Negative,' said Scant. 'If there's another one, it must be switched off.'

'We could always return to Zito's compound,' said Merv. 'We have a dozen more charges there.'

Opal leaned forward in her seat, punching Merv's shoulders with her tiny fists. 'Idiot. Moron. Halfwit. Are you in some kind of stupidity competition? Is that it? If we return to Zito's, the orebody will be too deep by the time we return. Not to mention the fact that Captain Short will present the LEP with her version of events and they will have to investigate, at the very least. We must get closer and we must detonate. Even if we miss the probe window, at least we shall destroy any witnesses against me.'

The stealth shuttle had proximity sensors linked into the navigating software, which meant that Opal and company did not have to worry about colliding with the chute wall or stalactites.

'How long before we're in detonation range?' Opal barked. To be honest, it was more of a yip.

Merv did some quick calculations. 'Three minutes. No more.'

'How deep will they be at that point?'

A few more sums. 'Hundred and fifty-five miles.'

Opal pinched her nose. 'It could work. Presuming they have both charges, the resulting explosion, even if not directed as we planned, may be enough to blow a crack in the wall. It's our only option. If it fails, at least we have time to regroup. As soon as they hit one zero five, send the detonate signal. Send it continuously. We may get lucky.'

Merv flipped a plastic safety cover off the detonate button. Only seconds to go.

Artemis's insides were trying to force their way out through his throat.

'This heap needs new gyroscopes,' he said.

Holly barely nodded, she was too busy concentrating on a particularly tricky series of jinks and loops in the chute.

Artemis consulted the dashboard's readout.

'We're at a depth of one zero five now. Opal will be trying to detonate. She's closing fast.'

Mulch stuck his head through from the passenger section. 'Is all this jiggling about really necessary? I've had a lot to eat recently.'

'Nearly there,' said Artemis. 'The ride is just about over. Tell Butler to open the bag.'

'OK. Are you sure Opal will do what she's supposed to?'

Artemis smiled reassuringly. 'Of course I am. It's human nature, and Opal is a human now. Remember? Now, Holly. Pull over.'

Mervall tapped the readout. 'You're not going to believe this, Op– Miss Koboi.'

The merest hint of a smile flickered across Opal's lips. 'Don't tell me. They have stopped.'

Merv shook his head, astounded. 'Yes, they are hovering at a hundred and twenty-four miles. Why would they do that?'

'There's no point trying to explain it, Mervall. Just keep sending the detonation signal, but slow us down. I don't want to be too close when we get a connection.'

She drummed her nails on the hand-held communicator left behind by the dwarf. Any second now.

A red call light flashed on the communicator, accompanied by a slight vibration. Opal smiled, flipping open the walkie-talkie's screen.

Artemis's pale face filled the tiny screen. He was trying to smile, but it was obviously forced. 'Opal, I am giving you one chance to surrender. We have disarmed your charges and the LEP are on their way. It would be better for you to turn yourself over to Captain Short than shoot it out with an armed LEP ship.'

Opal clapped her hands. 'Bravo, Master Fowl, what a wonderful fiction. Now, why don't I tell you the real truth? You have realized that the charges cannot be disarmed. The mere fact that I can receive your communication's signal means that my detonation signal will soon penetrate your shields. You cannot jettison the explosives or I will set them off in the chute, exactly as I had originally planned. Then I will simply fire a few heat-seekers at your craft. And if you attempt further flight, then I will follow and penetrate your shields before you clear the parallel stretch. You are not in communication with the LEP. If you were, we would have picked up your broadcast. So your only alternative is this pathetic bluff. And it is pathetic. You are obviously attempting to stall me until the orebody passes your depth.'

'So you refuse to surrender?'

Opal pretended to think about it, tapping her chin with a manicured nail. 'Why, yes. I think I will fight on, against all odds. And by the way, please don't look directly at the screen, it's bad for my skin.'

Artemis sighed dramatically. 'Well, if we have to go, at least we'll go on full stomachs.'

This was an unusually cavalier comment to make with seconds to live, even for a human. 'Full stomachs?'

'Yes,' said Artemis. 'Mulch took something else from your shuttle.'

He picked up a small chocolate-covered ball, wiggling it in front of the screen.

312

'My truffles?' gasped Opal. 'You took them. That's just mean.'

Artemis popped the treat into his mouth, chewing slowly. 'They really are divine. I can see why you missed them in the clinic. We're going to have to work really hard to eat all we took before you blow us to smithereens.'

Opal hissed, catlike. 'Killing you will be so easy.' She turned to Merv. 'Do we have a signal yet?'

'Nothing, Miss Koboi. But soon. If we have communications, it can't be long now.'

Holly squeezed her head into the viewfinder. One cheek was swollen with truffles. 'They really melt in the mouth, Opal. The condemned crew's final meal.'

Opal actually poked the screen with her nail. 'You survived twice, Short. You won't do it again, I guarantee it.'

Holly laughed. 'You should see Mulch. He's shovelling those truffles down his gullet.'

Opal was livid. 'Any signal?' Even now, with certain destruction only moments away, they were still mocking her.

'Not yet. Soon.'

'Keep trying. Keep your finger on that button.'

Opal unstrapped herself, striding through to the lounge. The dwarf couldn't have carried all the truffles *and* the explosives. Surely not. She had been so looking forward to a handful of the heavenly chocolate, once Haven was destroyed.

She knelt on the carpet, worming her hand underneath the seam to the hidden catch. It popped beneath her fingers, and the booty box's lid slid up and back.

There was not a single truffle left in the box. Instead, there were two shaped charges. For a moment Opal could not understand what she was seeing. Then it became terrifyingly clear. Artemis had never stolen the charges, he had simply told the dwarf to move them. Once in the booty box, they could not be detected or detonated. As long as the lid was sealed. She had opened the box herself. Artemis had goaded her into sealing her own fate.

The blood drained from Opal's face. 'Mervall,' she screamed. 'The detonation signal!'

'Don't worry, Miss Koboi,' the pixie shouted from the cockpit. 'We just got contact. Nothing can stop it now.'

Green countdown clocks activated on both charges and began counting back from twenty. A standard mining fuse.

Opal lurched into the cockpit. She had been tricked. Duped. Now the charges would detonate uselessly at seventy-four and a half miles, well above the parallel stretch. Of course, her own shuttle would be destroyed and she would be left stranded, ready to be scooped up by the LEP. At least, that was the theory. But Opal Koboi never left herself without options.

She strapped herself into a seat in the cockpit.

'I advise you to strap yourselves in,' she said curtly to

314

the Brill brothers. 'You have failed me. Enjoy prison.'

Merv and Scant barely had time to buckle up before Opal activated the ejector gel-pods under their seats. They were immediately immersed in a bubble of amber impact-gel and ejected through panels that had opened in the hull.

The impact-gel bubbles had no power source and relied on the initial gas propulsion to get them out of harm's way. The gel was fireproof, blast-resistant and contained enough oxygen for thirty minutes' shallow breathing. Merv and Scant were catapulted through black space until they came into contact with the chute wall. The gel stuck to the rocky surface, leaving the Brill brothers stranded, thousands of miles from home.

Opal, meanwhile, was rapidly keying codes into the shuttle's computer. She had less than ten seconds left to complete her final act of aggression. Artemis Fowl may have beaten her this time, but he wouldn't live to gloat about it.

Opal expertly activated and launched two heat-seeking plasma rockets from the nose tubes, then launched her own escape pod. No impact-gel for Opal Koboi. She had, of course, included a luxury pod in the ship's design. Just one, though, no need for the help to travel in comfort. In fact, Opal didn't care what happened to the Brill brothers, one way or the other. They were of no further use to her.

She opened the throttles wide, ignoring safety regulations. After all, who cared if she scorched the shuttle's hull? It was about to get a lot more than just scorched. The pod streaked towards the surface at over five hundred miles per hour. Pretty fast, but not fast enough to completely escape the shockwave from the two shaped charges.

The stealth shuttle exploded in a flash of multicoloured light. Holly pulled the LEP shuttle close to the wall, to avoid falling debris. After the shockwaves had passed, the shuttle's occupants waited in silence for the computer to run a scan on the stretch of chute above them. Eventually three red dots appeared on the three-dimensional representation of the chute. Two were static, while the other was moving rapidly towards the surface.

'They made it,' sighed Artemis. 'I have no doubt that the moving dot is Opal. We should pick her up.'

'We should,' said Holly, not looking as happy as one might have expected. 'But we won't.'

Artemis picked up on Holly's tone. 'Why not? What's wrong?'

'That's wrong,' said Holly, pointing to the screen. Two more dots had appeared on the screen and were moving towards them at extreme speed. The computer identified the dots as missiles, then quickly ran a match in its database.

'Heat-seeking plasma rockets. Locked on to our engines.'

Mulch shook his head. 'That Koboi is a bitter little pixie. She couldn't let it go.'

Artemis stared at the screen, as if he could destroy the missiles through concentration. 'I should have anticipated this.'

Butler poked his massive head past his charge's shoulders. 'Do you have any hot waffle to draw the missiles away?'

'This is a transport shuttle,' replied Holly. 'We were lucky to have shields.'

'The missiles are coming after our heat signature?'

'Yes,' said Holly, hoping there was an idea on the way.

'Is there any way to significantly alter that signature?'

An option occurred to Holly then. It was so extreme that she didn't bother running it past the shuttle's other occupants.

'There is one way,' she said, and turned off the engines.

The shuttle dropped like a rock through the chute. Holly tried to manoeuvre using the flaps, but without propulsion it was like trying to steer an anchor.

There was no time for fear or panic. There was only time to hang on to something and try to keep your last meal inside your body.

Holly gritted her teeth, swallowing the panic that was trying to claw its way out, as she fought the steering wheel. If she could keep the flaps centred, then they shouldn't collide with the chute walls. At least this way they had a chance.

She flicked her eyes towards the readouts. The core temperature of the craft was dropping, but would it be quick enough? This section of the chute was reasonably straight, but there was a kink coming up in thirty miles and they would crash into it like a fly hitting an elephant.

Butler crawled up towards the rear of the ship. On the way he snagged two fire extinguishers and popped their pins. He tossed the extinguishers into the engine room and closed the door. Through the hatch he could see the extinguishers cartwheeling, covering the engine with freezing foam.

The engine temperature dropped another notch.

The missiles were closer now, and gaining.

Holly opened all the vents wide, flooding the shuttle with cool air. Another notch towards green on the temperature readout.

'Come on,' she said through rippling lips. 'A few more degrees.'

They hurtled down and down, spinning into blackness. Little by little the ship was drifting to starboard. Soon it would smash into the kink that rose to meet them. Holly's finger hovered over the ignition. She would wait until the last possible moment.

The engines cooled even further. They were efficient energy-saving units. When they were not in use, they quickly funnelled excess heat to the life-support batteries. But still the missiles held their course.

The kink in the chute wall appeared in their headlights. It was bigger than an average mountain and was composed of hard, unforgiving rock. If the shuttle impacted, it would crumple like a tin can.

Artemis squeezed words from between his lips. 'Not working. Engines.'

'Wait,' Holly replied.

The flaps were vibrating now, and the shuttle went into a tumble. They could see the heat-seekers roaring up behind them, which were now in front of them, then behind them again.

They were close to the rock now. Too close. If Holly delayed just one more second, she would not have sufficient room to manoeuvre. She punched the ignition, veering to port at the last millisecond. The bow plates sent up an arc of sparks as they scraped along the rocky outcrop. Then they were free, zooming into the black void. That is, if you count being pursued by two heat-seekers as being free.

The engine temperature was still dropping and would be for maybe half a minute while the turbines heated up. Would it be enough? Holly punched the rear camera view up on the front screen. The rockets were still coming. Unrelenting. Purple fuel burning in their wake. Three seconds to impact. Then two.

Then they lost contact, veering away from their target. One went over the top, the other under the keel.

'It worked,' sighed Artemis, releasing a breath he didn't realize he'd been holding.

'Well done, soldier,' grinned Butler, ruffling Holly's hair.

Mulch poked his head through from the passenger area. His face was slightly green. 'I had a little accident,' he said. No one enquired further.

'Let's not celebrate just yet,' said Holly, checking her instruments. 'Those missiles should have detonated against the chute wall, but they didn't. I can think of only one reason why they wouldn't keep travelling in a straight line.'

'If they acquired another target,' offered Butler.

A red dot appeared on the plasma screen. The two missiles were heading directly for it.

'Exactly. That's an LEP supersonic attack shuttle, and, as far as they're concerned, we've just opened fire on them.'

Major Trouble Kelp was behind the wheel of the LEP attack shuttle. The craft was travelling at over three times the speed of sound, booming along the chute like a silver needle. Supersonic flights were very rarely cleared, as they could cause cave-ins and, in rare cases, be detected by human seismographic equipment.

The shuttle's interior was filled with impact-gel to dampen the otherwise bone-breaking vibration. Major Kelp was suspended in the gel in a modified pilot's suit. The ship's controls were connected directly to his gloves, and the video ran into his helmet.

Foaly was in constant contact from Police Plaza.

'Be advised that the stolen shuttle is back in the chute,' he informed Trouble. 'It's hovering at one twenty-four miles.'

'I have it,' said Trouble, locating the dot on his radar. He felt his heart race. There was a chance that Holly was alive, and aboard that shuttle. And if that were true, he would do whatever it took to bring her home safely.

A sunburst of white, yellow and orange flared on his scopes.

'We have an explosion of some kind. Was it the stolen shuttle?'

'No, Trouble. It came from nowhere. There was nothing there. Watch out for debris.'

The screen was streaked with dozens of jagged yellow lines as hot metal shards plummeted towards the centre of the Earth. Trouble activated the nose lasers, ready for anything that might head his way. It was unlikely that his vessel would be threatened – the chute was wider than the average city at this depth. The debris from the explosion would not spread more than a mile. He had plenty of room to steer himself out of harm's way.

Unless some of the debris followed him. Two of the yellow streaks were veering unnaturally in his direction. The on-board computer ran a scan. Both items had propulsion and guidance systems. Missiles.

'I am under fire,' he said into his microphone. 'Two missiles incoming.'

Had Holly fired on him? Was it true what Sool had said? Had she really gone bad?

Trouble reached into the air, tapping a virtual screen. He touched the representations for both missiles, targeting them for destruction. As soon as they came into range, the computer would hit them with a beam of laser fire. Trouble steered into the middle of the chute so that the lasers would have the longest possible line of fire. Lasers were only any good in a straight line.

Three minutes later, the missiles powered around the bend in the chute. Trouble barely spared them a glance, and the computer loosed two quick bursts, dispatching the missiles efficiently. Major Kelp flew straight through the shockwave, insulated by layers of impact-gel.

Another screen opened in his visor. It was the newly promoted Commander Ark Sool. 'Major, you are authorized to return fire. Use all necessary force.'

Trouble scowled. 'But, Commander, Holly may be on board.'

Sool raised a hand, silencing all objections. 'Captain Short has made her allegiances clear. Fire at will.'

Foaly could not remain silent. 'Hold your fire, Trouble. You know Holly isn't behind all of this. Somehow Opal Koboi fired those missiles.'

Sool pounded the desk. 'How can you be so blind to the truth, donkey boy? What does Short have to do to convince you she's a traitor? Send you an e-mail? She has murdered her commander, allied herself with a felon and fired on an LEP shuttle. Blast her out of the air.'

'No!' insisted Foaly. 'It sounds bad, I grant you. But there must be another explanation. Just give Holly a chance to tell us what it is.'

Sool was apoplectic. 'Shut up, Foaly! What are you doing, giving tactical orders? You are a civilian, now get off the line.'

'Trouble, listen to me,' began Foaly, but that was all he managed to say before Sool cut him off.

'Now,' said the commander, calming himself, 'you have your orders. Fire on that shuttle.'

The stolen shuttle was actually in view now. Trouble magnified its image in his visor and immediately noticed three things. First, the shuttle's communications mast was missing. Secondly, this was a transport shuttle and not rigged for missiles and, thirdly, he could actually see Holly Short in the cockpit, her face drawn and defiant.

'Commander Sool,' he said. 'I think we have some extenuating circumstances here.'

⊗□·ℛ·◊⅊·◉ℛ℧·⊗ℛ☃·℧♙⚭◊➤

'I said fire,' screeched Sool. 'You will obey me.'

'Yes, sir,' said Trouble, and fired.

Holly had watched the radar screen, following Opal's missiles through unblinking eyes. Her fingers had gripped the steering wheel until the rubber squeaked. She did not relax until the needle-like attack shuttle destroyed the missiles and coasted through the wreckage.

'No problem,' she said, smiling, bright-eyed, at the rest of the crew.

'Not for him,' said Artemis. 'But perhaps for us.'

The attack shuttle hovered off their port bow, sleek and deadly, bathing them in a dozen spotlights. Holly squinted into the pale light, trying to see who was in the captain's chair. A tube opened in the nose and a metallic cone nosed out.

'That's not good,' said Mulch. 'They're going to fire at us.'

But, strangely, Holly smiled. *It is good,* she thought. *Someone down there likes me.*

The communications spike travelled the short distance between the two shuttles, burying itself in the stolen craft's hull. A quick-drying sealant erupted from nozzles at the base of the spike, sealing the breach, and the nose cone unscrewed itself, dropping to the floor with a clang. Underneath was a conical speaker.

Trouble Kelp's voice filled the room. 'Captain Short, I have orders to blow you out of the air. Orders which I'd just as soon disobey. So start talking, and give me enough information to save both our careers.'

So Holly talked. She gave Trouble the condensed version: how this entire affair had been orchestrated by Opal, and how they could pick her up if they searched the chute.

'That's enough to keep you alive for now,' said Trouble. 'Though officially you, and any other shuttle occupants, are under arrest until we find Opal Koboi.'

Artemis cleared his throat. 'Excuse me. I don't believe you have any jurisdiction over humans. It would be illegal to arrest me or my associate.'

Trouble sighed. Over the speaker it sounded like a rasp of sandpaper. 'Let me guess: Artemis Fowl, right? I should have known. You people are becoming quite the team. Well, let's say you are a guest of the LEP, if that makes you any happier. Now, a Retrieval Squad is in the chute and they will take care of Opal and her associates. You follow me back to Haven.'

Holly wanted to object. She wanted to catch Opal herself. She wanted the personal pleasure of tossing the poisonous pixie into an actual gaol cell. But their position was precarious enough as it was, so for once she decided to follow orders.

CHAPTER II: **A LAST GOODBYE**

ONCE they reached Haven, a squad of LEP foot soldiers boarded the shuttle to secure the prisoners. The police swaggered on board, barking orders, then they saw Butler and their cockiness evaporated like rainwater off a hot highway. They had been told that the human was big. But this was more than big. This was monstrous. Mountainous.

Butler smiled apologetically. 'Don't worry, little fairies. I have this effect on most humans too.'

The police breathed a collective sigh of relief when Butler agreed to go quietly. They might possibly have subdued him if he had put up a fight, but then the massive Mud Man could have fallen on someone.

The detainees were housed in the shuttle port's

executive lounge, evicting several grumbling lawyers and businessfairies. It was all very civil: good food, clean clothes (not for Butler) and entertainment centres. But they were under guard nevertheless.

Half an hour later, Foaly burst into the lounge. 'Holly!' he said, wrapping a hairy arm round the elf. 'I am so happy that you're alive.'

'Me too, Foaly,' grinned Holly.

'A little "Hello" wouldn't hurt,' said Mulch sulkily. '"How are you, Mulch? Long time no see, Mulch. Here's your medal, Mulch."'

'Oh all right,' said Foaly, wrapping the other hairy arm around the equally hairy dwarf. 'Nice to see you too, Mulch, even if you did sink one of my subs. And no, no medal.'

'Because of the sub,' argued Mulch. 'If I hadn't done it, your bones would be buried under a hundred million tonnes of molten iron right now.'

'Good point,' noted the centaur. 'I'll mention it at your hearing.' He turned to Artemis. 'I see you managed to cheat the mind wipe, Artemis.'

Artemis smiled. 'A good thing for all of us.'

'Indeed. I'll never make the mistake of trying to wipe you again.' He took Artemis's hand and shook it warmly. 'You've been a friend to the People. You too, Butler.'

The bodyguard was sitting, hunched, on a sofa, elbows

on knees. 'You can repay me by building a room I can
stand up in.'

'I'm sorry about this,' said Foaly apologetically. 'We
don't have rooms for people your size. Sool wants you all
kept here until your story can be verified.'

'How are things going?' asked Holly.

Foaly pulled a file from inside his shirt. 'I'm not actually
supposed to be here, but I thought you'd like an update.'

They crowded round a table while Foaly laid out the
reports.

'We found the Brill brothers on the chute wall.
They're singing like stinkworms – so much for loyalty to
their employer. Forensics have collected enough pieces
of the stealth shuttle to prove its existence.'

Holly clapped her hands. 'That's it then.'

'It's not airtight,' Artemis corrected her. 'Without
Opal we could still be responsible for everything. The
Brills could be lying to protect us. Do you have her?'

Foaly clenched his fists. 'Well, yes and no. Her escape
pod was ruptured by the blast, so we could trace it. But
by the time we reached the crash site on the surface,
she had disappeared. We ran a thermal on the area and
isolated Opal's footprints. We followed them to a small
rustic homestead in the wine region near Bari. We can
actually see her on satellite, but an insertion is going to
take time to organize. She's ours, and we will get her. But
it may take a week.'

Holly's face was dark with rage. 'She'd better enjoy that week, because it will be the best of the rest of her life.'

Near Bari, Italy

Opal Koboi's craft limped to the surface, leaking plasma gouts through its cracked generator. Opal was well aware that this plasma was as good as a trail of arrows for Foaly. She must ditch the craft as soon as possible and find somewhere to lie low until she could access some of her funds.

She cleared the shuttle port and made it nearly ten miles across country before her engines seized utterly, forcing her to ditch in a vineyard. When she clambered out of the pod, Opal found a tall, tanned woman of perhaps forty waiting for her with a shovel and a furious expression on her face.

'These are my vines,' said the woman in Italian. 'The vines are my life. Who are you to crash here in your little aeroplane and destroy everything I have?'

Opal thought fast. 'Where is your family?' she asked. 'Your husband?'

The woman blew a strand of hair from her eyes. 'No family. No husband. I work the vines alone. I'm the last in the line. These vines mean more to me than my life, and certainly more to me than yours.'

'You're not alone,' said Opal and she turned on the hypnotic fairy *mesmer*. 'You have me now. I am your daughter, Belinda.'

Why not? she reasoned. *If it worked once . . .*

'Bel-inda,' said the woman slowly. 'I have a daughter?'

'That's right,' agreed Opal. 'Belinda. Remember. We work these vines together. I help make the wine.'

'You help me?'

Opal scowled. Humans never got something the first time.

'Yes,' she said, barely concealing her impatience. 'I help you. I work beside you.'

The woman's eyes cleared suddenly. 'Belinda. What are you doing, standing there? Get a shovel and clean up this mess. When you finish here, you must prepare dinner.'

Opal's heart skipped a beat. Manual labour? Not likely. Other people did that sort of thing.

'On second thoughts,' she said, pushing the *mesmer* as hard as she could. 'I am your pampered daughter Belinda. You never allow me to do any work, in case it roughens my hands. You're saving me for a rich husband.'

That should take care of it. She would hide out with this woman for a few hours and then escape to the city.

But a surprise was coming Opal's way. 'That's my Belinda,' said the woman. 'Always dreaming. Now take this shovel, girl, or you'll go to bed hungry.'

Opal's cheeks flushed red. 'Didn't you hear me, crone? I do not do physical work. You will serve me. That is your purpose in life.'

The Italian lady advanced on her tiny daughter. 'Now listen here, Belinda. I'm trying not to hear these poisonous words coming out of your mouth, but it is difficult. We both work the vines, that is the way it has always been. Now take the shovel, or I will lock you in your room with a hundred potatoes to peel and none to eat.'

Opal was dumbstruck. She could not understand what was happening. Even strong-minded humans were putty before the *mesmer*. What was happening here?

The simple truth was that Opal had been too clever for her own good. By placing a human pituitary gland in her own skull, she had effectively humanized herself. Gradually, the human growth hormone was overpowering the magic in her system. It was Opal's bad fortune that she had used her last drop of magic to convince this woman that she was her daughter. Now she was without magic, and was a virtual prisoner in the Italian lady's vineyard. And, what's more, she was being forced to work, and that was even worse than being in a coma.

'Hurry!' shouted the woman. 'There is rain forecast, and we have a lot to do.'

Opal took the shovel, resting the blade on the dry earth. It was taller than she was, and its handle was pitted and worn.

'What should I do with this shovel?'

'Crack the earth with the blade, then dig an irrigation trench between these two frames. And after dinner, I need you to wash by hand some of the laundry that I have taken in this week. It's Carmine's, and you know what his washing is like.' The lady grimaced, leaving Opal in no doubt as to the state of this person Carmine's clothing.

The Italian lady picked up a second shovel and began to dig beside Opal.

'Don't frown so, Belinda. Work is good for the character. After a few more years, you will see that.'

Opal swung the shovel, dealing the earth a pathetic blow that barely raised a sliver of clay. Already her hands were sore from holding the tool. In an hour she would be a mass of aches and blisters. Maybe the LEP would come and take her away.

Her wish was to be granted – but not until a week later, by which time her nails were cracked and brown and her skin was rough with welts. She had peeled countless potatoes and waited on her new mother hand and foot. Opal was also horrified to discover that her adopted parent kept pigs, and that cleaning out the sty was another one of her seemingly endless duties. By the time the LEPretrieval team came for her, she was almost happy to see them.

E7, Haven City

Julius Root's recycling ceremony was held the day after Artemis and Holly arrived in Haven City. All the brass turned up for the commitment ceremony. All the brass, but not Captain Holly Short. Commander Sool refused to allow her to attend the commitment, even under armed guard. The Tribunal investigating the case had not yet made its decision and, until it did, Holly was a suspect in a murder investigation.

So she sat in the executive lounge, watching the commitment ceremony on the big screen. Of all the things Sool had done to her, this was the worst. Julius Root had been her closest friend, and here she was, watching his recycling on a screen, while all the higher-ups attended, looking sad for the cameras.

She covered her face with her hands when they lowered an empty casket into the ornate stone decomposition vat. Had there been any actual remains, the bone and tissue would have completely broken down and nourished the earth.

Tears leaked out between Holly's fingers, flowing over her hands.

Artemis sat beside her, a gentle hand placed on her shoulder. 'Julius would have been proud of you. Haven is here today because of what you did.'

Holly sniffed. 'Maybe. Maybe if I had been a little smarter, Julius would be here today too.'

'Maybe, but I don't think so. I have been thinking about it, and there was no way out of that chute. Not without prior knowledge.'

Holly lowered her hands. 'Thanks, Artemis. That's a nice thing to say. You're not going soft, are you?'

Artemis was genuinely puzzled. 'I honestly don't know. Half of me wants to be a criminal, and the other half wants to be a normal teenager. I feel like I have two conflicting personalities and a head full of memories that aren't really mine yet. It's a strange feeling, not to know who you are exactly.'

'Don't worry, Mud Boy,' said Holly. 'I'll keep a close eye on you, to make sure you stay on the straight and narrow.'

'I have two parents and a bodyguard already trying to do that.'

'Well then, maybe it's time to let them.'

The lounge's doors slid open and Foaly clopped in excitedly, followed by Commander Sool and a couple of flunkies. Sool was obviously not as thrilled to be in the room as the centaur, and had brought the extra officers along just in case Butler got agitated.

Foaly grabbed Holly by the shoulders. 'You're clear,' he beamed. 'The Tribunal voted seven to one in your favour.'

Holly scowled at Sool. 'Let me guess which one.'

Sool bristled. 'I am still your superior officer, Short. I want to see that reflected in your attitude. You may have escaped this charge, but I will be watching you like a hawk from now on.'

Mulch clicked his fingers in front of Foaly's face. 'Hey, pony boy. Over here. What about me? Am I a free dwarf?'

'Well, the Tribunal decided to go after you for the grand theft auto.'

'What?' spluttered Mulch. 'After I saved the entire city?'

'But,' continued Foaly, 'considering the time already served for an illegal search, they're prepared to call it even. No medal, I'm sorry to say.'

Mulch slapped the centaur's haunch. 'You couldn't just say that, could you? You had to draw it out.'

Holly had not stopped scowling at Sool. 'Let me tell you what Julius told me shortly before he died,' she said.

'Please do,' said Sool, his words dripping with sarcasm. 'I find everything you say fascinating.'

'Julius told me, more or less, that my job was to serve the People, and that I should do that any way I could.'

'Smart fairy. I do hope you intend honouring those words.'

Holly ripped the LEP badge from her shoulder. 'I do. With you looking over my shoulder on every shift, I won't be able to help anyone, so I've decided to go it alone.' She tossed the badge on the table. 'I quit.'

Sool chuckled. 'If this is a bluff, it won't work. I'll be glad to see the back of you.'

'Holly, don't do this,' pleaded Foaly. 'The force needs you. I need you.'

Holly patted his flank. 'They accused me of murdering Julius. How can I stay? Don't worry, old friend. I won't be far away.' She nodded at Mulch. 'Are you coming?'

'What, me?'

Holly grinned. 'You're a free dwarf now, and every private detective needs a partner. Someone with underworld connections.'

Mulch's chest swelled. 'Mulch Diggums, private detective. I like that. Hey, I'm not a sidekick, am I? Because the sidekick always gets it.'

'No. You're a fully fledged partner. Whatever we make, we split.'

Holly turned to Artemis next.

'We did it again, Mud Boy. We saved the world, or at least stopped two worlds colliding.'

Artemis nodded. 'It doesn't get any easier. Maybe someone else should take a turn.'

Holly punched him playfully in the arm. 'Who else has our style?' Then she leaned in and whispered for his ears only, 'I'll be in touch. Maybe you might be interested in some consultancy work?'

Artemis cocked one brow and gave a slight nod. It was all the answer she needed.

Butler usually stood to say goodbye, but on this occasion he had to make do with kneeling. Holly was barely visible inside the hug he gave her.

'Until the next crisis,' she said.

'Or maybe you could just visit,' he replied.

'Getting a visa will be more difficult, now that I'm a civilian.'

'You're sure about this?'

Holly frowned. 'No. I'm torn.' She nodded at Artemis. 'But who isn't?'

Artemis treated Sool to his most scornful gaze. 'Congratulations, Commander, you have managed to alienate the LEP's finest officer.'

'Listen here, human,' began Sool, but Butler growled and the words withered in the commander's throat. The gnome stepped quickly behind the larger of his officers. 'Send them home. Now.'

The officers drew their sidearms, aimed and fired. A tranquillizer pellet stuck to Artemis's neck, dissolving instantly. The officers hit Butler with four, not taking any chances.

Artemis could hear Holly protesting as his vision blurred like an Impressionist painting. Like *The Fairy Thief*.

'There's no need for that, Sool,' she said, catching Artemis's elbow. 'They've seen the chute already. You could have returned them conscious.'

Sool's voice sounded as though he were speaking from the bottom of a well. 'I'm not taking any chances, Captain, I mean, *Miss* Short. Humans are violent creatures by nature, especially when they are being transported.'

Artemis felt Holly's hand on his chest. Under his jacket, slipping something into his pocket. But he couldn't ask what because his tongue would not obey him. All he could do with his mouth was breathe. He heard a thump behind him.

Butler's gone, he concluded. *Just me left.*

And then he was gone too.

FOWL MANOR

Artemis came to gradually. He felt well and rested, and all his memories were in place. Then again, maybe they weren't. How would he know?

He opened his eyes and saw the fresco on the ceiling above. He was back in his own room.

Artemis did not move for several moments. It wasn't that he couldn't move, it was just that lying here like this seemed utterly luxurious. There were no pixies after him, or trolls homing in on his scent, or fairy tribunals judging him. He could lie here and simply think. His favourite occupation.

Artemis Fowl had a big decision to make. Which way would his life go from here? The decision was his. He could not blame circumstances or peer pressure. He was his own person, and intelligent enough to realize it.

The solitary life of crime no longer appealed to him as completely as it had. He had no desire to create victims. And yet there was still something about the thrill of executing a brilliant plan that attracted him. Maybe there was a way to combine his criminal genius with his new-found morals. Some people deserved to be stolen from. He could be like a modern-day Robin Hood: steal from the rich and give to the poor. Well, maybe just steal from the rich. One step at a time.

Something vibrated in his jacket pocket. Artemis reached in and pulled out a fairy communicator. One of the pair they had planted in Opal Koboi's shuttle. Artemis had a vague memory of Holly sliding something into his pocket just before he passed out. She obviously wanted to stay in touch.

Artemis stood up, opening the device, and Holly's smiling face appeared on the screen.

'You got home safely, then. Sorry about the sedatives. Sool is a pig.'

'Forget about it. No harm done.'

'You have changed. Once upon a time, Artemis Fowl would have vowed revenge.'

'Once upon a time.'

Holly glanced around her. 'Listen, I can't stay on long. I had to bolt on a pirate booster to this thing, just to get a signal. This call is costing me a fortune. I need a favour.'

Artemis groaned. 'No one ever calls me to say hello.'

'Next time. I promise.'

'I'll hold you to it. What's the favour?'

'Mulch and I have our first client. He's an art dealer who's had a picture stolen. Frankly, I'm flummoxed, so I thought I'd ask an expert.'

Artemis smiled. 'I suppose I do have some expertise in the area of stolen art. Tell me what happened.'

'The thing is. There's no way in or out of this exhibition without detection. The painting is just gone. Not even warlocks have that kind of magic.'

Artemis heard footsteps on the stairs.

'Hang on a second, Holly. Someone's coming.'

Butler burst in through the door, pistol drawn.

'I just woke up,' he said. 'Are you all right?'

'Fine,' said Artemis. 'You can put that away.'

'I was half hoping Sool was still here, so I could scare him a little.' Butler crossed to the window, pulling aside the net curtains. 'There's a car coming up the avenue. It's your parents back from the spa in Westmeath. We'd better get our stories straight. Why did we come home from Germany?'

Artemis thought quickly. 'Let's just say I felt homesick. I missed being my parents' son. That's true enough.'

340

Butler smiled. 'I like that excuse. Hopefully you won't need to use it again.'

'I don't intend to.'

Butler held out a rolled-up canvas. 'And what about this? Have you decided what you should do with it?'

Artemis took *The Fairy Thief*, spreading it on the bed before him. It really was beautiful. 'Yes, old friend. I have decided to do what I should do. Now, can you stall my parents at the door? I need to take this call.'

Butler nodded and ran down the stairs three at a time.

Artemis returned to the communicator.

'Now, Holly, about your little problem. Have you considered the fact that the picture you seek may still be in the room, and our thief may have simply moved it?'

'That's the first thing I thought of. Come on, Artemis, you're supposed to be a genius. Use your brain.'

Artemis scratched his chin. He was finding it difficult to concentrate. He heard tyres crunching on the drive, and then his mother's voice laughing as she climbed from the car.

'Arty?' she called. 'Come down. We need to see you.'

'Come down, Arty boy,' shouted his father. 'Welcome us home.'

Artemis found that he was smiling. 'Holly, can you call me back later? I'm busy right now.'

Holly tried to scowl. 'OK. Five hours, and you'd better have some suggestions for me.'

⊗ ⚶ • ⬡⬡⬡ ⬡⬡⬡ ⬡ • ⬡ ⬡ ⬡⬡⬡⬡ • ⬡⬡ •

'Don't worry, I will. And also my consultant's bill.'

'Some things never change,' said Holly, and closed the link.

Artemis quickly locked the communicator in his room safe, then ran to the stairs. His mother was at the bottom of the steps, and her arms were open wide.

⬡□⬡·⬡⬡⬡⬡·⬡⬡⬡·⬡⬡⬡

EPILOGUE

An article from the Irish Times,
by Eugene Driscoll,
Culture Correspondent

Last week the art world was left reeling following the discovery of a lost painting by Pascal Hervé, the French Impressionist master. The rumoured existence of *The Fairy Thief* (oil on canvas) was confirmed when the painting was sent to the Louvre gallery in Paris. Someone, presumably an art lover, actually used the regular mail service to post the priceless masterpiece to the curator. The authenticity of the work has been confirmed by six independent experts.

A spokesman for the Louvre has stated that the picture will be exhibited within the next month. So, for the first time in almost a century, everyday art lovers will be able to enjoy Hervé's masterpiece.

But perhaps the most tantalizing part of this whole

affair is the typed note that came with *The Fairy Thief*. The note read simply – *More to follow*.

Is someone out there reclaiming lost or stolen masters for the people? If so, collectors beware. No secret vault is safe. This correspondent waits with bated breath. *More to follow*. Art lovers all over the world certainly hope so!

HOW DO YOU FOLLOW THAT?
HERE'S A SNEAK PREVIEW OF WHAT
ARTEMIS GETS UP TO NEXT IN . . .

ARTEMIS FOWL

AND THE LOST COLONY

Did you think Artemis would just retire
in his bed slippers and never be heard of again?
Not a chance.

Holly Short's career as an elfin private investigator was not working out as well as she'd hoped. This was mainly because the Lower Elements' most popular current events show had run not one but two specials on her over the past few months. It was difficult to go undercover when her face was forever popping up on cable reruns.

'Surgery?' suggested a voice in her head.

This voice was not the first sign of madness; it was her partner, Mulch Diggums, communicating from his mike to her earpiece.

'What?' she said, her voice carrying to her own microphone, a tiny flesh-coloured chip glued to her throat.

'I'm looking at a poster of your famous face, and I'm thinking that you should have some cosmetic surgery if we want to stay in business. And I mean real business, not this bounty-hunting game. Bounty hunters are the lowest of the low.'

Holly sighed. Her dwarf partner was right. Even criminals were considered more trustworthy than bounty hunters.

'A few implants and a reshaped nose and even your best friend wouldn't recognize you,' continued Mulch Diggums. 'It's not as if you're a beauty queen.'

'Forget it,' said Holly. She was fond of the face she had. It reminded her of her mother's.

'What about a skin spray? You could go green, disguise yourself as a sprite.'

'Mulch? Are you in position?' snapped Holly.

'Yep,' came the dwarf's reply. 'Any sign of the pixie?'

'No, he's not up and about yet, but he will be soon. So stop the chatter and just get ready.'

'Hey, we're partners now. No more criminal and police officer. I don't have to take orders from you.'

'Get ready, *please*.'

'No problem. Mulch Diggums, lowlife bounty hunter, signing off.'

Holly sighed. Sometimes she missed the discipline of the Lower Elements Police Reconnaissance Division. When an order was given, it was followed. Although if she was honest, Holly had to admit she had got herself into trouble more than once for disobeying a direct command. She had only survived in LEPrecon for as long as she had because of a few high-profile arrests. *And* because of her mentor, Commander Julius Root.

Holly felt her heart lurch as she remembered, for the thousandth time, that Julius was dead. She could go for hours without thinking about it, then it would hit her. Every time like the first time.

She had quit the LEP because Julius's replacement had actually accused her of murdering the Commander. Holly figured with a boss like that, she could do the fairy People more good outside the system. It was starting to look like she had been dead wrong. In her time as LEPrecon Captain she had been involved in putting down a goblin revolution, thwarting a plan to expose the subterranean fairy culture to the humans and reclaiming stolen fairy technology from a Mud Man in Chicago. Now she was tracking a fish smuggler who had skipped out on his bail. Not exactly national security stuff.

'What about shin extensions?' said Mulch, interrupting her thoughts. 'You could be taller in hours.'

Holly smiled. As irritating as her partner was, he could always cheer her up. Also, as a dwarf, Mulch had special talents which came in very handy in their new line of business. Until recently, he had used these skills to break *into* houses and *out* of prisons, but now he was on the side of the angels, or so he swore. Unfortunately, all fairies knew that a dwarf's vow to a non-dwarf wasn't worth the spit-sodden handshake that sealed the deal.

'Maybe you could get a brain extension,' Holly retorted.

Mulch chortled. 'Oh, brilliant. I must write that one down in my witty retorts book.'

Holly was trying to come up with an actual witty retort when their target appeared at the motel-room door. He was a harmless-looking pixie, barely half a metre high, but you didn't have to be tall to drive a lorry of fish. The smuggling bosses hired pixies as drivers and couriers because they looked so innocent and childlike. Holly had read this pixie's jacket, and she knew that he was anything but innocent.

Doodah Day had been smuggling livestock to illegal restaurants for over a century. In smuggling circles he was something of a legend. As an ex-criminal, Mulch was privy to criminal folklore and was able to supply Holly with all kinds of useful information that wouldn't find its way into an LEP report. For instance, Doodah had once made the heavily patrolled Atlantis—Haven run in under six hours without losing a fish from the tank.

Doodah had been arrested in the Atlantis Trench by a squad of LEP water sprites. He had skipped out en route from a holding cell to the courthouse, and now Holly had tracked him here. The bounty on Doodah Day was enough to pay six months' rent on their office. The plaque on the door read: *Short and Diggums. Private Investigators.*

Doodah Day stepped out of his room, scowling at the world in general. He zipped his jacket then headed south towards the shopping district. Holly stayed twenty steps back, hiding her face underneath a hood. This street had traditionally been a rough spot, but the Council were putting millions of ingots into a major revamp. In five years, there would be no more goblin ghetto. Huge yellow multimixers were chewing up old pavement and laying down brand-new paths behind them. Overhead, public service sprites unhooked burned-out sunstrips from the tunnel ceiling and replaced them with new molecule models.

The pixie followed the same route that he had for the past three days. He strolled down the road to the nearest plaza, picked up a carton of vole curry at a kiosk, then bought a ticket to the twenty-four-hour movie theatre. If he stayed true to form, then Doodah would be in there for at least eight hours.

Not if I can help it, thought Holly. She was determined to get this case wrapped by close of business. It wouldn't be easy. Doodah was small, but he was fast. Without weapons or restraints, it would be almost impossible to contain him. *Almost* impossible, but there was a way.

Holly bought a ticket from the gnome attendant, then settled into a seat two rows behind the target. The theatre was pretty quiet at this time of day. There were maybe fifty patrons besides themselves. Most of them weren't even wearing theatre goggles. This was just somewhere to put in a few hours between meals.

The theatre was running *The Hill of Taillte* trilogy nonstop. The trilogy told a cinematic version of the events surrounding the Hill of Taillte battle, where the humans had finally forced the fairies underground. The final part of the trilogy had cleaned up at the AMP awards a couple of years ago. The effects were splendid and there was even a special edition interactive version, where the player could become one of the minor characters.

Looking at the movie now, Holly felt the same pang of loss as she always did. The People should be living above ground; instead, they were stuck in this technologically advanced cave.

Holly watched the sweeping aerial views and slowmotion battles for forty minutes, then she moved into the aisle and threw off her hood. In her LEP days she would simply have come up behind the pixie and stuck her Neutrino 3000 in his back, but civilians were not allowed to carry weapons of any kind, and so a more subtle strategy would have to be employed.

She called the pixie from the aisle.

'Hey, you. Aren't you Doodah Day?'

The pixie jumped from his seat, which did not make him any taller. He fixed his fiercest scowl on his features and threw it Holly's way. 'Who wants to know?'

'The LEP,' replied Holly. Technically, she had not identified herself as a member of the LEP, which would be impersonating a police officer.

Doodah squinted at her. 'I know you. You're that female elf. The one who tackled the goblins. I've seen you on digital. You're not LEP any more.'

Holly felt her heartbeat speed up. It was good to be back in action. Any kind of action.

'Maybe not, Doodah, but I'm still here to bring you in. Are you going to come quietly?'

'And spend a few centuries in the Atlantis pen? What do you think?' said Doodah Day, dropping to his knees.

The little pixie was gone like a stone from a sling, crawling under the seats, jinking left and right.

Holly pulled up her hood and ran towards the fire exit. That's where Doodah would be going. He went this way every day. Every good criminal checks the exit routes in whatever building he visits.

Doodah was at the exit before her, crashing through the door like a dog through a hatch. All Holly could see was the blue blur of his jumpsuit.

'Target on the move,' she said, knowing her throat mike would pick up whatever she said. 'Coming your way.'

I hope, thought Holly, but she didn't say it.

In theory Doodah would make for his bolt-hole, a small storage unit over on Crystal, which was kitted out with a small cot and air-conditioning unit. When the pixie got there, Mulch would be waiting. It was a classic human hunting technique. Beat the grass and be ready when the bird flies. Of course, if you were human, you shot the bird then ate it. Mulch's method of capture was less terminal, but equally revolting.

Holly stuck close, but not too close. She could hear the pitter-patter of the pixie's tiny feet scurrying along the theatre's carpet, but she couldn't see the little fellow. She didn't want to see him. It was vital that Doodah believed he had got away, otherwise he wouldn't make for his bolt-hole.

In her LEP days there would have been no need for this kind of close-up pursuit. She would have had complete access to five thousand surveillance cameras dotted throughout Haven, not to mention a hundred other gadgets and gimmicks from the LEP surveillance arsenal. Now there was just her and Mulch. Four eyes and some special dwarf talents.

The main door was still flapping when Holly reached it. Just inside, an outraged gnome was flat on his behind, covered with nettle smoothie.

'A little kid,' he complained to an usher. 'Or a pixie. It had a big head, I know that much. Hit me right in the gut.'

Holly skirted the pair, shouldering her way on to the plaza outside. Outside, relatively speaking. Everything was inside when you lived in a tunnel. Overhead, the sunstrips were set to mid-morning. She could trace Doodah's progress by the trail of chaos in his wake. The vole kiosk was overturned. Lumpy grey-green curry congealed on the flagstones. And lumpy grey-green footsteps led to the plaza's northern corner. So far, Doodah was behaving very predictably.

Holly shouldered through the ragged line of curry customers, keeping her eyes on the pixie's footsteps.

'Two minutes,' she said, for Mulch's benefit.

There was no reply, but there shouldn't be, not if the dwarf was in position.

Doodah should take the next service alley and cut across to Crystal. Next time they were going after a gnome. Pixies were too fast. The fairy Council did not really like bounty hunters and tried to make life as difficult for them as possible. There was no such thing as a licensed firearm outside the LEP. Anyone with a weapon, without a badge, was going to prison.

Holly rounded the corner expecting to see the tail end of a pixie blur. Instead, she saw a ten-tonne yellow multimixer bearing down on her. Obviously, Doodah Day had finished being predictable.

'D'Arvit!' swore Holly, diving to one side. The multimixer's front rotor chewed through the plaza's paving, spitting it out at the rear in centimetre-perfect slabs. She rolled into a crouch, reaching for the Neutrino blaster, which had been on her hip until recently. All she found was air.

The multimixer was swinging round for a second run, bucking and hissing like a mechanical Jurassic carnivore. Giant pistons thumped, and rotor blades carved scythe-like through whatever surface fell beneath their blades. Debris was shovelled into the machine's belly, to be processed and shaped by heated plates.

It reminds me a bit of Mulch, thought Holly. Funny what crosses your mind when your life is in danger.

She back-pedalled away from the mixer. Yes, it was big, but it was slow and unwieldy. Holly glanced upwards to the cab, and there was Doodah, expertly manipulating the gears. His hands flashed across the knobs and levers, dragging the metal behemoth towards Holly.

All around was pandemonium. Shoppers howling, emergency klaxons sounding. But Holly couldn't worry about that now. Priority one: stay alive. Terrifying as this situation might be to the general public, Holly had years of LEP training and experience. She'd escaped the grasp of far quicker enemies than this multimixer.

As it turned out, Holly was mistaken. The multimixer was slow as a whole, but some of its parts were lightning fast. For example, the containment paddles, two three-metre-high walls of steel that slotted out on either side of the front rotor to contain any debris that might be thrown up by the rotor blades.

Doodah Day, an instinctive driver of any vehicle, saw his opportunity and took it. He overrode the safety and deployed the paddles. Four pneumatic pumps instantly pressurized and literally blew the paddles into the wall on both sides of Holly. They bit deep, sinking fifteen centimetres into the stone.

Holly's confidence drained down into her boots. She was trapped with a hundred curved strip blades tearing up the ground before her.

'Wings,' said Holly, but only her LEP suit had wings, and she had given up the right to wear that.

The paddles contained the vortex created by the blades and turned it back on itself. The vibration was terrific. Holly felt her teeth shake in her gums. She could see ten of everything. Her whole world was bad reception. Beneath her feet the blades greedily chewed the pavement. Holly jumped at the left-hand paddle, but it was well lubricated and afforded her no purchase. Her luck was equally bad with the other paddle. The only other possible avenue was straight ahead, and that wasn't really an option, not with the deadly rotor waiting.

Holly shouted at Doodah, maybe her mouth formed actual words. She couldn't be certain, not with the shaking and the noise. Blades snicked through the air, grabbing for her. With each pass they tore strips from the ground beneath her feet.There wasn't much ground left. Soon she would be feeding the multimixer. She would be shredded, passed through the machine's innards and finally laid as a paving slab. Holly Short would literally be part of the city.

There was nothing to do. Nothing. Mulch was too far away to be of any assistance, and it wasn't likely that any civilian would attempt to mount a rogue mixer, even if they had known she was trapped between the paddles.

As the blades closed in, Holly gazed towards the computer-generated sky. It would have been nice to die on the surface. Feeling the heat of the real sun warming her brow. It would have been nice.

Then the rotor stopped. Holly was sprayed with a shower of half-digested debris from the mixer's stomach. A few stone slivers scratched her skin, but that was the extent of her injury.

Holly wiped the grime from her face and looked up. Her ears rang with the engine's aftershock, and her eyes watered from the dust that settled on her like dirty snow.

Doodah peered down at her from the cab. His face was pale but fierce.

'Leave me alone!' he shouted. His voice seemed weak and tinny to Holly's damaged eardrums.

'Just leave me alone!'

And he was gone, scurrying down the access ladder, maybe heading for his bolt-hole.

Holly leaned against one of the paddles, allowing herself a moment to recover. Tiny sparks of magic blossomed on her many cuts, sealing them. Her ears popped, whined and flexed as the magic automatically targeted her eardrums.

In seconds, Holly's hearing was back to normal.

She had to get out of here. And there was only one way. Over the rotor. Past the blades. Holly tipped one gingerly with a finger. A droplet of blood oozed from a tiny cut, only to be sucked back in by a blue spark of magic. Those blades would cut her to ribbons if she slipped, and there wouldn't be enough magic under the world to stitch her back together again. But the rotor was her only way out, otherwise she would have to sit it out here until LEP traffic arrived. It would be bad enough causing this kind of damage with the weight of LEP public liability insurance behind her, but as a freelancer she'd probably be thrown in jail for a couple of months while the courts decided what to charge her with.

Holly threaded her fingers between the blades, gripping the first bar on the rotor. It would be just like climbing a ladder. A very sharp, potentially fatal ladder. She stepped on a lower bar and boosted herself up. The rotor groaned and dropped fifteen centimetres. Holly held on, because it was safer than letting go. Blades quivered two centimetres from her limbs. Slow and steady. No false moves. One bar at a time, Holly climbed the rotor. Twice a blade nicked her flesh, but the wounds were not serious and were quickly sealed by blue sparks. After a brief eternity of utter concentration, Holly pulled herself on to the hood. The bonnet was filthy and hot, but at least it wasn't sharper than a centaur's tongue.

'He went that way,' said a voice from ground level. Holly looked down to see a large frowning gnome in a city services uniform pointing towards Crystal.

'He went that way,' repeated the gnome. 'The pixie who threw me out of my mixer.'

Holly stared at the burly public services guy. 'That tiny pixie threw *you* out?'

The gnome almost blushed. 'I was getting out anyway; he just tipped me over.' He suddenly forgot all about his embarrassment. 'Hey, aren't you Polly something? Polly Little? That's it. The LEP hero.'

Holly climbed down the cab ladder. 'Polly Little. That's me.'

Holly landed running, her boots crunching on pebbles of crushed pavement.

'Mulch,' she said. 'Doodah is coming your way. Be careful. He's a lot more dangerous than we thought.'

Dangerous? Maybe, maybe not. He hadn't killed her when he'd had the chance. It would seem that the pixie had no stomach for murder.

Doodah's stunt with the multimixer had caused chaos in the plaza. Traffic police, nicknamed Wheelies, were pouring in and civilians were pouring out. Holly counted at least six LEPtraffic magna-bikes and two cruisers. She was keeping her head down, when one of the traffic officers hopped off his bike and grabbed her shoulder.

'Did you see what happened, missy?'

Missy? Holly was tempted to twist the hand on her shoulder and flip the officer into a nearby recycler. But this was not the time for outrage – she needed to redirect his attention.

'Why, thank goodness you're here, Officer,' she twittered in a voice at least an octave higher than her normal tones. 'Over there, by the multimixer. There's blood everywhere.'

'Blood!' exclaimed the Wheelie, delighted to hear it. 'Everywhere?'

'Absolutely everywhere.'

The traffic cop dropped Holly's shoulder. 'Thank you, missy. I'll handle it from here.'

He strode purposefully towards the multimixer, then turned back.

'Excuse me, missy,' he said, recognition glimmering in his eye, just out of reach. 'Don't I know you?'

But the hooded elf had disappeared.

Ah well, thought the Wheelie. *I should probably go and look at the blood everywhere.*

Holly ran towards Crystal Street, though she felt sure there was no need for haste. Doodah had either decided that there was too much heat on him to reveal his bolthole, or Mulch had him. Either way it was out of her control. Once again, she lamented the loss of LEP backup. In her Recon days, all it would have taken was a quick order into her helmet microphone, and every street in the area would be cordoned off.

She skirted a street-cleaning robot, turning on to Crystal. The narrow street was a service lane for the main shopping plaza, and consisted mostly of delivery bays. The rest of the units were rented out for storage. Holly was surprised to find Doodah directly in front of her, rummaging in his pocket, presumably for the access chip to his unit. Something must have held him up for a minute. Maybe he had ducked behind a crate to avoid the Wheelies. Whatever. She had another shot at him.

Doodah looked up, and all Holly could do was wave. 'Morning,' she said.

Doodah shook a tiny fist at her. 'Don't you have better things to do, elf? All I do is smuggle a few fish.'

The question cut Holly deeply. Was this really the best way to help the People? Surely Commander Root had wanted more from her? In the past few months she had gone from top-priority surface operations to chasing down fish smugglers in a back alley. That was quite a drop.

She showed Doodah her hands. 'I don't want you to get hurt, so stand perfectly still.'

Doodah chuckled. 'Hurt? By you? Not likely.'

'No,' said Holly. 'Not by me. By him.' She pointed at the patch of mud under Doodah's feet.

'Him?' Doodah looked down suspiciously, suspecting

a trap. His suspicions were absolutely correct. The ground beneath his feet fizzled slightly as the surface earth shivered and bounced.

'What?' said Doodah, lifting one foot. He would doubtless have stepped off the patch, if he'd had time. But what happened next, happened very quickly.

THE PEOPLE –
A SPOTTER'S GUIDE

There are many different types of fairy and, with each one, it's important to know what you are dealing with. This is just some of the information collected by Artemis Fowl during his adventures. It is confidential and must *not* fall into the wrong hands. The future of the People depends on it.

ELVES

Distinguishing features: About one metre tall. Pointy ears. Brown skin. Red hair.
Character: Intelligent. Strong sense of right and wrong. Very loyal. Sarcastic sense of humour, although that might just be a particular female LEP officer.
Loves: Flying, either in a craft or with wings.
Situations to avoid: They really don't like it if you kidnap them and take their gold.

DWARFS

Distinguishing features: Short, round and hairy. Large tombstone teeth – good for grinding . . . well, anything really. Unhingable jaws enabling them to excavate tunnels. Sensitive beard hair. Skin capable of acting like suction cups when dehydrated. Smelly.
Character: Sensitive. Intelligent. Criminal tendencies.
Loves: Gold and precious gems. Tunnelling. The dark.
Situations to avoid: Being in a confined space with them when they have been tunnelling and have a build-up of trapped air. If they reach for the bum flap on their trousers, get out of there . . .

TROLLS

Distinguishing features: Huge – as big as an elephant. Light-sensitive eyes. Hate noise. Hairy with dreadlocks. Retractable claws. Teeth! – lots and lots of teeth. Tusks like a wild boar (a really wild boar). Green tongue. Exceptionally strong. Weak point at the base of the skull.
Character: Very, very stupid – the troll has a tiny brain. Mean and bad-tempered.
Loves: Eating – anything. A couple of cows would make a light snack.
Situations to avoid: Are you joking? If you even think a troll is near, run like the wind.

Goblins

Distinguishing features:
Scaly. Lidless eyes – they lick
their eyeballs to keep them moist.
Able to throw fireballs. They
go on all fours when speed is
important. Forked tongue. Less
than a metre tall. Slimy, fireproof skin.
Character: Not clever,
but cunning. Argumentative.
Ambitious. Power-hungry.
Loves: Fire. A good argument.
Power.
Situations to avoid: Don't get
in the way if they're throwing
a fireball.

Sprites

Distinguishing features:
About one metre tall. Pointy ears.
Green skin. Wings.
Character: Average intelligence.
Generally happy-go-lucky
attitude.
Loves: Flying – more than
anything else under or above
the Earth.
Situations to avoid: Watch out
for low-flying sprites – they don't
always look where they're going.

Centaurs

Distinguishing features:
Half-man, half-pony. Hairy –
obviously! Hooves can get
very dry.
Character: Extremely
intelligent. Vain. Paranoid. Kind.
Computer geeks.
Loves: Showing off. Inventing.
Situations to avoid: They aren't
very dangerous physically, but
they will sulk if you criticize their
latest invention, mess with their
hard drive or borrow their hoof
moisturizer.

Pixies

Distinguishing features:
About one metre tall. Pointy ears.
Apart from their ears and their
height, pixies look almost human.
Character: Extremely
intelligent. No morals. Cunning.
Ambitious. Greedy.
Loves: Power and money.
Chocolate.
Situations to avoid: Never get
on the wrong side of a pixie,
especially one as clever and
ruthless as Opal Koboi, unless
you are as brilliant as Artemis
Fowl, of course.

OPAL KOBOI

Mind Control — 91
— mastered the art of reaching Gola Schweem's cleansing coma state at the age of fourteen

Greed — 92
— insatiable desire for power and money

Weaknesses — 80
— genius IQ brings with it mental health problems, bordering on the schizophrenic

Morality — 0
— non-existent

Height — 100
— one metre

FOWL FILE

ILLUSTRATION COPYRIGHT © KEV WALKER ·

BRIEF ENCOVNTERS WITH...
OPAL KOBOI

I must admit that I have never talked to Opal Koboi face to face. I begged and pleaded with my fairy contacts, but there was nothing anyone could do. Opal Koboi is fairy public enemy number one, and there is no way a human is going to get within a thousand kilometres of her. Foaly did manage to slip me a snippet of video from her trial. I watched it with interest on a little fairy player he loaned me. Wonderful thing. The sensor is so powerful that I can watch DVDs belonging to my neighbour while they're still on his shelf.

So, anyway, back to Opal. She doesn't look dangerous. This little doll-faced pixie. If you saw her on the street, you'd help her find her mother. But look into her eyes, and the madness there is frightening. During the trial, the prosecutor asked her: Why, Miss Koboi? Why did you do it?

And she turned those cold, dead eyes on him and said: I did it because nobody thought it was possible. It was obvious to me, and to everyone in the courtroom that Opal Koboi did not care about all the lives that could have been lost. Not one whit.

Having seen that video, I'm glad I have never talked to Opal. I never want to.

Eoin Colfer

Enter Artemis Fowl's wicked world at
artemisfowl.co.uk

Enter the LEPrecon Demon Tracking Centre

See Artemis Fowl conniving in colour

Download profiles, games and top-secret info

Join Colfer Confidential for sneak previews of Eoin Colfer's new books, exclusive competitions, event announcements and exclusive downloads!

 artemisfowl.co.uk

ARTEMIS FOWL

THE GRAPHIC NOVEL

Of course, it had started with the Internet.
But then it always does.

Alien abductions. UFO sightings. Leylines. Ancient stone circles.

And the People.
It always came back to the People.

Trawling through gigs of data, he had compiled a database from the thousands of references to fairies he'd found from countries all over the world.

Each human civilization had its own term for the People. But there was no doubt that the reports referred to the same hidden race.

Many stories whispered of a special book carried by each fairy.

It was their bible containing the history of their race. It also contained their laws, their rules... and their weaknesses.

RELIVE THE ADVENTURE, THE MAGIC,
THE MIND-BLOWING TECHNOLOGY,
THE BEGINNING.
AS YOU'VE NEVER SEEN IT BEFORE.

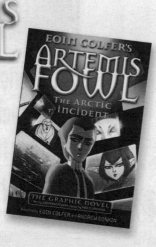

THE GRAPHIC NOVEL

Text copyright © Eoin Colfer, 2007. Adapted by Andrew Donkin. Illustrations copyright © Giovanni Rigano and Paolo Lamanna, 2007

My name is Moon. Fletcher Moon. And I'm a private detective.
I thought I'd seen it all. I was wrong.
Very wrong.

From the megaselling biographer of Artemis Fowl

A curious young detective.
A notorious criminal family. And a pretty girl.
It all adds up to just one thing . . . trouble.

With a capital T.

puffin.co.uk

halfmooninvestigations.co.uk

FOR CONOR BROEKHART THE ONLY WAY OUT. . . IS UP.

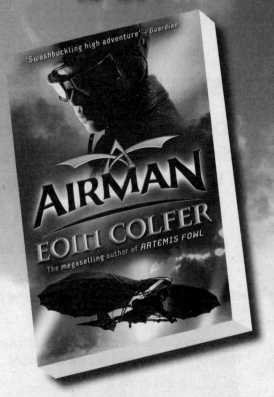

THE BRAND-NEW SWASHBUCKLING ADVENTURE FROM

EOIN COLFER

GO TO ISITABIRD.CO.UK TO SEE THE RACE FOR FLIGHT.

COVER ILLUSTRATION BY STEVE STONE

Your story starts here . . .

Do you **love books** and
discovering new stories?
Then **www.puffin.co.uk**
is the place for you . . .

- Thrilling adventures, fantastic fiction
  and laugh-out-loud fun

- Brilliant videos featuring your favourite authors
  and characters

- Exciting competitions, news, activities,
  the Puffin blog and SO MUCH more . . .

www.puffin.co.uk